# GOLDEN HILLS HAUNTING

## M.D. Neu

Although this novel is a work of fiction, many of the stories and events are based on actual occurrences gathered from several members of the community who wish to remain unnamed. To them, I dedicate this novel.

# ~ Chapter One ~

When I decided to sit down and write our story, I wasn't sure where to open, and I'm still not. Since things didn't begin all bad, they kicked off slowly. Which makes finding the starting point difficult. I guess when we questioned what was happening in our neighborhood was the day Alejandro came home not feeling well. We'd been in our house for about four months, everything had been unpacked, and our new place felt like a home. Even Chloe, our daughter, had managed to make friends in the neighborhood. We'd had family and friends over and even managed to pull off a big party: our housewarming, which thinking back now should have been our first warning given what happened that day. I digress. Alejandro rarely came home from the office sick, but on that day, I wasn't sure I'd ever seen him so ill.

We were lucky, of course. He was unwell, but he wasn't as bad as some of our neighbors. By the time we got Alejandro settled in bed to rest, three different ambulances had shown up on our cul-de-sac dealing with numerous medical emergencies at various houses. By that evening, almost every home in our circle had been visited by emergency services. The media didn't catch wind of the story for a few more days, not until the EPA showed up. Hell, everyone arrived, PG&E, San Jose Water, representatives from the housing development, the County, basically every government organization you might throw a rock at. The weeks that followed were only the beginning of our nightmare.

This new house had been our dream, one we had been

working toward for years and we needed the change desperately. Our home was the second finished on our street and we were the second family to move in. Yes, we were going to be living around construction for a couple more weeks, but for this house, the daily construction would be worth it, especially at the price we paid. In this valley, these homes were an outright steal. Chloe, in theory, would be at school during the day or off with friends or at therapy. Alejandro and I both worked so we wouldn't be around during the day when a majority of the construction commenced. Well, except for me. I still worked from home three days a week, but I could manage the noise; I had my music. The only real problem: the traffic as people were moving in and construction teams came and went. We imagined we'd be able to deal with the building and the neighborhood, but we were wrong.

The cause of the mystery illnesses. What a joke. It wasn't a gas leak or anything in the water or the dirt. We were all looking for the wrong things. At the time, no one ever contemplated we were under attack from the supernatural or paranormal or whatever you want to call a bunch of pissed off spirits and a horde of Demons thrown in for good measure.

But is that when everything commenced?

I don't think so.

We should have known something was off when we went to the sales center, about three months prior to our moving in. Let me start from before we moved in and go from there. Knowing how things began will help paint a full picture.

Our new neighborhood, our new home, was an infill neighborhood, one of those small groupings of houses that are built on a subdivided parcel of land. They do that a lot in San Jose, with housing being an issue. It's funny, there wasn't even a model home to look at. There was a portable sales office with floor plans and finishes to pick from. How we got the house didn't matter to us; getting the house was what mattered. Chloe needed the change, especially with all she had been dealing with. So, when I found out they were building this infill community, I told Alejandro and we understood we would have to move promptly. After seeing the information, the next day we called out from work and drove to Evergreen to check the location.

The area had everything we were looking for. Chloe could walk to the school, Chaboya Middle School, and she would have to make new friends, but we understood she'd manage. Chloe was social despite the trouble she had when we first got her. There were parks and a creek, plus several trails for hiking and biking. Down Fowler Road at Ruby Avenue a quaint Evergreen Village had been established with shops, restaurants, and larger stores. We couldn't have asked for a better neighborhood.

If we only knew.

I pulled up the information on my cell and called to ensure they were open, and as Alejandro drove, I sat on my phone pointing out directions. We located the sales center and, after parking, we made our way in. The sales center wasn't much more than a portable building that you see being used for schools or construction sites, which this area now fit.

"What do you think?" Alejandro asked as he opened the door to the car.

"The area is great." I glanced at my phone, frowning. "Service here sucks." I held up my phone, adjusting my glasses as well, thinking it might be my eyes. It wasn't.

He shrugged. "There aren't going to be too many homes. And this is Silicon Valley. We make the tech for everyone else and you know none of it will work here." He scoffed and pointed to all the wooden frames going up and a few slabs still not built on.

"Hi," we heard from the trailer. A woman in dark pants and blue blouse stood, waving, every part of her made up with impeccable make-up, hair, and nails. She even had a bright, wide grin. "You must be Kyle and Alejandro."

"That we are," I answered as we walked over.

"Welcome to Golden Hills." She reached the bottom of the steps of the trailer. "I'm Janet, I'm glad to see you here checking out our new homes." Janet smiled.

"Not much to check out, is there?" Alejandro waved around the construction zone.

She beamed. "Not yet, but if you wait for them to finish, they'll be sold. In fact, three of the houses are already spoken for. Why don't you come in? I can show you the information, and you can see how big the lots are. You won't find any other homes or lots in this area that are comparable, especially at the prices we're offering... and the incentives."

About halfway down the street, a builder rushed out of the house and tossed his tools in his truck, then jumped in the cab. He revved the engine and made his way up the street toward us, stopping at Janet. He rolled down his window.

"You tell Mel to go fuck himself if he thinks I'm going to keep dealing with this shit. I'm out of here." He rolled up the window and took off like a bat out of hell.

"What was that about?" I glanced at where the guy had come from. The house gave the impression of being fine. In fact, the home was one of the ones that appeared the farthest along.

Janet frowned and her face grew pale. "Nothing..." Her voice cracked. "I'm sorry, that was unprofessional. We've had a lot of issues with our builders, and poor Mel, he's so busy, he's hardly here to oversee the work, but don't let that dissuade you. These homes are built to the highest standard and have a fifteen-year contractors' warranty covering everything, which is five years more than the state requires." She beamed, but from what I noted, her expression came across as forced. "We also have several other incentives that you're not going to find with any other development or builder."

I adjusted my glasses again and peeked over at Alejandro, who smiled at me as we made our way into the sales office. By the end of our visit, we had made the decision to buy. The incentives were impressive, as Janet had promised when we arrived, but we told Janet we wanted to bring Chloe to get her take and ensure our daughter had a say. We also wanted Chloe to be involved with picking out the finishes for our new dream home since our move had been because of her and her situation at her current, soon to be former, school.

That Saturday, we made our way from our townhome in Campbell to the building site of what would be our new home.

"Are you excited?" I glanced over my shoulder at Chloe.

"I guess," she mumbled up from her phone. "I'll be glad to have a bigger room. And I'll be glad to be away from…" She peeked over at me, her eyes big and bright, but sadly, there were hints of tears there. This last year had been hell for her.

She didn't need to say anything more. Chloe had been bullied at school. We did all we could for her, and the school, to their credit, did what they could, but kids can be cruel and even with everything being done, Chloe still had a hard time. At least she had us and her therapist. We all agreed this move would be a good thing. The move doubtlessly wouldn't be soon enough, but as parents, you do the best you can.

"And you get to help us pick all the finishes…" I did what I could to be as uplifting as possible.

"Assuming you like the house," Alejandro added. "We won't proceed unless you are in complete agreement."

"Exactly," I agreed.

"If you say so." Chloe glanced at her phone.

Once at the Golden Hills construction site, we pulled into a makeshift parking lot, where the sales trailer and guest parking sat and would later be turned into the community park they would be building. It would be nice since the lots, despite being called large and spacious, weren't. Outside the trailer two men stood, one dressed in dress slacks and a button-down shirt, the other in jeans, work boots, and a flannel shirt. We had arrived in time to watch what appeared to be a heated conversation.

"I wonder what's happening there?" I waggled my head toward the two men.

"Construction drama." Alejandro parked the car.

"I understand there are deadlines," the guy in jeans countered. "I'm doing the best I can. Some of my crews refuse to return and word is getting…"

The man in the dress clothes held up a hand. "We'll talk about this later." He glanced our way. "Hi, you must be Kyle and Alejandro." His face beamed, holding a polished smile. "And that must be Chloe." He waved. "Janet told me to expect you today."

"Isn't Janet here?" I asked as my husband, daughter, and I made our way over to them.

"She's working at one of our other sites." His voice dripped with an off-putting charm. I wasn't sure how his demeanor struck me. "I'm Lee and this is Mel, our construction head."

"The homes are coming along," Alejandro commented, bobbing his head at the street. "I'm surprised to see all the progress in such a short amount of time. You must be pushing your crews."

"We're trying. We should be a lot farther along…" Mel glanced around the site. Only a few workers were present, but the ones on site were busy. "If you'll excuse me," he headed off to one of the homes still being framed out.

"Poor Mel. We need to get him more help." Lee continued his grin as he scrutinized the foreman's retreat to the homes.

"I guess there are labor issues in every industry," I commented. Even at my office, we were having a hard time finding staff. I kept telling management we needed to pay more, but they didn't want to listen, so we still had positions to fill. I peered around at all the homes. At present, nine of the ten homes lay in various stages of construction. Three, at the end of the street, from what we noticed appeared a lot farther along than the others.

"So, Chloe, I understand you have to make some decisions today." Lee beamed at our daughter.

"I suppose." She peeked up from her cell phone. "Papa, my phone's not working again."

"We'll sort it out at home," Alejandro raised his eyebrows towards her. "Now put your phone away and pay attention to Lee."

She huffed, but did as she was told.

I peeked at my phone. Nothing. There was no cell service again, which annoyed me, given that we had service on the drive over here. Maybe all the tools and construction going on had affected the service in the area.

Once in the sales center, we viewed a map of the new development with all the homes and how they would be placed on the street. The street was a cul-de-sac with a small park at the entrance of the neighborhood where the sales center currently sat.

"As you can see, since you were here a few days ago, we sold two more homes, but we have a hold on the two you were interested in." Lee smiled, pointing to the map showing the street and the lots with their planned homes. "Which I guess is what we are here to talk about today."

Lee pulled out all the details on the homes and all the various samples. "Are you ready to have some fun?" He glanced at Chloe, then at Alejandro and me.

I pulled off my glasses, removing a couple of spots as we all leaned in. As crazy as this all seemed, we were excited, as we got our new home soon enough so we would have the ability to pick all the finishes and even which house style and upgrades we wanted. Of the three floor plans we had on offer, we had decided that one of the two stories would be the best for us, especially if we wanted to adopt another kid, which was the current plan. So, I was relieved when Chloe instantly pushed the single story to the side.

"I like this one." She pointed to the biggest house. I wasn't surprised. If I remembered correctly, the home Chloe picked was also the house the construction worker left from a couple of days ago.

"And why do you like that one?" Alejandro asked, genuinely curious. He was good with Chloe. The two understood each other, which pleased me.

She twisted her mouth to the left and right. "Well, I know you want to adopt another kid, and this house has an office, so when dad works from home he's not in the dining room. Plus, this home feels better."

"What about the one with the loft? We thought that might make a great place for you and your friends..." I pointed to the floorplan. "We can make the space a great hang out area for you."

She tapped her lips. "Well, I think the kitchen is better in this one, plus I like the island and I think the kitchen is bigger, and we like to cook, so..."

I pulled off my glasses. "Well, Papa, what do you think?"

"I think Chloe picked our house."

"Really?" Chloe's voice rose as she glanced between us.

"You're picking this one?" She pointed. "Can we turn one of the extra bedrooms into a hangout room?"

"We'll talk about it." I laughed as I put my glasses on.

"Well, this home is a great choice. Now we have to figure out all the rest of your finishes and what upgrades you want. As you know, we are at a point where we'll need to get these choices made so we don't have any additional delays." Lee pulled out more samples and catalogs for us to look through.

Over the next hour and a half we picked cabinets, countertops, flooring, and all our other finishes, including deciding and splurging on the two-tone walls, so they wouldn't be boring beige. By the time we finished, exhaustion filled every part of my body and I needed dinner. With the help of my phone I found a great Japanese place down the street, and Japanese happened to be one of the few foods we all agreed on.

We were happy that day. I only wish that feeling would have lasted.

# ~ Chapter Two ~

During the time between buying the new house and fixing up our townhouse to be rented once we moved, time sped up and slowed down. We got updates from Lee about the construction process and some of the delays they continued to have. Mainly they were having trouble with the building crews. We found out that Mel had left, and they had a new construction manager, but he only lasted a few weeks. You would have assumed all the small things would have registered with us, but they never did, not until much later. We also never heard from Janet again and only worked with Lee. Even our lender had some issues with the paperwork, not on our end, but from the builder, which struck us as odd, considering the builder was a huge company and had tons of construction projects all over the country and state. Occasionally, we would drive over to the work site and see how the construction progressed. Despite all the delays and headaches, our new home came along and began to turn into everything we had hoped the house would be.

More importantly, Chloe appeared happy. She wasn't having as many issues at school as before and her therapist reported that she was maturing and getting better.

When June came, we were ready to move in. All the inspections had been signed off on and all the financial work on our end had wrapped up. Getting the keys had been a huge relief. Alejandro and I were lucky; when we got married and moved in together, he had a condo downtown already and I had my townhouse in Campbell, so we were able to sell his condo—my townhouse was bigger—and fix things up. With the extra money from the sale of his condo, we'd use the money for our new dream house. Luckily, my husband worked as a Controller for a tech company and he was a wiz with money. I wasn't too bad either, but where our finances were involved I realized who to defer too. Keeping the townhouse was something we agreed on, especially since the extra income would be a godsend and help us build up, not just our nest egg, and in the long run, we both wanted to help our kids like our parents helped us. The money would also help Chloe's college fund and assist us when we began the adoption process for our next child.

With the new home in Evergreen, we'd start the process again.

The day the movers pulled up at our new house, our neighborhood looked nothing like what we had first showed up to in February. Our home was the second one ready for move in, and the other eight weren't far behind. Landscaping had begun on several homes and it appeared that most of the homes were being finished up. I had been worried about construction noise, but that seem like a nonissue now.

*Thank goodness.*

As the sun began dipping behind the other homes, and the reds, yellows, and oranges would soon commence to replace the blues of the day, we were in a mess of furniture and boxes. If it wasn't for the knock at the front door, I think we would have all collapsed where we were, only to dig ourselves out the next morning.

"I got it." I glanced at my watch. My glasses were filthy again. I pulled them off and gave them a quick clean. Returning them to my face, I scanned my watch; a bit after seven. It felt a lot later, I deliberated, as I made my way from the kitchen to the front door. My new, shiny, chocolate-brown door. I ran a hand over the smooth finish, enjoying the feel. I opened the door and standing in front of me was a brown-haired woman wearing a bright blue Saree and a man in blue jeans and a bright blue shirt matching the Saree in color but not in style. He held a tray covered with aluminum foil.

"Hello," I greeted the strangers.

"We're Mr. and Mrs. Patil." The woman smiled. "We're your neighbors." She pointed to the house across the street and one over. The house with the lights on and similar in style to ours, except with a different façade.

"Oh, hi," I greeted as Chloe and Alejandro appeared from behind.

"We noticed you moving in today and I figured—well, Deepa and I agreed you might not feel like cooking, so I made you butter chicken, naan, and rice. I didn't make the food too spicy and kept the food simplish." He held out the tray. "I hope you like Indian food."

"Like it? We love it. Thank you." I took the tray of delights. "Please, come in." I stepped to the side, the smashing of packing paper filling the hall. "I'm Kyle. This is my husband Alejandro and our daughter Chloe."

"Oh, we don't want to be a bother. We wanted to welcome you." Deepa gestured to all the boxes in our hall. "I know how hard moving is. Then having to think about food and everything that goes with dinner can be a headache. Plus, Hari is an amazing chef, and he enjoys showing off." She laughed.

"Well, it smells wonderful." My stomach gurgled in agreement and anticipation of what promised to be something delicious.

"Please, come in. We aren't going to do too much more today." Alejandro gestured down the hall toward the dining area, pushing some of the packing paper out of his way. "Plus, the dining table is all set up... I don't know where the dishes are yet, though." He raked a hand through his mussed hair. "But we'll have places to sit, at least."

"We have paper plates from lunch. They're on the counter," Chloe announced. "Do you have any kids?" she followed up.

Deepa laughed. "Hari and I have two sons, but they are older, I'm afraid."

Chloe frowned, heading to the kitchen.

"Do they live with you?" I asked as we made our way to the dining room. Alejandro and I were doing our best to make sure the path was clear.

"You went with the home office conversion." Hari pointed. "That's smart. We had the space made into the fifth bedroom for when our parents come and stay," he continued as they passed by the office.

"Since I work from home half the time, having the office was key for us."

Hari shook his head in agreement.

"Neil's in college." Deepa returned the conversation to their children. "And Vyan's at Evergreen Valley High School. He's going to be a Junior in the fall, but he's with friends today. You know teens."

"Oh, yes." Alejandro glanced toward Chloe. "She's growing up."

"They do that." Deepa beamed and took a seat at our cherry wood table. "Is Chloe your only child?"

"We're planning on adopting again, perhaps a boy this time, but we'll take—"

As everyone took their seats and settled in around the dining table, the lights in the chandelier began to flicker and flash, followed by the lights in the kitchen. The light show moved between the lights in the kitchen and the dining room; all the other lights on in the house were unaffected.

"What the heck?" Alejandro stood and walked to the light switch, and flicked the toggle a couple of times.

"We've been having issues with our lights since we moved in." Deepa frowned. "We called the builder, and they've sent out two different people, but they still can't find the issue."

"I hope this isn't an omen of things to come."

Hari laughed. "It's a new house. These things happen. I'm glad we're not the only ones. I can see Deepa trying to engineer something new. As things were, she had a lot of requests when it came to the solar, back-up batteries, and all her computer needs."

As abruptly as the lights began to flash, they stopped. The rest of the early evening we enjoyed our first meal with the Patils and were happy to have gotten to know our new neighbors.

If the odd occurrences would have stopped with the lights that would have been great, but we weren't going to be that lucky. None of us were.

# ~ Chapter Three ~

Over the next ten days, we had crews from the builder in our home repairing the electrical, even though they couldn't find anything wrong. They had to replace the refrigerator and gas cooktop, and replace one of the battery backs-ups connected to the house's solar system. Most recently, they came to look at the water in the shower in the primary bedroom, as the water never got hot. All these minor annoyances were nothing that we considered, as this was a new house and there were always issues with new things. At least, that's what we told ourselves.

Since I had flexibility in my work schedule, I'd been making good use of my new office, despite the trouble with our internet connection and cell service. The only thing that kept me sane was hearing from Deepa that they were having continued issues at their house as well. And we weren't the only ones, it would seem. Even the builders were having issues, crews coming out to work for a couple of days, and not returning.

But today, today was for Alejandro and I. Chloe had gone with two good friends from Campbell over to the beach for a beach day. We knew the parents well and felt comfortable with letting our daughter spend the day with them, and she had her phone, so if there were any issues, she'd contact us, but we didn't anticipate any trouble.

"There you are." Alejandro stood at the door to my office. "What're you doing?"

"I'm getting caught up on some messages." I pushed my

glasses up on my face.

"Working on the weekend." Alejandro tsked. "That needs to change. What have we said about work-life balance?"

"I know." I stopped typing. "With everything happening here and the move, I can't seem to catch up."

Alejandro continued to study me from the door. He wore his gray shorts and a black tee-shirt, his dark hair messed from all the work he had been doing getting the house in order. He was determined to have all the boxes unpacked by the end of the weekend.

"How goes the unpacking? Have you left anything for me? Are we going to be set for our housewarming?"

Alejandro laughed, pointing to the boxes in my new office. "I got the kitchen all unpacked. That basically leaves Chloe's room and a few more boxes in our bedroom. In fact…" He moved over to me, pulled off my glasses and rested them on my desk next to my phone. "I thought we might go up there and take care of a few packages we've been ignoring the last week or so." He stretched down and brushed his hand over my crotch, ensuring he had my attention, which he did.

"Well, I guess I can pull myself away and assist you with some much-needed emptying of loads."

He leaned in and gave me a quick kiss, slipping his hand up my thigh between the fabric of my shorts and my skin, finding his way to my crotch and giving my bulge a squeeze. I leaned back, giving him better access, but instead of him rubbing my dick, he pulled out his hand, took mine, pulling me from my chair. We hurriedly made our way from the office up to our bedroom where, much to my surprise, Alejandro had a couple of ocean mist candles lit, the blinds pulled shut, and our duvet pulled down, waiting for us.

"Oh, sneaky." I beamed at him, giving him another kiss. "Looks like someone was planning."

"Who, me?" Alejandro placed a hand on his chest, feigning innocence. "I don't know what you mean." He stepped over and pulled at my Tina Turner tee-shirt, making quick work of the fabric, "God, I love your chest, all your red chest hair. I'm so jealous."

"And I'm jealous of that beautiful head of hair of yours." I ran my fingers through his dark mop of hair. "And your smooth chest."

He chuckled and commenced unfastening the strings to my shorts. I didn't need any more of an invitation and made fast work of his shirt, shorts, and underwear. "Beautiful," I whispered, taking in his smooth body, a small amount of trimmed hair spreading out from his shaft, the hair not reaching far in any direction, but enough to make him look all the more appealing.

Alejandro pulled down my briefs and gave my stiffening cock a squeeze. "You feel so good." He kissed me again.

I cupped his balls in my hand as I rubbed the tip of his dick. I loved how his cock fell over his balls as he got hard. The first time we fooled around and I found out his dick curved down, I couldn't help but continue to play with it through the fabric of his pants. What I didn't realize was how sensitive he was, especially when I played with both his dick and balls at the same time. He came so fast that night. Not only did he gush with seamen but embarrassment and frustration with the mess he made in his underwear and jeans. But I loved feeling him erupt and witnessing the ecstasy on his face, and any time I'd be able to do that for him, I would. However, I wanted more today.

We kissed again and made our way to the bed. We knew each other's bodies as if they were our own. Alejandro hadn't been lying when he said we'd been abstaining for a while, with getting the townhouse ready for the renters, packing, moving, and now unpacking, as well as dealing with the various issues going on with the house. We had been neglecting each other, and that was never a good thing. One of the biggest reasons relationships fail is the couple starts to ignore each other not only in the bedroom, but outside the bedroom, finding ways to take care of their needs in other ways.

On our bed, Alejandro's hand slowly moved up and down my dick. I hadn't been this hard in a while, and the sensation sent bolts of energy to every part of my body. I wasted no time finding his cock and putting my own hand to work again as we continued to kiss. I inhaled the scent of Alejandro and ocean mist. His aroma made its way deep into me, touching my very soul. I needed to breathe, but didn't want him to stop. I also didn't want to come too hastily. We had the whole afternoon to enjoy each other, and I didn't want to rush.

I pulled away from our kiss and gazed deep into his dark eyes. "I love you so much."

He kissed me again. "I love you too." He pushed me onto the pillow and kissed my cheeks. Alejandro moved to my neck and made his way to my chest and my overly sensitive nipples, which he loved to suck on as he stroked me.

A chuckle of pleasure escaped my lips. "If you keep doing that, I'm not going to last long."

He smiled up at me. "Well, we can't have that." He shifted his position so his hard cock was staring me in the face. "Let's see who can last the longest," he teased, eagerly taking me into his mouth. With a gasp, I didn't hesitate and rapidly took his hefty cock into my mouth. For Alejandro's shorter stature, the one area he wasn't small in was his dick and balls. I remembered the first time we had actually been together and fooling around. I had felt completely inadequate compared to him, but after getting to know him and what he liked and enjoyed, I didn't worry about how our bodies were built differently. I learned simply to enjoy him and his body as he did mine.

I felt him getting close and, during my own brief moments of clarity, I imagined I may outlast him, which would be a nice change. Not that I, or we, kept track of such things. Well, maybe I did. I liked to ensure he was satisfied before I finished, but as much as my mind wanted that, my body often had other plans. So, when I would make him finish first, that always made me happy.

There was a crash from somewhere downstairs.

I pulled away. "What the hell!"

"Don't stop." Alejandro moaned. "That feels so good." He went to work on me.

Another crash from downstairs clawed its way into our ears, and this time he stopped and we both shared a look.

"Did you lock the doors?" I asked.

"Before I found you."

"Fuck!" I huffed. "Where's the bat?" I whispered as I pulled away.

"Closet." He eyed the direction of our walk-in. I got up and pulled on my pants, foregoing my briefs. "Stay here."

"Fuck that." Alejandro moved off the bed and pulled on his shorts. Both our dicks as hard as stone, luckily mine slowly deflated, but not quickly enough for the situation.

We moved to the closet and I got the bat before we both headed to the stairs. "Get your phone," I instructed.

He pointed downstairs.

I frowned. Mine was in the office with my glasses. I shook my head and moved down the stairs, hearing another bang. This one was much louder, shaking the whole house. "Jesus."

"An earthquake?" Alejandro glanced around the staircase.

"No." We continued down to where the noise had come from.

21

At the bottom of the landing, I checked to my left and didn't see anyone. The front door was closed and, I presumed, locked. When I glanced to the right and the family room, a person all in black rushed by making their way into the dining room and kitchen. "What the hell? Stop!" I yelled.

Alejandro and I rushed toward the intruder and the kitchen, but there was nothing. No one.

"Where'd they go?" Alejandro asked.

"Get your phone and call the cops." He snatched up his phone from the dining table, and we moved to the office where I grabbed my glasses and phone. Not wanting to take any chances, we made our way to the front porch. The afternoon was bright and the neighborhood quieter than any neighborhood on a Saturday afternoon should be.

By the time the police arrived, Alejandro and I weren't sure what we observed, but we witnessed someone. Someone had gotten into the house, possibly from the back door or garage. I wasn't wearing my glasses at the time so my sight wasn't reliable, and all Alejandro mentioned seeing was a tall person in dark clothing, with some kind of cloak and hat, that he couldn't make out any features of, and he assumed based on height that the person was a man, but who knew.

"Well, Mr. and Mr. Del Rosario," Officer Lancey rested a hand on her holster. "We checked the house and all the doors and windows." She shook her head. "We didn't find anyone, but the sliding door was unlocked. Nothing was broken either. You sure you heard three large bangs?"

"It shook the stairs," I stated.

"But I locked that door," Alejandro insisted. "I know I did. That's why I left my phone on the dining table."

Officer Lancey raised a hand. "A lot of times people think they do something but don't. Like autopilot, they go and find that they never did what they set out to do."

"Look, Officer… Lancey, is it? I don't know about you…" he lowered his voice so only she and I would hear his words—not like anyone else was around, but still. "When you and your partner are about to engage in… well… you know… make love." His face was red. And, given the heat on my neck, I had no doubt I was as red, if not redder, than him. "Do you leave doors open, or do you make damn sure they are locked?"

The officer cleared her throat. "As I mentioned, the sliding door was unlocked, so maybe they got in that way. Sliding doors are easy to pick. My suggestion is to get yourselves a solid wooden dowel and put it in the track so the door is harder to open. I see you have a security alarm, so that's good."

"We're not going to arm the system when we're home," I argued with a shake of my head.

"No, but maybe get some cameras," the officer pushed her hand into her pocket. "Take my card. It has the case number and how to contact me. If anything is missing, let me know for our files. This should be all you need for your insurance, assuming you find anything broken or missing." She glanced around. "Maybe you heard something out here. Maybe that's what shook your house and made all the noise."

"Maybe!" I huffed.

Alejandro took the card.

"We'll bump up patrols, but…" she trailed off.

"I'll be happy once they finish construction and everyone else moves in," I declared with a glance up the street, seeing Lancey's partner walking around. He was a Latino guy with dark hair and broad shoulders.

"I'm sorry this ruined your afternoon." Her tone was warm and kind.

I frowned as Alejandro rubbed his chin.

"Give us a call if anything else happens." Officer Lancey

glanced around, peeking toward her partner. "Are any other folks moved in yet?"

"The Patils are across the street, but they're away this weekend, visiting their son…" I laughed. "I told them we'd watch the house." My stomach dropped. "You don't think anyone broke in there, do you?"

"I'll go walk around the house and ensure everything's okay."

"Thank you," Alejandro replied.

With a final gesture at us, the officer left us on our front porch. We didn't move as she walked around and checked the Patils' home. Once she got in her patrol car, she drove slowly down the rest of the street, checking the homes at the end of the cul-de-sac. They were finished and ready to be moved into. She picked up her partner and the two sat in the car, not leaving.

"They're going to be a while, so let's get dressed and go to the hardware store. I want to pick up a camera system for the house and a dowel for the sliding door and maybe another lock for the garage door." Alejandro huffed, glancing at the front door. "I can't believe this." He headed to the door.

"Sounds like a plan." I straightened up from leaning on the porch pillar. "I don't want to tell Chloe. I don't want her to worry."

"We'll need to tell her something," Alejandro countered. "I don't want her to be scared, but I don't want her to feel like we're hiding things from her."

"We'll figure it out." I glanced around the yard at the bright sunny day; the new trees, the freshly planted lawn, and flower bed, all drought resistant and new. Everything looked so perfect. "Who the hell would try to break into a house during the day? It doesn't make any sense."

"People are crazy. I wish I got a better look at them."

Alejandro extended out his hand to me. "I'm sorry about today. Maybe we can finish tonight, but I'm not in the mood anymore, unless you are."

I shook my head. There was no worse boner killer than someone trying to break into your house when you're at your most vulnerable.

I peeked over my shoulder at the parked patrol car. There was no point watching the officers drive around or do their paperwork, so I took Alejandro's hand and we made our way into the house. That was our first interaction with the San Jose Police Department and Officer Danielle Lancey. I wish I could say that this encounter was our last, but nothing in life is ever that simple. Not for us, and not for poor Officer Lancey.

# ~ Chapter Four ~

"Hamburger buns?"

"Check."

"Soda?"

"Check."

"Cupcakes?"

"Dad, we have everything." Chloe beamed at me.

"Are you excited to see your grandparents?" I glanced around the kitchen, seeing that everything was ready. I spent the whole night before pulling out everything we were going to need for the housewarming today. Alejandro got on my case about how I turned into a pain in the ass before a party, but I couldn't help it. This was the first big shindig in our new home, and I wanted everything to be great.

"The coals are looking good." Alejandro walked in from the backyard.

"Are you sure we're going to have enough?"

"Watch out, psycho dad is in full force, Papa," Chloe teased.

"Hey, that's not nice," I chided.

"Do we want to bet on how early your grandparents are going to be?" Alejandro smiled.

"Well, we know it won't be your family." I gave Alejandro the side eye. You could offer his family a million dollars and all they had to do to claim the money was show up on time, and you would never have to worry about paying them. It was impossible for them to be anything less than thirty minutes late.

"Not fair, they've gotten a lot better."

"True, especially since we ate Christmas dinner without them so all they had was dessert when they finally arrived an hour and a half late," I countered, forcing a big-ass snarky smirk on my face.

Alejandro's eyes narrowed on me.

"You're not going to fight again, are you?" Chloe glanced between Alejandro and me. "That's all you guys have been doing since we moved in."

"We're not going to fight," I huffed at our daughter. We had been on edge since we moved in that was fair enough, but that was because we had a lot to do, and setting up the house and still having the construction going on didn't help matters.

"We're playing." Alejandro's eyes opened wide as his lips parted, revealing the whites of his teeth, which were highlighted by his white button-down shirt. He always looked great in white shirts, and no matter what we were doing, he always managed to keep them perfectly clean. I'm not sure how he accomplishes that. If I even considered the idea of wearing a white shirt, or shorts for that matter, I would see a stain on what I was wearing.

"Okay," Chloe declared, but her set jaw showed she didn't believe me.

"Plus, I told them the party started at eleven," Alejandro stated.

I was about to remind him we did the same thing for Christmas and they were still late. However, a knock from the front door caught all our attentions.

"Saved by the door," Alejandro commented as he and Chloe rushed to the door.

That's the problem with being with someone as long as Alejandro and I had been together. You know what to say to irk the other person, and he must have known I was about to say something, so I was grateful for the door keeping my mouth shut.

"Hi George, hi Diana," Alejandro greeted.

"Alejandro, how many times do we have to tell you to call us mom and dad?" My mother hugged him. "The house is beautiful."

"Too bad about all the construction still going on," my father commented as they walked in. "The park isn't even finished."

"Hi, mom." I hugged my mother, then gave my dad a hug. "It's been nothing but delays and construction issues."

"We got you boys a little something." My mom handed me an envelope. "Maybe use it for the house or your trip."

"Thanks, mom." I pocketed the envelope. The gift was money, which I appreciated, and we would find a good use for the cash. I can't speak for everyone, but being an only child had perks.

"Now I know we're early, but I figured you can put us to work."

"Come on, Grandad and Nan…" Chloe pulled their hands. "I want to show you my rooms."

"Rooms?" my dad asked, looking at me.

"We'll let Chloe explain." I gestured to our daughter, observing as she pulled my parents up to the second floor. "Show them the rest of the house while you're up there," I called after them.

"What'd your mom give us?" Alejandro asked, his voice hushed.

I went to pull the envelope out of my back pocket as we moved to the kitchen, but it was gone. "An envelope…" I trailed off, checking my pockets as we got into the kitchen. "But I…"

"You mean this envelope?" Alejandro picked the envelope

up from the counter.

"Oh, funny." I pinched my lips together. "You pulled the envelope from my pocket, making me think I lost it."

"'Cause I have nothing better to do." Alejandro huffed and handed me the envelope after peeking in. "Cash. Nice."

I pulled the cash from the envelope and put the bills in my pocket, shaking my head. There was a ring of the doorbell, stopping us from saying anything more, or saying something we might regret later.

As our guests continued to arrive, our house filled with conversation and laughter. We had each invited our families and co-workers and friends. We also invited the Patil family and the Chen family who lived next door to us, who were the third family to move in. I was pleased to see that Carmelita and James, Alejandro's parents, were not the last to arrive. That honor fell to his sister, Ana. Although, to be fair, she did have two kids with her, and sadly, her husband Lee wasn't much help, assuming he even bothered to show up to these types of events.

"Sorry we were later than we wanted to be, but the chicken adobo took longer than I expected." Carmelita stepped from the cooktop, glancing at the lumpias in the oven. "And the lumpias are always best hot. We really try."

"Oh, Carmelita, you and James are great, and the adobo and lumpia are always a huge hit, you know that." I continued to pull food out of the refrigerator.

"How are Angelo and Aaron?"

"You know boys, they have their own lives with their girlfriends." She shook her head. "I'm so happy Alejandro and you stayed close to us."

"And what about Anthony? How's he liking San Diego?"

She shrugged. "When he calls, he says he's fine, but I don't like him so far away."

"Alejandro sent me in. The burgers and dogs are about ready." Carter held a beer in his hand.

"Excellent." I wiped my hands, going to the dining table.

"Need some help?" Sara placed her red cup on the counter.

"Please," I responded. Sara and Carter, Jacky's mom and dad, had been wonderful. Getting to know them through Jacky helped Chloe, and Sara had been an excellent resource for things I never pondered to even worry about with Chloe, like silk pillow cases, hair wraps, and more skin lotion than conceivable. Plus, they were a lot of fun and Carter and Alejandro both worked in finance. Well, Carter worked in payroll, but to my mind payroll was part of finance.

"Did you hear that Dan is having to go to court again? That poor man is never going to be rid of his awful wife," Sara declared.

"And Maggie is stuck in the middle." Carter shook his head, moving the fruit tray.

"Well, if he needs anything, I hope he knows to—"

"Alejandro! Kyle!" Carmelita yelled from the kitchen.

"Oh, god!" I rushed over and all conversation stopped as every set of eyes fell onto the cooktop. Our gas range was ablaze with fire. Flames touched the hood and almost to the ceiling. Carmelita tried to cover the flames with the lid to her pot, but it did nothing. I hurried to the door of the garage and grabbed the fire extinguisher, making short work of the flames and, sadly, the chicken adobo.

My mom held Carmelita. "Did you see it?" Carmelita's voice shook. "Did you see it?"

I shook my head at my mother. We didn't need a panic on our hands. The fire was bad enough. "Yes, we all saw those dreadful flames. Truly terrifying, but the fire's out now." My mom had an English "everything is fine" face firmly in place, for which I was grateful.

"I've made that recipe for fifty years and it's never done that."

"It's fine." My mom rubbed Carmelita's shoulder. "I can't tell you how many times I've almost burned down our home when I've baked." She laughed. "I'll never make it as a baker or even get close to being in one of those baking competitions."

"Don't worry, everything is all good." I smiled, pulling the pot to the sink and turning on the faucet. I also ensured the cooktop was off, so nothing else might catch a blaze. I glanced at all our guests gathering around the kitchen and smiled as I pulled open the kitchen window. "What a way to break in our new house. Right?" I beamed. "Good thing we have lots of burgers and hotdogs, and we still have the wonderful lumpias, which should be about ready." There were several laughs and people restarted their conversations, enjoying the party, or at least pretending to.

Hari walked over to me.

"Mom, why don't you take Carmelita out to the patio so she can get some fresh air? While I finish cleaning this up."

"That shouldn't have happened." Carmelita continued her defense. "And you saw it, right? How could anyone miss that hideous face."

"That was the fire," my mother soothed.

"I was talking to Carmelita about her recipe." Hari's voice was low. "There's nothing that should have done that and that kind of gas range shouldn't flare like that." Hari's eyes were large. "And I've seen my fair share of kitchen fires in the restaurant."

"I've never seen anything catch like that." Sara picked up her red cup, and her hand trembled. "And I swear, I noticed a face in those flames, something evil." She shuddered and glanced at both Hari and me.

"Pareidolia." I smiled. "You know how our brains work."

I forced a laugh. I didn't want to admit to seeing the face as well. My mind tickled with a memory of that weekend in Boulder Creek with Reza when we were dating, but that was a lifetime ago, before I had met Alejandro and we never saw anything like that, never.

"If you say so." Sara took Carter by the arm. "Where's Jacky?"

"Up with Chloe and the other kids." Carter pointed to the hallway.

They moved away, and once they were out of earshot. I turned to Hari. "That's a brand-new cooktop. The original cooktop we had when we moved in damn near caught the whole kitchen on fire."

Hari took my arm. "The face, I saw it, too."

Despite almost burning down our kitchen, the rest of the party went well. I still had the feeling that our friends and family were more than a little shaken by what they witnessed, or imagined they had seen. After everything was cleaned up and Alejandro and I were relaxing in front of the TV, Chloe hold up in her room. I got five text messages and two phone calls about the evil face in the flames and asking if everything was okay with us and our home. I wasn't sure how to respond, so I played it off and reassured everyone that everything was fine. I told them I had already left a message for the builder to come and check the gas line to the range and that we wouldn't be using the cooktop until it was thoroughly checked out...

Again...

I left that part out.

"I can't understand why everyone is making such a big deal out of the fire." Alejandro scrutinized me as I put my phone on the coffee table.

"You didn't see it." I shook my head. "I didn't want your poor mom to freak out any more than she already was, but that face, the image, that whatever, isn't something I'm going to so easily forget, either." I sighed.

"What?"

"You remember that story I told you about Reza and me? And what happened at the cabin?"

"Oh, yes, I remember all about you and *him*…"

"Alejandro, come on," I snarled.

"Relax," Alejandro countered with a wave of his hand. "I'm teasing." The words he spoke didn't match the expression on his face, but I didn't want to argue. Everything that happened with Reza happened before we actually met.

*But even then, we never experienced anything like this, like that face.*

"Anyway, all these things happening…"

Alejandro laughed.

"You don't think—"

"I think…" Alejandro raised a hand. "Your imagination is running wild." His voice faltered as he grasped a hand to me. "You said so yourself. Pareidolia. And the rest…" He shrugged. "It's a new house, and with all the construction issues and changes in labor, I'm surprised the house is in as good a shape as it is."

I gestured and glanced over my shoulder to the kitchen and the range with a shake of my head. That wasn't the only time we would see that face, but god, I wish it was.

# ~ Chapter Five ~

With the housewarming out of the way, things had become normal. The construction in the neighborhood finished, the sales center had been removed, and the landscaping of the new community park finished up. We and the Patils had the opportunity to welcome the Johnsons and their kids who live next to the Patils, and occupied the house right next to the park. We viewed Mr. and Mrs. Williams move in as well as the Martins, Walkers, Gills, and Harrises. Within a few days, the park was filled with kids out playing, a rare event in the age of cellphones, and they appeared to all get along. There were a couple of kids around Chloe's age, so with fingers crossed, I hoped they would all be at the same school. Everyone seemed nice, even the Martins, who stayed to themselves for the most part. Not everyone's interested in being buddy-buddy with their neighbors, even when you all have a shared trauma.

I found out later that part of the reason they moved out was they decided to get a divorce. I guess Golden Hills Court proved to be too much for them. I wasn't all that surprised. There were times I wanted to pick up and leave Alejandro. How much are people supposed to take?

Now that we had our family routine, and the move-in officially ended with the last of the boxes in the recycle bin, things were good. I worked in my home office three days a week, so when Alejandro walked through the door pale and on the brink of collapse, relief filled every pore in my body that I had been home that day.

The door opened, and I got up from my office chair. "Chloe, is that you?" I called, turning the corner. "Oh god, Alejandro, what's wrong?" I rushed over.

He held up a hand at me. "Don't get too close. I think I have the flu or something, maybe one of the variants. I don't know." He coughed and struggled to gulp down some air.

"Never mind that. Let's get you undressed and upstairs." I touched his arm, and his skin burned under my fingers. "Let's get you in the shower first and see if we can cool you down." I helped him up to our room. I stripped my husband naked and moved him to the bathroom and turned on the shower, keeping the water cool, but not cold. I placed my glasses on the counter and tugged off my shirt and sweats in case he couldn't stand and needed my help in the shower. Once under the cool water, he came to life.

"How are you feeling?"

"A bit better." He stood under the shower, allowing himself to be engulfed by the chilled water. "The water is cold, but..."

I moved to our counter and put my glasses on. I dug through the drawers, pulling out Aspirin and the cold and flu medications. Once the meds were out and I put my clothes back on, I grabbed a towel for Alejandro. I snapped my fingers. "Where's the thermometer?"

"Chloe's bathroom, I think. Wasn't it with the medicines?" Alejandro asked between sprays of water.

"Are you going to be okay?"

"I'm feeling a bit better, not so hot."

I headed out of our room to Chloe's bathroom and searched for the thermometer. I wanted to take Alejandro's temperature and make sure we didn't need to get him to the hospital. I couldn't find the device in any of her drawers, so I headed into our bathroom, hearing the water stop. Once I returned,

Alejandro wrapped himself in his towel. "The thermometer wasn't in her bathroom."

Alejandro shook his head.

I glanced at the counter and, resting inside our basket of hand towels, was the thermometer. "What the hell? Did you do this?" I grabbed the gadget from the towels.

"Do what?" Alejandro turned and faced me.

I held up the thermometer. "It was with the towels."

"No. I assumed you couldn't find it?"

"I couldn't. Come on," I pointed, and we moved to the bed.

Alejandro pulled on his pajama bottoms and lay on the bed. "Oh, better." He exhaled.

"Open up." I demanded and stuck the stick of a device into his mouth.

As I got the medication for Alejandro and a cup of water, the beep-beep broke the silence. His temperature taken, I returned to our room and placed everything on the nightstand. "Take these," I instructed and pulled out the thermometer. "99 degrees." I frowned. "There is no way you're only 99 degrees." I felt his forehead. He was still warm, but not as hot as before the shower. I bit my upper lip.

"Maybe I got overheated," Alejandro commented through sips of water. He had taken the Aspirin and the other cold and flu meds I pulled out for him.

I shook my head. I wasn't a doctor or a nurse, but I've been sick plenty and getting through the pandemic I recognized a fever; we all did. "I'll go and make you something to eat and fill up a big glass of water for you. Is there anything special you want?"

"Grilled cheese, maybe? I'm not that hungry."

"Okay."

I made my way out of our bedroom and headed

downstairs. In the kitchen, I pulled out everything to make a grilled cheese and grabbed one of our big glasses. I filled the container with cool water from the refrigerator and a few ice cubes; I didn't want the water too cold. After I got everything assembled and put on a plate, I headed up to our bedroom where Alejandro lay fast asleep. I inhaled, relieved. I ran a hand over his forehead; he still emitted warmth, but not too bad. I placed the plate with the sandwich on the nightstand, along with the glass of water. I figured he would be fine for a while, so I went back to work.

By the time I shut down my computer, I noticed a key unlocking the door and eyed my phone, tapping the device to activate the machine to see the clock. Chloe was home.

"Hey there, how were Jacky and Maggie? Did you have fun getting your hair done?" I went over and greeted her with a hug. "Did Jacky's mom want to come in?"

"No, she seemed to be in a hurry to leave."

"Well, I hope you thanked her for taking you." I smiled. "You know I could've done your braids for you."

Chloe rolled her eyes.

"Sorry, I forgot. My braid work isn't nearly as good," I teased. "Papa isn't feeling well, he's upstairs resting. Let's be quiet and not bother him."

"Weird," Chloe uttered through biting her lower lip.

"What?"

"When I got home, there was an ambulance outside the house next to the Patils'."

"Really?" I wandered to the front door, peeking outside. Sure enough, an ambulance was pulling away.

"I hope it's nothing serious." As the first ambulance headed off down Yerba Buena, a second ambulance arrived.

Chloe joined me at the front door. "What's happening?"

"I... I'm not sure." I waved over to Deepa. As she crossed

the street, she coughed and pulled her jacket tighter around her shoulders.

"I don't want to get too close." She stayed at the front of our driveway. "I'm not feeling very well, and neither is Vyan."

"Neither is Alejandro. He's upstairs."

"I talked to Dayo. She seemed really frazzled and upset. She shared that her and Fred were arguing about the new home and all the issues they've been having, especially with the sewage smell that they can't get rid of. Anyway, she told me Fred collapsed. Apparently he wasn't feeling well either."

"And now the Martins." I spotted the paramedics rush to the front door. "What's going on?"

Deepa shook her head. "I don't know, but I'm gonna get inside. I hope Alejandro feels better."

I stood in disbelief as I surveyed our neighborhood. Was this normal? Were we looking at the opening of another pandemic? I moved myself and Chloe into the house, closing and locking the door behind us.

"Dad, what's happening?" Chloe's bright eyes were wide. "We're not going to have to be locked down again, are we?"

I forced what I hoped was a pleasant expression on my face. "No. It's a summer cold or flu, but let's not take any chances. Go wash your hands and send Jacky a text thanking her and her mom for taking you out today. Let them know that your papa isn't feeling well, but that you feel fine and we agreed they should know."

"Alright." She rushed off and I made my way up to our bedroom. Alejandro sat, nibbling on the cold sandwich.

"It's not as good cold." He smiled.

"I can heat it up if you want?"

"No." He put the sandwich down and finished off the water.

"How are you feeling?" I walked over, placing a hand on

his forehead. His skin felt cooler to the touch and his color had returned.

"Tired, like all the energy's been drained from me."

"Well, you're not the only one sick." I sat on the edge of our bed. "Deepa came by. She's not feeling well, and I guess Vyan is sick too. The Williams, you know the white guy and the woman from Sudan, the older couple. I guess he collapsed. And now there's an ambulance at the Martins'."

"You're kidding." He tried to sit up as he leaned on the pillows.

"Deepa mentioned something about a sewage smell at the Williams' home. I wonder if those gasses are responsible for getting everyone sick, but I've been home all day and I haven't smelled a thing."

"I think we would all smell that." Alejandro chuckled with a crinkle of his nose. "You can't miss the smell of poop everywhere." He waved a hand in front of his face.

"I don't know. It's crazy. And like I said, nothing here today."

"Well, that's good... I heard Chloe come back. How do her braids look?"

"Perfect. I told her I'd do her hair, but she laughed at me."

"Honey, I love you, you are talented and you do a better job than me with Chloe's hair, but neither of us are black girls and I think giving her this as a treat is worth the price and peace of mind. Plus, she has all the babysitting money, so..." He shrugged.

"I know, I feel bad. I hated that she had to teach us about what she needed for her hair and how she needed to wrap her hair up for bed." I pulled off my glasses to look at the lenses. I would need to get my cloth.

Alejandro shifted on the bed. "But we learned."

He was right, we learned. I did a lot of research and talked to one of my office mates who had hair similar to Chloe's about what to do and what we can do to ensure she looked her best. I even had Chloe help me find the perfect shop for her to go to, which is where she met Jacky and Maggie.

I let Alejandro rest as I went to fix Chloe and myself something to eat for supper. I didn't feel like going all out, but I figured I'd do better than grilled cheese.

What happened over the next few hours, I couldn't believe. I never, in my life, had been that scared. After Chloe and I finished supper, more sirens filled the quiet of our home, so Chloe and I went to my office and peeked out the window. There were two more ambulances and a couple of police cars. Chloe and I shared a look. "Go play on your phone," I suggested.

"Dad, what's happening?"

"I don't know. I'm going to check on Alejandro, and I'll find out."

Chloe bit her lip. We both made our way upstairs, Chloe to her room and me to our bedroom to check on Alejandro. His eyes were closed and his head tilted off to the side. No color filled his face. "No!" I shouted and rushed over to him. "Alejandro." I called, patting his cheek. "Alejandro, baby, wake up." Tears filled my eyes, but he didn't seem to wake up. I did something I swore I would never do, and I slapped my husband as tears occupied my eyes. "Alejandro!"

"Daddy," Chloe called from behind me.

"Alejandro, wake up," I demanded, now shaking him. "Chloe, go—"

"Jesus." Alejandro's voice came out soft as he raised a hand to massage his cheek. "What the hell?"

I hugged him so tight. "Thank God."

"What? I was asleep."

"Chloe, come sit with your papa. I'm going to talk to

the police or paramedics and find out what the fuck is going on here."

"What?" Alejandro shifted.

Chloe rushed over and sat with Alejandro.

"I'll be right back."

I left our room and made my way downstairs to the front door. As I opened the door, Officer Lancey stood about to knock. Medical gloves engulfed her hands, and a mask covered her mouth and nose.

"Jesus," I yelped and took a step back.

"Good evening, Mr. Del Rosario. I didn't mean to startle you," the officer declared. "As you can see, there is a lot of excitement happening."

"What's going on?" I questioned. "There have been two ambulances earlier today and now all this. I have Alejandro upstairs sick and a daughter who's terrified."

Officer Lancey held up a blue gloved hand, her mask a tight fit around her nose and mouth. "That's what we're trying to find out. You said your husband isn't feeling well?"

"He came home from work today with a fever, and he's been resting, but..." I shook my head. "I worried he died or something. He had no color, and he lay there like a corpse. I slapped him and he woke up. I know that sounds crazy."

"How are you and your daughter feeling?" the officer asked.

"Fine. I've been home all day. Is it some kind of gas leak or something?"

"We're not sure."

"Should we take Alejandro to the doctor?"

"You said he's awake?"

"Yes."

"I'm going to ask the IC to have someone come and check

your house and your husband. Okay?"

"Jesus. Yes."

"What's happening?" Alejandro uttered from behind me, giving me a start.

"Mr. Del Rosario, your husband says you haven't been feeling well today?"

"No, I was burning up at work—"

"Where is your office? Was anyone else sick?"

"No, just me." Alejandro shook his head. "I work downtown on Second Street. Why?"

Officer Lancey made some notes. "You came home?" she prompted.

"I came home and soaked in a cold shower and took some meds, and I've been resting until a little bit ago."

"And you're feeling better?" the officer asked.

"That's right." He leaned against the wall. He still appeared paler than normal.

The officer spoke into her walkie and I left the door open as I took Alejandro into my office to sit down. Within a couple of minutes, a pair of paramedics—also masked and gloved up—were in our home, checking Alejandro. After what seemed like hours, the lead paramedic spoke. "Everything seems fine. I can't find anything wrong. Have you ever been diagnosed with anemia?"

"No." Alejandro shook his head.

"It's almost certainly like you thought…"

There was a scream from upstairs, followed by feet running down the stairs. I don't think I would've been able to move any faster if I had wings. I met Chloe halfway at the landing on the staircase.

"Chloe, what's wrong?"

"There's someone in my room. I was… Daddy, there's someone in my room, I saw them."

Officer Lancey spoke from behind me. "Take her downstairs. I'll check."

"Come on." I pulled Chloe's hand. "Let's let the officer do her job." I wrapped an arm around my daughter and pulled her downstairs.

"What's happening?" Alejandro demanded as the paramedics scanned us before checking on him again.

"Someone's in Chloe's room, we think."

"They were bigger than me. He had a funny hat on his head and some kind of long coat that came to here." She pointed to her knees. "Something hung from his side, but I didn't see. I couldn't see his face." She inhaled and I did my best to wipe at her tears. "They tried to grab me." She hiccupped, pulling closer to me.

"And you ran and screamed for help like you're supposed to." I hugged her, trying to fill her with all the strength and love I had.

We all waited in my office for Officer Lancey to return. When she reappeared, she shook her head. "Is it possible you mistook all the lights outside seeing a shadow?"

"My lights were on, there weren't any shadows. I was on my phone and…" She stopped. "Papa, it wasn't dark and I swear I'm not making it up."

"We believe you." Alejandro met my gaze. What Chloe had described sounded a lot like what we had both seen when we assumed someone broke into our house when we moved in.

"Okay," I declared. "Chloe, it's okay. Whoever was there is gone now. Right, Officer Lancey?"

"I checked the whole upstairs and no one is…"

Loud footsteps banged from our second floor and one of the doors slammed, causing everyone to jump. "Get them out of here now," Officer Lancey instructed to the paramedics.

It didn't take much instruction on our part. Chloe, Alejandro, the two paramedics, and I were out of my office on the sidewalk as two more officers rushed into our house.

"Papa, Daddy, what's going on?" Chloe asked.

"I don't know, but the police'll figure it out." Alejandro took our daughter's hand.

"Like they did the last time someone broke in," I snipped. I couldn't help my reaction. This was the second time someone got into our house and terrorized our family.

As the police searched our home, everyone in the neighborhood congregated out of their homes, either talking to emergency services or each other. Our street resembled a disaster zone, like we were hit by a twister or an earthquake, but there was no destruction; everything appeared ordinary and undamaged. By the time we were allowed in our house, none of us were sure what had happened. But that wasn't the end. The next day, we had people from PG&E, the San Jose Water Company, and the builders there checking everyone's homes. The invasion was awful and with all these people in and out of our homes we didn't have a moments peace. Finally, when the EPA showed up and people from the County came, they claimed to have found nothing. They tested the water, they examined the air, the ground, they ran tests for days, but no one identified why so many people got ill all of a sudden.

Even though that should have bothered me the most, it didn't. What bothered me the most was when Officer Lancey left our home that night, she came up to Alejandro and I after finishing the search of our home, not finding anything. The officers found our solid wood laundry room door busted, split down the middle, as if someone tried to break out into the hall. She couldn't explain how the door fractured in that way. She also told us that the first time she went up there, the door appeared fine and she had intentionally opened the door and left it open after she checked the rest of the upstairs.

I remember her taking my hand and her words chilled me to the core. "I'm sorry I can't do more. I don't think you're dealing with a *physical* intruder. Good luck." The words and how she squeezed my hand, not to mention how pale her face was even behind the mask. That's the thing that really got me. Her gaze met mine, as if she was holding back something; fear or terror, if I had to guess. Her words and her reaction were enough for me to never want to go into our house again, but I did. We all did. I believe that was our biggest mistake.

# ~ Chapter Six ~

After dealing with the media circus for the next couple of days and the constant questions from the various agencies as they tried to find a cause for the illnesses, we were glad to see things settle down. Once the media got bored with our local story, we were replaced by yet another mass shooting. I had to ask myself if we, as a country, were ever going to pull our heads out of our butts and find a way to deal with all this gun violence and mental illness affecting so many people. Regardless, I, well, we, were glad to see our street quiet again. Instead of replacing the door to the laundry room right away, we took the door off the hinges and rested the two pieces in the garage. I placed a call to the builder to find the cost of a replacement door and they stated they would replace our door at no charge, which, given all we've been through, was a nice offer. When I talked to Alejandro, he suggested we wait and see if anything else might need to be replaced.

As I clicked away on my keyboard, in the distance, a dog's barking pulled my attention to my office window and I peeked out. I noted how the sun beat down on the plants and street right beyond where I sat. A rumble and roar of a car shattered the rhythm of the neighborhood as it boomed down Yerba Buena. Our house lay relatively quiet today with Chloe out with her friends, so I was feeling productive. Now, if I could make these virtual meetings vanish. Since lockdown, people had become cyber meeting junkies, items that should easily be a phone call or email were now virtual meetings. Time was wasted, but that's how things worked these days. I moved from my chair to close the office window, glancing around my office, ensuring all my knickknacks and photos were in place and appeared neat. As I dropped into my chair, I pulled at the bottom of my shirt so it lay flat on my shoulders, guaranteeing when my image filled the screen that I appeared put together. Today I even wore jeans.

*I'm so over dressed for this meeting. I should go put on my basketball shorts.*

My lips pulled up in a smile at the notion. I pondered how many people only wore their underwear or pajama bottoms from the waist down while their upper half was dressed up. I glanced at the clock on my screen and peeked toward the ceiling. "Here we go," I muttered to no one and opened up my meeting invite. Within moments, familiar faces populated my screen. And another grin filled my face, not at seeing my co-workers, but at the idea that off-screen they were all in sweatpants, PJs, or potentially nothing at all. I greeted a few people before muting my mic and waited for the meeting to launch.

Like all virtual meetings, this one bled into all the others I had been on. I'm sure at one point there was a point to the meeting, but after twenty minutes the point and purpose of the meeting were lost on me. To be fair, not all meetings were a waste of time, but given how many meetings I had been a part of, I wasn't feeling today's.

My office grew a bit chilly as the meeting continued, which was fine. The AC helped keep me awake, and I hated being hot and sweaty.

The first ding of a private message pulled my attention from the meeting; however, I didn't have time to respond before my co-worker Larry mentioned me. "Kyle, you need to mute your mic, please," he declared.

"What?"

"Kyle, there is a lot of chatting and laughing, so maybe you need to close your office doors," Joan said.

I checked my mic. My computer was unmuted, but I'd have sworn I hit the mute button. "Sorry everyone, but the noise isn't coming from me. There's no one here."

Several people studied me.

I muted my mic again and responded in the chat:

*Better?*

No one was talking and everyone appeared to be watching me.

"Who's yelling?" Larry asked.

"Was that a scream?" Joan commented.

I peered around my office; nothing. Whatever came through the speakers wasn't something I noticed, but they were still saying the noise came from me and my computer. They might be picking up something from outside, or a cell phone. I got up and opened my office window… but nothing. No barking dog, no kids out playing in the park, no cars. Everything was quiet. Almost too quiet.

I moved to my computer and shook my head, and again I noticed my mic was active.

"I'm really sorry, everyone. I don't know what's happening. I'm not hearing what you're hearing, maybe it's inter—"

A boom from upstairs got my attention and I jumped. "I heard that." I glanced at my monitor. I faced the hallway and no one was there. Kids' feet ran down the stairs, forcing me to step further into the hall. Maybe Chloe came home and I didn't notice.

"Chloe?" I called out. "When did you get…" I expected to see her on the landing of the stairs, but nothing. Instead of seeing anyone, the sound of running down the stairs right toward me forced me to move. Two distinct sets of feet, one set smaller and one larger. My movements were a mix between a jump and run as I backed into the wall. "What the hell?" I shouted.

"Kyle, get out of there," someone shouted from my monitor. Whatever they were hearing, I now experienced, too.

I glanced around the hall and moved immediately into the dining room. I turned toward the kitchen, but there was no one. I focused toward the family room, nada. The house had again fallen silent. Only the banging of my heart in my head echoed in my home. I inhaled with another survey of the space, satisfied. I moved into my office.

"Did you see that?" someone shouted and pointed at their screen.

"Kyle, is there's someone in the house with you?"

"Call the police," another of my co-workers shouted.

"Kyle." Larry called my name. "Kyle."

I focused and inhaled as deep as possible, releasing a lung full of air, forcing myself to calm down.

"What's going on?" Wayne asked. "Are you okay?"

"Did you see anything?" Maria pointed as she asked. "I swear I spotted a woman and a boy. She wore a short skirt made of animal skin or plant fibers, or something very indigenous. I couldn't see, could you? And the little boy had on shorts or something, and they both had long black hair."

"I watched them rush by the camera," Larry commented. "I would swear they were Native American."

"I... I didn't see... I heard... what are you saying?" I asked, glancing at the monitor. "I swear there were people running, but I didn't see anything. Are you guys messing with me?"

"I can assure you." Joan's frown was countered by her large focused eyes. "We are not messing with you and I'm wondering the same thing about you."

"No. I swear I wasn't doing any of this." I forced my face and my beating heart to relax. "Sorry about all this craziness. I wish I had an explanation. My neighbor across the street is a software engineer, so maybe it's something she's working on." I shrugged, not believing my own words, but I didn't have any other explanation.

"Do you need to leave the meeting?" Joan asked, as she tried to refocus our conversation.

"No. Let's continue." I forced out the air in my lungs as I spoke. I also took the opportunity to pull out my headset, plugged the device in, and adjusted the settings. I hoped this would solve the problem for my co-workers and for me.

I'm not sure what happened during the rest of the meeting and I don't think my co-workers wanted to press me on the matter. The meeting came to an end and, when I checked my instant messages, I had several notes from some of the people I'm close with and a few who had been to our housewarming. They were all concerned for Alejandro, and Chloe, and me. I'm still not sure what I had experienced during that meeting, but I decided from then on I would only wear my headphones during my meetings. No more pulling from my computer mic and speakers; I didn't want to get in trouble.

After that meeting I did some digging around on social media, seeing if I may be able to find information on Reza. I remembered how fascinated he was with the supernatural and I had no doubt, at the time, he would go into the field. However, after we broke up, we lost touch. It wasn't like we had a bad breakup, but we moved in different directions. And Social Media wasn't like it is today. Unfortunately, I didn't find what I was looking for that afternoon.

*I should ask Chloe she'd be able to find the information in a heartbeat.*

Somehow, I managed to finish out my work day. I had

to wonder if what I experienced had something to do with Alejandro and the rest of the neighborhood getting sick. But how were they linked? How might any of this be happening?

I turned off my phone and put the device on my night-stand. I focused on watching Alejandro crawl in next to me. "Are you sure about the noises? It sounds crazy."

"You read the messages from my co-workers. I have no idea what they witnessed, because I didn't see anything, but I heard something. The running was insane. Like when we caught the guy in the house. I'm not making this up."

"I never said you were."

"I know…" I raked a hand through my hair. I didn't see the point in mentioning my limited social media research for Reza. Not like I found anything, still I didn't want to upset Alejandro. "Everyone had to point out to me at first what was going on. I didn't hear anything."

"Did you say anything to Chloe?"

"No way. It would freak her out." I shook my head.

"Good." Alejandro shifted in our bed, pulling at the comforter and letting one of his feet hang out. "She's been dealing with enough."

"Haven't we all?" I frowned.

"Come here." Alejandro pulled me close to him and wrapped an arm around me. The warmth from his body filled me with comfort. Here with him was the best I had felt since my work meeting. "Maybe you should keep your camera off from now on." He kissed my forehead.

"I know you're teasing, but Joan sent me an email suggesting the same thing."

"She did?" He faced me.

"Yep. I think she assumed that I was messing with every-one. I told her I would, and that I would wear my headphones."

"Hopefully that'll help." He sighed.

"Maybe I should start going to the office more," I suggested. I didn't want to; I enjoyed the flexibility of working at home. I was able to take care of things here at home and not have to worry about being away from the office.

"And what about Chloe?" Alejandro asked.

"Well, she's twelve." I inhaled deeply, snuggling next to him. "But no, maybe I'll wait until she's starts school."

Alejandro kissed the top of my head again. "It'll be fine."

I glanced at our bedroom door and peeked around our room. What was happening here?

We didn't know what we were in for. After the initial shock and surprise had worn off from my work ordeal, no one said much to me, but I always had a feeling that everyone focused more on me and my virtual window than on any agenda item. A benefit of the encounter had been the number of virtual meetings I received decreased—at least, for a couple of months. The meetings were replaced instead by an uptick in emails and phone calls, which I was honestly fine with.

Since that ghostly virtual meeting, only my close work friends asked about what was happening at our house. They were worried for us. I never shared everything with them. I comprehended how crazy our encounters sounded. Everyone else at the office and who were on call with me that day, I suspected, were happy to live in blissful ignorance. I was jealous. I wish that had been an option for us, but we weren't that lucky. As far as work went, I made sure I kept my camera off and my headphones on for meetings, unless I had to present materials or report on my projects. Luckily, I suppose, I never had an encounter while I attended a work meeting again. For me, work remained my safe space, most of the time.

# ~ Chapter Seven ~

By the middle of July, we were planning our trip to Hawaii. We would be staying at the Aulani for a week, and I couldn't wait. Chloe had been doing more babysitting and getting to know all the kids on our street. Her hustle impressed me. Still, with everything going on not only at work with the loss of one of my co-workers, but with everyone in our house on edge, we'd been at each other's throats for the smallest things. I was annoyed as I turned down our street. Traffic had been ridiculous on the drive home, which we should have considered before moving here. Unfortunately, what greeted me wasn't a nice, quiet street, but a street partially blocked by a moving van in front of the Williams' home. Inhaling several times to cool my temper, I got out of my car, hit in the face with the warm summer day. I noticed Dayo barking orders in the front yard of her house.

I put on what I hoped was a warm smile. "Hi." I waved. "Everything okay?"

"No!" Dayo snapped, wiping her brow. "This house is bad. I'm leaving." She waved a finger at me. "I tell Fred I didn't want move here, but he no listen. Now I go." She sneered at the house.

"Well, we're sorry to see you and your husband leave."

"Not husband, only me. Maybe he get smart and come, but he stay… foolish man. Let him deal with little children and *shabah*. Not me, I no leave my country to deal with…" She waved her hands.

"Oh," I uttered, not sure what more to say and honestly

53

not in the mood to listen to her. Also, if she was unhappy about the kids in the neighborhood, maybe they should have moved to a condo or townhouse. Anyway, clearly, they weren't getting along and she had had enough.

"Take care," I waved.

She muttered something under her breath.

Turning to my house, I waved at the camera over our garage. It was a joke. I couldn't believe Alejandro wasted money on the dumb thing. The cameras were always going off during the day, triggered by nothing but a shadow or a bird or squirrel. The incessant notifications on my phone got to the point where I turned them off. If Alejandro wanted the cameras so badly, he'd deal with all the messages. I had other things to worry about and take care of.

So, I waved at the camera. I did it every time I got home, especially hearing that the device was recording me. I glanced over at the park, seeing Chloe out with a couple of neighbor kids. I was pretty sure she was with Miguel and Cynthia and the boy from the end of the street—I couldn't remember his name. Also hanging around with them were the Chens' kids and a dog. At least she was making friends, even if they were sitting on the grass looking at their phones while the dog ran around trying to get their attention. I'm glad I grew up when I did. I deliberated if we were being foolish for getting her a cell phone at this age. Only time would tell.

"Maybe we should get a dog. Or a cat," I commented to no one as I pulled out my keys to open the door, only to find the door unlocked and ajar. I huffed, my nerves already frayed. I don't know how many times I had to tell Chloe to lock and close the door, especially after the break-in when we moved in. Sure, she was in the park across the street, but still, something might have happened.

"Jesus." I shivered. The house was impossibly cold. I

stopped at the thermostat, and the device showed 70 degrees. I shook my head. There was no way the house was 70—more like 50, but I didn't want to open the windows because outside we were hovering over 90 degrees.

*The AC's probably on the fritz again.*

I shook my head and placed my keys and phone on the small table by the front door. I made my way to the kitchen to pull things out for dinner. I wanted something simple and fresh. I opened the refrigerator and pulled out a bag of mixed greens and some other veggies. My plan was to make a big grilled chicken salad. The meal wasn't fancy, but we had everything we needed in the house, and eating in was a hell of a lot better than eating out, which I felt like we had been doing too much of these past few weeks.

I stopped and headed to the foyer to grab my phone to turn on some music. At the table, both my phone and keys were gone.

"What the hell?" I glanced at the tray I always left them on, nothing. I checked the floor. I walked into my office and checked my desk… nothing.

"Great!"

I went to the powder room. Not finding anything there, I commenced my search. By the time the front door opened and closed, I was beyond frustrated. I had been up and down the stairs multiple times and was in the process of checking under our bed.

"Hello," the familiar voice of our daughter met my stressed ears.

Chloe had gotten home.

"Where have you been, young lady?" I demanded as I moved from our bedroom.

"I was at the park. Didn't you see me?"

"And why the hell did you leave the front door open?"

I barked at my daughter. I had no idea where all this anger came from, but I was tired of games and being disrespected in my own home.

"Dad, I didn't—"

"Enough! Give me your phone."

"What?"

"I said, give me your phone. You've lost your phone and tablet privilege, young lady. Now hand it over."

"But I... I locked the door. I—"

"God dammit, Chloe! Give me your fucking phone right now, and I want my keys and phone this instant!" I demanded. "And get upstairs to your room, and if you're lucky, I'll call you when dinner's ready."

I burned with anger. I didn't see or hear Alejandro come through the door and I'm so glad he did. I wasn't sure what I was going to do to Chloe. Looking back, I'm terrified that I might have actually hurt her in that moment.

"What's going on?" Alejandro met us at the stairs.

"Papa, I swear I locked the door." Her eyes were so big and white. She was terrified. "I was at the park and I didn't take Dad's phone or his keys. I just got home, honest."

He smiled at her. "You're fine. Go watch TV." He ran a hand over her head and smiled as she rushed off.

"No surprise you're taking her side!" I shouted. "This doesn't surprise me in the least. You two always off and plotting and laughing at me. You think I don't know, but I do. I see a lot more than you think I do, Alejandro," I continued to yell at him. "And don't think I've missed those Social Media pages you watch, when you don't think I notice. Trust me I notice."

"Kyle, what're you talking about? Our daughter is upset and your keys and phone..." He pointed to the table by the front door. "Right where you leave them every day. What's wrong with you?"

"But I—" One would have hoped I would have calmed down, but as I glanced at the table where my keys and phone sat, venom continued to pour from my mouth, each word meant to deliver as much poison as possible. I wanted to wound them. "You're both fucking with me, aren't you? This is bullshit. No wonder Dayo said what she said about the neighborhood kids. They're all brats, including Chloe." I stormed past him, snatching my keys and phone. "I'm going out. Do whatever the fuck you want for dinner. I don't give a shit. In fact, why don't you take her out for ice cream, like you do after her therapy appointments, thinking I don't know. You realize I see the charges on the banking statement, right?"

"Kyle…" Alejandro stood frozen in place, the pain from my words hitting as hard and direct as I intended. His expression shifted as sadness and confusion found a home on his face.

"There're times like now where I miss Reza, or the other guys before you," I snarled. "They all knew their way around the bedroom and could really make my toes curl, not like you with that fucking deformed banana dick of yours."

I didn't hear him as I seized my things and slammed our entry door as I left. I needed to get out of our house and away from the two of them. They were always plotting. There was no way we'd ever all live in peace.

I didn't know where I was headed as I marched up the street and turned down Yerba Buena on my walk, but the farther I got from the house, the more my anger vanished and within ten minutes, I had no idea what had gotten into me. I stopped at the wooden fence where the establishment of the trail along the creek began, right next to the college. I leaned up against the wood, shaking my head as the banging in my chest and head slowed.

"Where did all that anger come from?" I questioned as I glanced around. The afternoon summer air was warm on my skin and the heat helped me feel a lot better. I continued to enjoy the afternoon air, but the longer I stood there, the more shame filled my heart for all I shouted and how I acted. Losing my cool over keys and a phone I overlooked, and the front door being unlocked.

I waited another half hour before I made my way home. I reached Golden Hills Court glancing down the street. Ten perfect new homes. With ten, now nine, families. From the outside, everything appeared flawless, but who knew what happened in each of those homes? Who understood what kind of darkness lay behind each of the new doors, behind the new windows and blinds? I stopped staring at everything and nothing all at the same time. The sky was crisp and clear; the air filled with subtle hints of alfalfa or grass. In the distance, a dog barked as several birds took to flight. I inhaled and walked to our front door and slowly opened the door. I had some apologies to make and a lot of crow to eat. I would need to start with Chloe. The poor thing doubtlessly thinks I hate her and nothing could be farther from the truth.

I slipped my phone in my pocket and placed my keys on the tray where they belonged. I moved down the hall toward our living space. I caught Alejandro's eye and mouthed the words: I'm sorry. Alejandro accepted my peace offering, and he dutifully continued putting together the salad. He motioned to Chloe sitting on the couch, flipping through the TV. I walked over to her. "May I speak with you?" My tone was soft and gentle.

She turned off the TV.

"Dad, I didn't take anything and I swear—"

"I know and I'm sorry." I relaxed my neck and shoulders. I wasn't mad anymore, flustered mainly at myself, and definitely embarrassed for my earlier behavior. "I was wrong to accuse you. If you say you locked the front door, you locked the door. I probably unlocked the door myself, not thinking."

"You believe me?" Her frown twisted into a bit of a pensive smile, but her eyes filled with relief.

"Absolutely. I was bothered and annoyed with Mrs. Williams. She said some things about the kids in the neighborhood as part of the reason she was leaving. And that bothered me, because you're such a great kid. Plus, and this is not an excuse, I had a long, difficult day at the office. One of my co-workers suddenly passed away."

"Oh, hon, when? Who?" Alejandro asked from the kitchen. "One of the guys from our San Diego office, last night, I think, we got the notice today. You never met him, but he was a good guy and we worked on a lot of projects together."

"I'm sorry, Dad," Chloe declared.

"You have nothing to apologize for. I took my bad feelings out on you and Papa. I'm the one who is sorry. I should know better. And I should know how to deal with my feelings."

Chloe pulled at the corner of the pillow, suddenly fascinated with the fabric. I understood what she wanted to ask before she found the words. "Can I still have my phone?" She glanced from the pillow over her shoulder to the dining table. "I haven't touched it since you told me not to. I swear, you can ask Papa."

"Oh Chloe, I'm sorry." I stretched over and hugged her. "Yes, you can have your phone, after dinner," I added. "I want to enjoy our family with none of our devices."

"Okay." She hugged me.

As I sat hugging my daughter, I reflected on the mix of lies I told her. I never realized how much we all lie on a daily basis. My lies weren't hurtful. Well, not to anyone but me, I suppose. I hadn't overlooked my keys or my phone; they weren't on the table. The front door was unlocked and open when I got home. I always try the handle before I put my key in, to ensure everything is okay and today nothing appeared okay. Checking the door had been something I've always done, since I was Chloe's age. I didn't like being surprised, especially after what happened with Reza and me. Or maybe I was afraid of someone or something being in the house. These were the modest lies I told myself. These lies didn't stop there. I continued to tell myself everything was fine in our new home. There was nothing wrong with the house or our neighborhood, but those lies… well, those lies did end up hurting people.

# ~ Chapter Eight ~

Flipping through my phone as we waited, I found a couple of images that always gave me a chuckle. I elbowed Alejandro and showed him my phone. He smiled and shook his head as he focused on his phone. Typically, I didn't attend Chloe's therapy sessions, but Dr. Wilson asked to see both of us. Honestly, I was grateful to be out of the house. Since my blow up, the three of us continued to trade barbs over the stupidest things. We were constantly squabbling and getting on each other's nerves. The only time we got along was when we were away from the house. We needed the vacation and, as a surprise, I upgraded Alejandro, Chloe, and myself to first class. It would be a nice treat and given all we'd been through we deserved the extra pampering.

"You sit here and wait?" I put my phone away.

Alejandro glanced over at me. "Pretty much. There're some magazines that you can flip through." He half-chuckled as he responded.

"I don't say this enough, especially lately, but thank you for doing this with her."

"Honestly, I don't mind." Alejandro put away his phone. "It gives me time to zone out and relax." He leaned his head back. "Sitting doing nothing honestly feels nice every now and then… you should try it."

I glanced at the leafy plant in the corner. If memory serves, the shrub was a China Doll. Whatever the plant's name, it was definitely pretty.

A click caught my attention as the door to the doctor's

office opened and Chloe walked out, her normal smile missing from her face and her shoulders drooped.

"How was your conversation?" I asked, worried that something terrible had happened in there.

She shrugged and took a seat, pulling out her phone.

"Kyle. Alejandro." Dr. Wilson stood at the office door, her honey brown hair hit right at her shoulders, and her hazel eyes peered at us through her glasses as she focused on us. "Care to join me?" She stepped to the side, her spring top hung loosely over her bigger frame. Not the most flattering cut, but the colors worked for her.

I stood up, peeked at Chloe, and glanced at Alejandro. He smiled, clearly used to this. We made our way into the doctor's office.

Dr. Wilson's office had a couch, a couple of soft-sided chairs, a desk with a high-back chair, and several bookcases, filled with hundreds of books. I swear the room looked more like a library than an office, but since she was a therapist, I figured she needed a lot of reference material. To one side, an area had been set up for a child to play and there lay a box of toys. Alejandro and I sat on the couch. The softness engulfed me.

Dr. Wilson sat in one of the soft sided chairs.

"Thank you both for agreeing to be here." Dr. Wilson's words had a hint of maybe a Boston accent or possibly North Eastern U.S. I couldn't quite place it, but if I remembered correctly, she originated from that part of the country. I wanted to say Bangor, or she may have been from somewhere outside of Providence.

"Anything to ensure Chloe is getting what she needs," Alejandro stated with a note of finality.

I bobbed my agreement, not completely sure what to say and still worrying about my daughter outside the door.

Dr. Wilson smiled. "Well, in general, Chloe is an amazing girl. Very sensitive, bright, and kind. You both should be proud."

"We like to think she's a great kid and we couldn't be prouder." My heart swelled with pride as the warmth of my affection for our daughter bubbled inside me. "But she didn't look happy and I don't think you'd call us both here to tell us how terrific our daughter is," I prodded. I didn't want to spend any more time with Dr. Wilson than we needed. Not that I had any issues with therapy, I didn't like wasting time, especially when it came to Chloe's mental health.

"No, you're right." Dr. Wilson shifted how she sat, crossing her right ankle over her left. "With the move and the new school year coming up, Chloe's mentioned to me that there has been a lot of tension in the house. That you all seem to be fighting, more than before."

Alejandro and I glanced at each other. I ran a hand over my chin, the stubble scratching my fingers and palm.

"There has been a lot of stress," Alejandro affirmed with a shake of his head as he spoke. "A bunch of us on our street got sick. The city assumed there might be something in the water, or dirt, or something."

"I remember that," Dr. Wilson admitted. "Several of your neighbors went to the hospital, at least according to the news."

"And they never figured out the cause." Alejandro frowned. Dr. Wilson made a few notes on her pad.

"There was also the break-in when we first moved in." I shook my head. "The police didn't find anything, and we weren't much help with the description." I pulled off my glasses. "We didn't want to lie to Chloe about what happened, especially when we got the cameras for the house." I focused on the doctor's bookshelf and deliberated if she had time to read all those books. "But we tried to keep our worry to a minimum," I added, focusing on the doctor.

"That's all important. Thank you for sharing, but I'm more interested in the arguments you've all been having. Chloe mentioned you left." Dr. Wilson leaned a bit forward, focusing on me.

I glanced at Alejandro, sat deeper into the sofa, and faced the doctor. "Not one of my finer moments. I lost my cool the other day at Chloe. I got home, and I assumed she left the front door unlocked, then I misplaced my keys and phone. The whole incident was stupid. But I got angry." I still couldn't believe the visceral hatred and anger I experienced at that moment. "We got into a bit of a fight, and I…well… I kind of stormed off and went for a walk to cool off." I licked my lips, trying to downplay the event despite the growing knot in my stomach. "But I came home, and we talked, and everything was good."

Dr. Wilson didn't say anything as she continued to study me.

"At least I imagined we were okay." I tapped my hands on my leg. "I really scared her?"

"That wasn't the only time. We all have been fighting a lot more, including Chloe. We assumed the fighting was because she's going to be a teenager; puberty and all." Alejandro raked a hand through his hair.

"How have her *periods* been for the two of you?" Dr. Wilson asked.

At the mention of Chloe menstruating, I wanted to crawl into a ball with my hands over my ears going, la la la la. But that wouldn't help.

"I mean, I guess okay." I forced out my words. "Her… ah… cycles haven't been super regular yet, but I think we're all getting the hang of things. That first time was…." I rubbed my eye. "Well, you can imagine."

Dr. Wilson tapped her pen on her notepad.

"Look, Dr. Wilson, Marsha, these fights aren't hormones. They happen all the time and over stupid things: lights left on, not tucking in the chairs in the dining room, leaving the water on in the bathroom, messing with the security cameras, the computer. It's all been petty, but in those moments..." Alejandro leaned forward. "You see red... it's terrifying."

"Given Chloe's past with her mother, and the abuse there, I think she's worried that..."

"Dr. Wilson," I had to interrupt. "We would never do that to Chloe. Never." I leaned in, focusing on the doctor's face. "She doesn't think we would... God... Alejandro." I dropped back, resting a hand on my forehead. Is that what she assumed? Is that how we're acting? The poor baby.

"I don't think Chloe's worried about anything like that." Dr. Wilson's voice filled with assurance. "But she's young and all the fighting, no matter how minimal, can trigger her, even if she's doing the fighting." She smiled. "Seeing how upset the two of you are about these events as adults? Imagine what it's like for Chloe."

"We're awful. This whole thing is terrible." My hand began tapping on my leg, and my stomach grew into a larger jumble of knots.

"Dr. Wilson..." Alejandro kicked off, not looking at me. "Can something in the house cause this?"

She leaned forward. "What do you mean?"

I glanced at Alejandro. He still wouldn't look at me. "Alejandro?"

"A few days ago, Kyle was on a work call and..."

"Alejandro, not now." I rested my hand on his knee. I didn't want to say anything to make the doctor think we were crazy, and my work story wasn't something I wanted shared with anyone who didn't need to know. As much as I respected Dr. Wilson, we didn't know her, and I didn't think she needed to hear this insane story.

"Kyle…" Dr. Wilson leaned closer to us and focusing on me again. "Did something happen at work that Chloe might have overheard? Is everything okay with your job?"

Alejandro glanced at me. "Tell her." He bit his bottom lip.

I licked my lips and sat on my hands to keep them from moving as I told her the story. "You're going to think I'm crazy…"

"Trust me, Kyle, I won't think you're crazy. I've listened to plenty in my career." She adjusted how she sat. A glow of encouragement radiated from her face as she encouraged me to open up.

I cleared my throat and told her what happened on my virtual call with work. How my co-workers heard noises coming from the house, noises I didn't hear. I didn't want to include the bit about them seeing a woman and a little boy, but I figured in for a penny, in for a pound. Before I stopped sharing, I provided many plausible explanations as to what happened. Even as I spoke these rationalizations I didn't believe them, but I also didn't want to end up in a mental hospital for observation.

"Have you seen anything… odd, Alejandro?" Dr. Wilson glanced at my husband.

I'm not sure if I witnessed relief on his face, but I noticed how pale he had become.

"Just… on the day someone broke into our house and when I was sick…" He rubbed his chin. "Look, what I thought I saw was undoubtedly a dream, but when I lay there sick, I swear there were several Native American people standing around me. Watching me." He focused on the floor, not looking at the doctor or me. "A woman and a boy, and two men and a little girl. They scrutinized me, like they were trying to figure out who… or what I was. I felt like I didn't belong there, I knew it, and I think they knew it too." He shook his head. "The woman and boy matched the description you gave me." He turned to me, his eyes as large as saucers.

"You never said." I wrapped my arm around Alejandro.

"I know how crazy all these things sound, but when you told me about the call and what your co-workers shared…" Alejandro faced the doctor. "Can something in our house be causing all this? Can there be something I don't… this is all crazy."

After what felt like hours of silence, Dr. Wilson spoke. "You're asking me if I think your home is haunted and affecting your moods and your family?" She leaned back, adjusting her glasses on her face. "Well, I've never seen any proof of ghosts that couldn't be explained away as a trick of the light or something completely mundane, like a gust of wind or a power surge."

"So, we're crazy and you're going to have them take Chloe from us." I shook my head. We shouldn't have disclosed anything. No one ever believes in these things actually happening. I pulled off my glasses rubbing the worry out of my eyes.

*Well, that's not true. But I didn't want to believe back then. I was the one who didn't believe.*

"I'd never say you're crazy, and I'm certainly not going to have anyone take Chloe from you." Dr. Wilson smiled and rested her hands on her lap. "You've moved into a new home. There's a lot of stress, and given the bullying Chloe went through at her last school, compounded with the arguments at home, I think your vac—"

"Papa! Dad!" Chloe yelled as something crashed from the lobby.

"What the…" Both Alejandro and I were at the door,

trying to open it with no success.

"It won't open." Alejandro banged on the door. "Chloe!" he shouted.

"The door doesn't have a lock." Dr. Wilson pushed past us and struggled with the door, playing with the handle. "I can't—" Another crash from behind the door, this one not as loud as the first one.

There was a scream from the lobby.

"Chloe!" I yelled, standing there, useless, as Alejandro and Dr. Wilson tried to open the stuck door.

"Dr. Wilson, the door!" Alejandro demanded.

"I'm trying," Dr. Wilson called out. "It won't. Chloe, sweetie, get away from the door. I can't open it with you holding the knob."

"Make it stop!" Chloe yelled. "Go away! Papa! Dad! I'm not at the door."

"Chloe, we're coming!" I found myself banging on the door.

"That's it," Alejandro bellowed. "Move."

I grabbed Dr. Wilson and pulled her out of the way as Alejandro took several steps.

"Chloe, get away from the door," Alejandro called out, glancing at Dr. Wilson, whose eyes were the size of saucers and her skin as pale as a white piece of paper. "We're going to…"

The door popped open with a click and the three of us rushed into the lobby. The box of tissues that had sat on the coffee table flew across the room, hitting the main door to the office. I scanned the room for Chloe. In the corner on the floor, Chloe hugged her knees to her chest with her head buried, hiding. I got to her as she grasped up to me. I snatched her off the floor, not sure where my strength came from. As we glanced around the lobby, every light was going crazy.

On

Off

On

Off

None of them were in sync, all flickering at different intervals.

"Dr. Wilson, what's happening?" Alejandro moved to Chloe and me. "What's going on?"

The China Doll, the leafy plant that was on the stand in the corner that I admired, now lay on the floor, dirt spilled from the container. Several of the magazines on the side table had been thrown about the room and were now scattered all over the floor. If the woman were any paler, I didn't know how.

"This shouldn't—" Dr. Wilson stammered. "The lights. My plant." Her voice broke. "The power."

The lights continued going crazy.

Chloe's head was firmly buried in my shoulder.

I shook my head. "We're getting out of—"

As quickly as the event commenced, everything ended. Silence filled the space. As I glanced around, nothing. It was over. I put Chloe down and the four of us stood amongst the chaos, taking in the room, the lights, and the doors.

"I was on my phone. When the plant fell over." Chloe swallowed and shook her head. "All at once the lights and the magazines… Papa, what's happening? Can we go home? I want to go home."

"Go on." I squeezed Alejandro's arm. "Get Chloe out of here. I'll be there shortly."

Alejandro examined me. "Are you sure?" His eyes were wide.

"I'll be right there."

I took several deep breaths as they left the office, trying

to calm my frayed nerves. I bent down and picked up the magazines, placing them on the side table. Dr. Wilson stood in the middle of her destroyed lobby as I moved to the plant and picked the greenery up and got the container and China Doll returned to the stand. Some dirt remained on the floor, but that'd get cleaned up later. I moved to the tissue box, picked the pink-colored box up and held it in my hands. "We all watched this fly at the door," I moved the box up and down. "A tissue box can't suddenly fly through the air."

"No." Dr. Wilson bit at her fingernail, not taking the tissue box.

"What's happening to us?"

"It must have been the wind from the window, or the AC." Dr. Wilson's gazed bounced around the space as color slowly returned to her face. "Yes, of course, the AC, it's been acting funny for weeks now, and the landlord hasn't gotten it repaired." The words barely audible.

"And the lights?" I asked, continuing to hold the box out, but the doctor wouldn't take it.

"Maybe a power surge. Or some kind of energy flicker."

"And your office door?" I examined her, waiting to hear what she would say next. "Three of us tried that door and the damn thing wouldn't open. We step back and pop…"

"I… I don't… panic… we all panicked." Dr. Wilson continued to work on her fingernail. "Trying to get to Chloe."

I bit my lips. What else was there to say or do? Predictably she had the same level of denial on her face as I knew I had on my own, or Alejandro on his, and what I witnessed on Chloe's. Our minds have a wonderful capacity to find a logical explanation where none exists. I put the tissue box on the coffee table and glanced at the doctor. I didn't know what to say to her as she stood there, shock filling her expression, but her color returned slowly. Still, she stood in the room like a statue.

"I'll see Chloe next week," Dr. Wilson's voice squeaked out.

"Are you sure?"

"Yes, I won't abandon her or any of you. Not now. I can't." Dr. Wilson's voice grew firmer and more determined as she walked over to me. "I'm scared. That terrified me, but I'm sure there is a logical explanation..." She swallowed. "And even if there isn't, I can't and will not abandon her, nor you."

"Thank you." I reached out and took the doctor's hand. "Thank you." There were tears dancing on the edges of my eyes.

"Be careful, Kyle. Please be careful." She squeezed my hand. "Has anything like this happened to you or Alejandro before?"

I froze as my gaze dropped to the floor. "Yes... once... a long time ago, but I refused to believe these events are related. I ignored the activity before, or tried to laugh it off as a fun adventure." I shook my head.

Dr. Wilson's gaze met mine. "I don't think you can afford to ignore this now."

With a final motion of thanks and agreement, I left the office, headed out to my husband and daughter. They needed me. We needed each other. And Dr. Wilson was correct, we couldn't afford to ignore any of this.

To Dr. Marsha Wilson's credit, she didn't forsake us. She kept her weekly appointments with Chloe and, if anything, our shared experience made Chloe's sessions easier because now Chloe realized, as we all did, that the doctor provided as much help as possible. Even if Dr. Wilson only listened and helped us deal with the emotional toll these events took on us, that was enough. I'll tell you now. Knowing you aren't crazy and that people believe you, at least on some level, makes a difference. We weren't alone in this, even though most of the time we believed we were. Dr. Wilson couldn't help us with our paranormal trouble, but she didn't shun us either, like some people did, and we were happy to have her support, especially once things got categorically bad.

# ~ Chapter Nine ~

Our trip couldn't come fast enough. The next few days had been tense. A few days after Dayo Williams moved out, right as I got home, Fred rushed out to his car, his clothes in hand. He tossed his wad of clothes in the back seat of his car and pulled out of the driveway. He barreled down the street, almost hitting the Patils' son's car. I couldn't believe him. I hardly talked to him, or his wife, but from what I noticed, that man appeared terrified. I continued to observe Derek across the street, still not understanding what I had witnessed.

"What was that all about?" I asked and walked to the end of our driveway.

"I don't know, man, maybe all the crazy shit happening here," he exclaimed.

"What'cha mean?"

"First, a bunch of us get sick, then all the problems with the electricity and Internet." He shook his head. "We've all had to replace our phones. And what about those smells… this place…"

"What smells?"

"Oh, you guys haven't had problems with sewage gas in your home? Mercedes been complaining to the builder for weeks. It's insane. Then the…" His voice quivered and he shook his head. "Anyway, we're thinking our dream home is cursed."

"Well, if it helps, we've been broken into twice and for whatever reason, the water in our house never gets hot. Well, that's not true; the water never gets hot for me." I raked a hand through my hair.

"You know the Martins…" He pointed to the house two doors from ours, on our side of the road.

"Not really. They don't talk much."

"No, I guess not." Derek continued. "Well, their daughter had a seizure and he had a heart attack, or what turned out to be an anxiety attack, on the same day. You know, the day everyone got sick."

"What?" I bit my upper lip. "Little Sammy. I had no idea about Ken either, but that day, we were going through it too."

"This place." He shook his head. "I'm heading to the store. All our dairy spoiled, again. We bought it two days ago."

My mouth opened. I didn't know what to say to that. "Take care. Let me know if you still want Chloe to babysit Jr. and Diane this weekend."

"Definitely. Mercedes and I need a break, and I think the kids do as well." Derek waved and got into his car.

I made my way into the house, glancing over my shoulder at our street. How unlucky could one group of people be? It was Wednesday and I would be home alone as Alejandro and Chloe were off at her therapy appointment. I inhaled. I felt frustration grow inside my stomach. The minute I got through the door, a seed of disdain that I didn't even know existed in my gut grew into a full grown tree. Instead of letting myself get worked up, I fired off a text to Alejandro that I was going for a bike ride.

Since my blow up at Chloe and our appointment with Dr. Wilson, I decided to work off some of my stress. I began biking again. I headed upstairs, changed out of my work clothes and put on my padded bike shorts and shirt.

My phone dinged and I walked over, grabbing the device, and checked the message:

Enjoy your ride. Don't hurt anything I might want to

play with later.

He ended the message with an eggplant emoji and winky emoji.

I laughed and responded:

Tease.

I slipped my phone in my shorts pocket and made my way downstairs to the garage. Grabbing my bike and helmet, I decided to bring the bike out the front door so I could make damn sure the entry was locked.

Out in the afternoon air, I was good. I made my way down Yerba Buena, through the college grounds and out to the hiking and biking trail. From there I crossed the bridge and headed down Ruby through the village square and along the road past the high school. I decided to tackle Norwood Avenue and head up Mt. Pleasant Road. The route I took was all uphill, not easy, but there weren't a lot of cars and the views up in the hills were worth the effort. Plus, I ended up meeting up with Ruby, so my ride made a nice circle. When all was said and done, the route I went ended up being about fifteen miles and was a great workout.

Once home and feeling exhausted, but in a good way, I expected Alejandro and Chloe to be home, and I was right. I dropped my bike on the porch and opened the front door. "I'm home."

"How was your ride?" Alejandro called from the kitchen.

"Good." I closed the door and headed into the kitchen, unstrapping my helmet. "Where's Chloe?"

"On her phone, in the house somewhere." Alejandro laughed.

"How was her session?"

Alejandro shook his head back and forth. "Good, I think. They both seemed fine when we left." He glanced at me and put the knife down he had used to cut some carrots. Walking over to me, he gave me a kiss, his hand finding the front of my bike shorts. "How are my boys? They going to be ready for me later tonight?"

I kissed him and took his hand, holding him there a moment, allowing him to feel my buck under his touch, signaling him on how ready things were already getting.

"Yum." He kissed me again and stepped away. "Go get cleaned up. Dinner'll be ready soon."

"Oh, such a tease." I adjusted myself in my shorts so my bits and bobs weren't super noticeable.

"No… I'm making you have your dinner before you get dessert."

I laughed and headed to the garage to put my bike and helmet away. Upstairs, I checked on Chloe; she was as Alejandro said. On her phone. "How was your appointment today? Does Dr. Wilson still think we're crazy?" I asked.

She shrugged.

"Oh, I talked to Mr. Johnson, and they may still need you to babysit Friday night."

"Why didn't he ask me?" Chloe snapped, tossing her phone to her side. "I don't need you to manage my schedule or my babysitting."

"Whoa, Chloe, I'm only relaying the message." I took a step away from her.

"Well, he should have asked me. He could've texted me. I might not be able to babysit Friday. Jacky may have us over for a sleepover."

"Okay then, after dinner, go and talk to Mr. Johnson and let him know."

She huffed.

"Why don't you ever invite Jacky and Maggie here? Include Cynthia too. Plus, we have plenty of room and I think having your friends over would be—"

"No one likes our house. We're too far away." Again, she snapped her response.

"Okay, well, I'm going to take a shower, so why don't you check your attitude before dinner, or you won't be doing anything this weekend."

"I hate you!" she snarled.

I wanted to reach out and slap the braids off her head, but I bit my tongue. My good mood was gone. Instead of saying any more, I turned and walked to our bedroom, closing the door to take my shower, "Well, if that's a good mood, I would hate to see a bad mood," I mumbled as I turned on the shower, pushing the water as hot as the nob would hopefully go, headed to the bedroom and slipped out of my biking outfit.

Finally, a hot shower, the water hitting each of my muscles making me tingle in all the right ways. As I lathered up, I found my hand spending more time cleaning my dick and my balls, but I won't lie, the feeling was everything I needed at the moment. How long since I did this in the shower? I speculated as I continued to massage myself.

"¿Qué estás haciendo?" Whenever Alejandro spoke Spanish, it made me harder. His ability to speak not only Tagalog but Spanish always impressed me. Sadly, I was lucky to speak English and some ASL on a good day.

Despite my aroused state, I jumped and stopped what I was doing at once. "God, you scared me." I turned around to peek at the door to the bathroom. "How long..." But he wasn't there. I frowned. Clearly, he was messing with me. Knowing him, he didn't want me to not be in the mood later, but luckily for him, and for me, I've never had an issue with being in the mood and always performed when called upon. Still, he was right. I figured I'd wait until later so we'd be able to take care of each other, so I finished rinsing off. By the time I dried off and got myself dressed, my arousal quieted as I returned to normal.

I stopped by Chloe's bedroom, but she was gone. So, I made my way downstairs and spotted Chloe on the couch on her phone and Alejandro in the kitchen.

"You gave me a start in the shower." I walked over to the kitchen island.

"What're you talking about?" Alejandro placed the pan with the three salmon steaks down on the cook top.

"Didn't you come upstairs while I was in the shower and sneak a peek?" I lifted my eyebrows and pointed at my crotch, ensuring only he'd see me.

"No, I've been here the whole time, finishing dinner." He shook his head.

"But I…" I trailed off. Maybe what I witnessed was my dirty mind playing tricks on me. My subconscious and my imagination wanting Alejandro to find me and join me.

"Chloe, come get ready for dinner," Alejandro called.

"Do I have to? I'm not hungry."

"It's salmon, and yes, you have to eat." Alejandro pointed to her chair at the dining table.

"Fine." She crawled off the couch and dragged herself to the table.

I didn't say anything. I had already been on the sharp end of that tongue today and had no interest in getting another tongue lashing from my daughter. Dinner was filled with a lot of huffing and annoyed looks. Every time Alejandro or I tried to say something, we were greeted with venom.

As we finished dinner, neither of us were happy with Chloe, but we said nothing more. She got up from the table and headed away.

"Hey, Chloe. Dishes." Alejandro gestured his head as he pointed toward the sink.

"Dad told me I have to go and talk to Mr. Johnson about babysitting this Friday."

"You're right. I'll take care of the dishes." I put my fork down next to my plate. "You go talk to the Johnsons."

"No." Alejandro wiped his mouth with his napkin. "You'll do the dishes like always and afterwards you can go and talk to the Johnsons, or you can surrender your phone for the rest of the night."

"God, you both suck!" She sneered at us.

I held up my hand and shook my head.

Alejandro inhaled, but said no more. The rest of the night was a tightrope act of watching what we say and how we respond. I'm ashamed to admit I was glad when our wonderful tween daughter headed off to bed, without a word to either of us.

When we turned in for bed, the light was out in Chloe's room, so we let her be. Once we were in bed, I glanced over at Alejandro. "You said she was in a good mood."

"She was. What happened between the two of you?"

"Nothing. I came up to take a shower, stopped by her bedroom, asked her about her appointment, and told her I talked to Derek... then, the wrath of Chloe. I even got an 'I hate you'."

"She said what?"

"It's fine. I know she didn't mean what she said. I think we've officially met our teenage daughter." I leaned deeper in bed.

"This is going to sound harsh," Alejandro lowered his voice and met my gaze. "But is it that time?"

"No, it's not that. That was two weeks ago." I closed my eyes. "Oh, also, none of her friends want to come here. They hate our house and think we're too far out."

"We realized this might happen."

"I had hoped we would be wrong."

Alejandro leaned in and gave me a kiss. "No more talk about our daughter. There is something I've been wanting to get my hands on all day."

I chuckled. "Oh, really?"

"Really." Wasting no time, Alejandro made quick work of my pajama buttons and had my dick in his mouth and balls in his hand. Given all we had been through the last couple of weeks, the bolts of energy filled me with bliss, being together and sharing ourselves with each other. We were in a frenzy as we brought pleasure to each other. When Alejandro stopped, I wanted to protest, until I caught the sound of the drawer opening and I realized he pulled out what he needed. In short order, he massaged my dick with lotion and I gasped. Alejandro climbed on top of me and took my cock deep into him. The tightness of him squeezed down on me warming me and causing me to thrust both willingly and involuntarily all at the same time. We were one and moved in synchronized motion. He was in complete control, and I loved it.

I loved him.

My hand found him and with each movement he made with me in him, I made an equal movement with my hand wrapped around him. Looking up, watching this beautiful man brought me so much pleasure that it overwhelmed me. There was nothing I wouldn't do for him and, in this moment, I recognized he felt the same. Whether we stayed like this for hours or minutes, this time was ours to share.

"You're going to make me come," Alejandro whispered in my ear as he kissed my cheek.

"You feel so good. I love being in you."

"I want to come when you come." Alejandro slid up my shaft and down again.

"Mmm," I moaned.

"Are you close?" he asked.

"God, yes."

"Good." His movements became harder and faster as he rode me. "I'm going... oh, man..."

As we came to a crescendo, I was there with him, with each of his thrusts he took all I had to give. With an additional push, his warmth landed on my stomach, chest, and reached my cheek. As he thrusted, more of his warmth landed on my chest, on my stomach, leaving me covered and enjoying every bit of his essence. He leaned down and we kissed in between gasping for air.

"Oh, baby, I needed you. I needed that." He laughed.

"I can tell." To emphasize my point, I reached up with my dry hand and wiped my cheek.

"I'll get some towels." He moved off me. A small chuckle of release escaped my lips as my slowly deflating dick rested, spent, off to the left side. That was the one thing I appreciated about my body, even after my orgasm I didn't fully deflate. My penis stayed quasi aroused for quite some time. Something Alejandro and all my past partners seemed to appreciate.

I lay there at peace, waiting for Alejandro to return. Soon enough, a warm, damp towel wrapped around my still semi stiff dick as he cleaned me off. He gave me another warm damp towel which I took and used on my cheek and hands. He managed to clean my chest and stomach as well.

"That was nice." I handed him the towels.

"Sex is always nice with you." Alejandro kissed me again. "You're amazing."

I laughed. "Well, you did all the work tonight."

"Nah, you were still amazing." He slipped on his PJs as I did the same.

"Well, if you want to go again, we certainly can..." I shifted so he could take in my dick. I bucked my cock showing him I could be ready to go again in short order.

He laughed.

"Except I think I want to do all the work."

"Oh, tempting, but I think I'm spent, so maybe in the morning." He snuggled next to me and closed his eyes. In short order, I joined him in sleep.

*****

I raised my hand to stop the red burning light from hurting my eyes. Peeking around, I found myself walking up the stairs of our house, copper assaulting my nose as I continued up the stairs. Everything was in a red glow, almost reminiscent of blood.

"Alejandro," I called. What I hoped would be worry in my voice sounded more like irritation.

Nothing.

I pursed my lips and waved my free hand in front of my face, trying to clear the scent of burning and copper away from my nose. I swallowed several times to keep myself from gagging. I missed the pleasant scents our home normally held, but in an odd way, this new fragrance slowly grew on me.

"Chloe," I exclaimed as I reached the top of the second-floor landing, rubbing my hand across my forehead, I smeared something there or wiped something off.

*Does it matter?*

I shook my head. "You guys are pissing me off!" I shouted. An anger unfamiliar to me grew from the pit of my stomach, like poisonous vines spreading to every part of my body, ending at my toes, fingers, and the tip of my dick. A tingle pulsed through my body; excitement.

"They need to be punished." The words filled my mind as heat rose up my neck and into my cheeks. I adjusted my cock as my dick hardened. The rush of power and energy inside me was unlike anything I had experienced before.

I moved over to our bedroom. "If you're lying around and not answering me, I'm gonna be pissed. And if you're lying around, you better greet me with your ass in the air, ready to be plowed." The anger in me was only matched by my current need for sex. Equal parts fury and lust filled every part of me. I opened the door and lying, greeting me in our bed…

I rubbed my cock and licked my lips.

"You better be ready for a pounding." I marched over to the bed and pulled the cover. Alejandro's eyes were wide open. No life in his gaze greeted me. I scanned his naked body, undeterred by the horror before me. There was probably still some life there. His body lay in a puddle of red crimson. His chest had been filleted, each of his organs removed, placed around him almost as if they were set to the points of a compass. Even his beautiful cock wasn't spared, which sent a burst of ire and disappointment through me.

"Well, fuck." I gave my dick a squeeze. "Maybe Chloe."

I pinched my lips together and let out a sigh. "You should have answered when I called." I inhaled the smell of death, savoring the perfume. "Who's going to clean up this mess?" I asked, before turning my back on him, leaving our room. "'Cause it ain't gonna be me."

"Chloe, get out here." I shouted. After she cleaned up that mess, I would give it to her. "You need to clean this mess up."

I marched to her bedroom door and pushed the door open. Inside her room on the floor, she lay in a pentagram drawn in blood. My head tilted to the right, then the left. I worked my mouth back and forth. Something was off about the design, and I couldn't put my finger on it. I don't know what annoyed me more: the sloppy workmanship, or the mess on the floor. Or perhaps it was a lack of finding any sexual relief.

*Everything is blurring together at the moment.*

I raised my hand, seeing the knife held in it, and stepped away. The blood-soaked knife dropped from my grip, hitting the floor with a wet thud.

*This isn't me.*

I peeked at the mirror. I stood, covered in blood. Their blood. The blood of my husband and daughter. "God in heaven, what's happening?"

"There is no god here," a voice called out.

I glanced around the space, screaming. "No! I couldn't have done this." My heart pounded in my chest and head. Every muscled screamed in pain. I wanted to vomit. Run, scream, and vomit.

"Oh, but you could," my reflection snarled at me. "Don't you want to get rid of them? Be free. They're holding you back, Kyle. They're keeping you from fulfilling your potential. You don't need them," the thing stealing my likeness in the mirror commented. It wasn't me. I wouldn't say those things. I loved my family. None of this was real.

It couldn't be.

*What's happening?*

My reflection laughed at me. "Oh Kyle, give in to your lust and your desires. Don't let them…" It pointed to the dead bloodied bodies of Alejandro and Chloe now flanking them. "Keep you from what you want… no need." The last word drawn out.

"No," I shouted, stepping from the image. "Alejandro! Chloe!" I backed away from the room and the images in the mirror, unable to look at what I had done to Chloe.

"What are you? Who are you?" I bellowed.

The only response I received was laughter from the three images.

I startled awake, pushing the awful images from my mind and crinkling my nose to hopefully vanquish the smell of copper in my nose.

*A dream. An awful dream.*

Unlike most dreams, the images remained fresh in my mind's eye. I needed to vanquish these images and thoughts from my brain. I opened my eyes. The beams of light coming from behind the blinds and curtains were a welcomed signal to my body that what I witnessed was all a horrific dream. One I hoped to never have again. Thanks to the terrible dream, I wanted to get up. I wanted to do something to cleanse my mind. A bike ride. As I shifted, the morning rays of light and my morning erection also signaled to my brain that I needed to get my day started. Being up early is great when you're with another morning person, but it can be a bit cumbersome when you're not. I rolled over and wrapped my arm around Alejandro, who was still blissfully alive and asleep. The warmth from his half-naked body pushed away the remnants of my dreadful dream and reminded me of the love we shared and how I'd never hurt him or Chloe. I inhaled his scent and, much like a good sherbet, my mind was being purified.

With an additional deep inhale, I adjusted my arm resting over his shoulder as my hand hung next to his chest. Sometimes, if I positioned myself right, my body would elicit a favorable response from him that we both would end up enjoying, and I needed the mental pallet cleanser after that dream. Unfortunately, this morning wasn't going to work in my favor as he snorted, taking a deep breath and shifting in our bed.

*Probably for the best. I doubt I'd be able to perform, given that nightmare.*

With a hint of a yawn, instead of attempting to wake him up and get his engine running, I decided to get myself up, ignoring the monster in my pajamas and intending to go for a bike ride. The ride would have to serve the same purpose as sex with my husband this morning.

*But first I got to pee.*

I made my way to the bathroom, did what I needed to do, and washed my hands and brushed my teeth. I always needed to brush my teeth first thing in the morning. I couldn't stand having funky teeth, tongue, and breath once I was up. There were even times I would also brush my teeth before bed, but I didn't do that nearly as much as my dentist would like. Either way, I needed to clean the 'nasty' out of my mouth.

I returned to our room, slipping off my PJs and grabbing my bike shorts and shirt.

"God, I love that fuzzy bum of yours." Alejandro's words came out groggily. But sensing his gaze as I put my clothes on, I shook my now covered booty for him.

"And you had the opportunity, but too late now. I'm going—" Screams turned my blood cold. As my head snapped in the direction of our daughter's room. This is not how we wanted to kick off our morning, especially after the dream I had. All the images rushed front and center in my mind. I reached the door first, but Alejandro stood next to me. "Chloe!" I yelled, reaching for the door handle.

I grabbed the knob on our door, but the door wouldn't open. "It's locked!" I shouted.

There was another scream from down the hall. "Daddy! Papa!" The terror radiating from Chloe's room made my heart drop and anger build up inside of me. My daughter needed me and I couldn't reach her fast enough.

I banged on the door. "We're here," I yelled. "Alejandro, the door!"

"I'm trying," he roared. "Move," he demanded and, as I got clear of the door, he bashed into the barrier with his shoulder, but again, the door wouldn't budge.

"Help!" Chloe bawled again.

"God! What's happening?" I roared. "First the nightmare, now this. God, please help us."

Alejandro spared a quick glance at me. I shook my head and tried the door again. Nothing. Alejandro grasped for the handle again, and this time the door popped open.

"What the hell?" he shouted, throwing the door open.

How our bedroom door opened didn't matter, as we were out and on our way. We rushed to Chloe's door and, again, the door wouldn't open. This time, we didn't hesitate. "Chloe, get away from the door," I shouted and, within seconds, her door shattered from its frame and we were in her room, with enough time to see her prone on top of the bed.

I can't say who got to her first, but we had her wrapped up in our arms, and by the time we were downstairs she shook and cried. We placed her on the sofa and sat on either side of her fussing about her, but not accomplishing anything by way of helping her. Instead, we showered her with our love and whatever strength we had.

"I woke up." She hiccupped. "Something was holding me down." She cried, forcing out each of the words. "I tried to fight, but I couldn't move. I tried to fight, but I couldn't. I called, and you didn't come and get me."

"Oh, baby, we tried." I wiped away her tears with my hand.

"Did you hear us?" Alejandro wrapped an arm around her, pulling her tight to him.

"I screamed and screamed, but it wouldn't let me go." She shook her head.

"Chloe, we're here and we got you." I hugged her, pushing

her silk multi-colored bonnet off her head.

"Ow, that hurts." Chloe pulled away from my hug as I rubbed her back.

"What?" I pulled away. "I'm sorry." I removed my hands.

"Papa, it really hurts." She moaned as she squirmed under our touch.

"Let's take a look." Alejandro backed away, raising his gaze and his brows in assurance. "Lift up your shirt?"

She moved to the side, turned and lifted up her shirt for us to look at.

"Honey, how'd you scratch yourself?" I asked, trying to work out how she'd managed the marks. I wasn't sure that even if she were double-jointed, self-inflicting these slashes would be possible to do herself.

"Kyle." Alejandro faced me, his eyes as large as saucers. Alejandro got up and rushed to the kitchen, then to the powder room. The door to the garage opened and closed. I examined the marks again. There were two sets of three deep claw marks down the middle of her back. The abrasions were an angry red color. These scratches—she couldn't have done this, could she? "God."

"Papa, what is it?" Chloe tried to turn her head to see.

"Some scratches, baby." I tried to push away any worry on my face and replace my expression with positivity and assuredness. "You must have caught your back when you were on your bed, or trying to move, but don't worry, we're going to get you cleaned up."

Chloe glanced at me. "Papa, they hurt."

"I know." My voice cracked as I spoke. "Daddy's getting some towels or bandages and some antiseptic." I again tried to keep my voice and words as neutral and calm as possible.

Alejandro returned with damp paper towels, handing them to me. "My God." He froze for a moment, stepping closer to Chloe. "How... What...?"

"I don't know, but we need..." I went to work on the wounds, wiping at the angry reds on her back. "Get your cellphone."

"It's upstairs." He countered.

I shot him a look, and he understood. "Get my glasses too, I can't see..." I almost cursed but that wasn't going to help anything, and I didn't like using foul language around Chloe despite my recent outbursts, and even though I had no delusions that she didn't already know them plus some new ones I didn't know.

Alejandro was off and I continued to work on her wounds. "Better?" I asked.

"A little," she replied.

I didn't know if we should call the police or an ambulance. How do you explain mystery scratch marks on your twelve-year-old daughter? How do you explain any of this? They would think we're insane, or at the very least, guilty of child abuse. No. we would take care of this ourselves.

*Somehow.*

I called over my shoulder, "Take pictures of the doors and the frames. There is no way those doors should have stuck like that."

"Dad, what's happening?" Chloe asked as she worked her bottom lip.

"I don't know." This was not a lie. I had no idea what was happening. Was she having a dream? Was she having a nightmare like I had? God, I hope she didn't have a terrible dream like that. Was it sleep paralysis? Possibly. Even the scratches might be somehow self-induced, but what about the doors? Why wouldn't they open? Like at the doctor's office. I cleared my worry before speaking. "You had a bad dream, and that's what scared you. When I have bad dreams, sometimes they make me feel like I can't move and I know how scary that feels."

*Did that happen to me this morning? Could I move?*

"But I was awake." Chloe frowned. "I know I was. I was scrolling through my phone."

I continued to clean up my daughter's cuts and when Alejandro came down, not only did he have his phone but mine as well, and the peroxide and Neosporin, along with my glasses hanging out of his mouth. I reached for my glasses, slipping them on. The glasses only made the marks look worse. "Honey, Papa is going to take some pictures of your back. Afterwards, we'll finish getting them all cleaned up. Once we're all cleaned up, how about we go out for a big breakfast? You pick."

Her grin slowly bloomed across her lips. "I'm sorry about last night. I don't know why I said those things. I'm sorry. I didn't mean them. Please tell me you're not mad at me."

"We were never mad at you." I kissed her shoulder.

"Good." A tear-filled smile eeked out over her face. "Sometimes, I get so angry and mad. I don't know why."

Alejandro glanced up from his phone. "We all get that way, Chloe." He checked the images on his camera, shaking his head. "But we have to learn to keep from saying and doing things that can hurt other people. Controlling our anger is part of becoming an adult."

I eyeballed Alejandro and smiled as he rubbed her shoulder. "There you go." I closed up the Neosporin and placed everything on the coffee table. "Feel better?"

She shifted her shoulders and moved her back as she licked her lips, tugging down her shirt. "Yep."

After we got everything cleaned up downstairs and upstairs, and once we got ourselves and our daughter calmed down, I made a note to keep records of everything happening to us and in our neighborhood. I made notes of the day, the time, the weather, all of it. When ready, I would fill in who was involved and if there were others around. Someone had to keep a record of all this, in case we needed the information for something, maybe a lawsuit against the builder. I didn't know for sure, but I wanted to have everything documented to the best of my abilities, including all the images we'd collect. No matter how big or small the incident. I would make a point to get to know all our neighbors and learn what I could from them as well. We already knew about some of what happened with the Williams, the Patils, and the Johnsons, and what happened the night everyone got sick. Maybe there was a pattern to all these events. I decided then and there that getting to the bottom of our neighborhood mystery would be my personal mission. My plan: learn everything possible about the neighborhood. For the first time since we moved in, I felt like I had a strategy and a course of action.

# ~ Chapter Ten ~

Nothing. Absolutely nothing. After the incident with Chloe and the moment I started going and documenting all the odd and annoying occurrences, things went quiet. Except for my calls to the builder. I got a lot of 'humidity' and 'the house settling' talk. When the door expert came out to replace the doors, she couldn't explain why our doors stuck and wouldn't open. She did say she was impressed with how well they held up against all our efforts. I wasn't sure how to take that. But by the time we left for our Hawaiian trip, I was happy to see our house and our neighborhood in the rearview mirror, at least for a short while.

Hawaii is always beautiful, and the resort had been perfect, so leaving hurt my soul. Even Chloe didn't want to go, but as with all things, our trip came to an end, and by the end of the first week of August, we had our memories and finished planning for Chloe's new school in a couple of weeks. Things continued, and we almost forgot about the past and our first three months in our new home.

"We have the whole night to ourselves." I glanced over at Alejandro.

"Well, not really," he countered. "We still have Chloe."

"She's over at the Johnson's babysitting…"

"And we're not planning on keeping our eyes on her and their house."

I laughed.

"Any luck finding Reza?"

Given all that had happened and with my research into

our house and neighborhood, I decided my best course of action was to let Alejandro know I planned on reaching out to Reza, since he had a lot of experience with the paranormal now. Unfortunately, for me, and by extension us, he had relocated to the East Coast with his husband, explaining why I had trouble tracking him down originally. I never figured he would leave the Bay Area, but then again, I never figured we would need paranormal help.

"I found his website, and I sent him a message, but no. Nothing yet."

"You think this might have something to do with what happened to the two of you back then? I mean, I know you said nothing bad happened, but... I don't know."

I shook my head, adding a shrug to show my uncertainty. Those events were nothing like this, yes things were strange and a little odd. Yes, Reza and I had a couple of minor disagreements, but those events brought us closer... in a way.

"You sure Chloe will be okay?" he asked, peeking down the hall.

Alejandro had become more protective of Chloe since things had happened and I didn't blame him, but Chloe was twelve and wanted to make her own money, and the Johnsons needed a babysitter so, why not. In fact, Chloe had picked up babysitting for the Johnsons, the Martins, and beginning next Saturday, she would watch the Gills' son for them. I was happy to see her excited and experiencing a taste of freedom, even if we were on the same street and could easily watch her, or go and get her if something happened.

"You don't think she's too young, do you?"

"Don't say that to her," my eyebrows raised as my cheeks pulled apart, raising my lips.

"I'm serious."

"No. I don't think she's too young to babysit and none

of the kids are babies, so it's fine. Plus, she's making twenty an hour and I'm happy to see her doing something other than watching videos on her phone or tablet." I pointed at Alejandro, who was watching videos on his phone.

"Ha ha." He put his phone down. "Twenty an hour, geez. I don't think my sister got that for watching us. Still, with everything happening..." He glanced at the entry hall.

"Hon, it's not even dark." I moved to the family room windows and pointed out to our backyard. Filled with bright summer light, the yard had some basic plantings from the builder. Another upgrade for the house that was included in the price (both front and backyard gardens and a bit of a patio, eight by eight), another nice feature. I always questioned if all these bonuses were because they realized something was wrong with this place.

"Fine. He placed his phone on the coffee table. "What did you want to do?"

"Oh, I can think of a few things." I waggled my eyebrows.

"Movie it is." Alejandro grabbed the remote control and turned on the TV. "You can make the popcorn while I find us something to watch."

We snuggled on the sofa and were halfway through the bowl of buttery popcorn, which was about fifteen minutes into the movie, and I may have already dozed off once. With a bang, we both jumped, almost flinging the bowl of popcorn to the floor, as we both rushed to our feet.

"Kyle! Alejandro!" a voice called out.

"What the..." Alejandro paused the movie as I made my way to the front door.

There was more pounding on the door. I opened the door to see Deepa, hand in the air, ready to bang on the door again. "Deepa, what's..."

She grabbed my arm and pulled me from the door to the

porch. "Look!" she yelled, pointing to the Johnsons' home.

The Johnsons' house erupted in an electric light show, every window burst with lights and yells from the inside.

"Chloe!" I bellowed.

This brought Alejandro to the door to join me.

"What's happening over there?" Deepa squeezed my arm as the three of us rushed across the street.

As we reached the front of the Johnsons' home, Hari and Vyan banged on the door trying to get in, and more screams found my ears. I stood on the grass observing the window, not able to believe what I witnessed.

"Chloe, open the door!" I shouted.

Alejandro had joined Hari and Vyan at the door, and the three of them continued to try the lock and pounded on the front door.

"We just got home." Deepa shook her head. "Hari finished at the restaurant. We saw the light going crazy, and then the screams...

Another shriek filled our ears, but this noise chilled me to the bone. That wasn't Chloe or Jr. or Diane. It was a woman—at least I imagined the shout was from a woman, but not like any female voice I ever noticed before.

"What is that?" I couldn't stop from yelling. "They're only children! Leave them alone!" I added, not caring how my voice sounded or how loud I yelled.

As my husband and neighbors continued to bang on the door, I continued to yell for the kids. Deepa's voice joined mine, thank goodness. Several of our neighbors were out of their homes, witnessing what we all observed. With all the yelling and banging, it was no wonder they picked up on what was happening. Another shriek filled our ears. Again not any of the kids—no child could make that kind of noise.

"We called 9-1-1," Mrs. Hernandez called out, Miguel,

Cynthia and JJ. all in tow, but they stopped at the Johnsons' driveway. "What's happening?" Lidia's voice elevated.

"Did you call the…" Another shout filled the neighborhood. I wasn't sure from whom.

"Papa! Daddy!" Chloe yelled from the upstairs. She banged on the second-floor window. If my memory was correct, that would be the loft for this home.

"Chloe!" I called out. "Open the window."

"Where are Jr. and Diane?" Deepa pointed

"I can't!" Chloe shouted. Two more faces appeared next to her at the window, crying and banging on the glass.

"I'm going to try the back door." Vyan pushed past Hari and Alejandro.

"Hari, go with him." Deepa pointed.

"You need to calm them down," Marsha declared. "When people are stressed, they can't always function."

I inhaled as much air as possible, not only to calm myself but to keep the panic from my words. "Chloe," My voice loud enough not to be overshadowed but hopefully not sounding as panic-stricken as my pounding heart and sweat-covered forehead played me out to be. "Take a breath honey, try to focus and open the window. You can do it," I shouted.

"Those poor children," Mrs. Hernandez uttered as prayers poured from her mouth. I glanced over my shoulder. By now, everyone was out of their homes, watching the light show and hearing the screams and yells coming from the Johnsons' home.

"Should we break the window?" Alejandro asked, stepping from the door and rushing to the powder room window.

"I'll get my tools." Mr. Martin ran off.

The house was going insane. Lights on and off and the screams that weren't the children continued to fill all our ears. A howl, not from the house but from the backyard, caught my ears. Within seconds, Vyan pulled Hari out.

"Something attacked Dad," Vyan yelled. "We got to the back door and something…" He shook his head. Deepa ran to her husband and helped pull him away from the house. By the time Mr. Martin appeared with his tools, he dropped them to the sidewalk, seeing Hari laid out on the lawn. Marsha was over helping Deepa and Vyan.

"Good lord." He froze, glancing at his wife, who held their daughter in place.

The sirens—I never imagined I would be so happy to hear sirens in my life—pulled up and poor Officer Lancey got out of her car. "God in heaven." She rushed over to us.

"We can't get in and something attacked Hari." I tried to focus on the officer and her partner. The poor Latino guy appeared as worried and, dare I say, frightened as the rest of us, as another screech reached all our ears. "Please, you have to help. Our daughter is in there with Jr. and Diane."

"Dannie, what are we going to do?" Her partner's eyes were on the house and the lights going on and off. Another scream caught all our attention and pulled Dannie and her partner into action.

"Do you have your neighbor's phone number?" he asked.

I stood there, frozen, watching my little girl trying to open the window, all these tiny fingers working the lock and banging on the window again.

Officer Lancey, Dannie, grabbed me. "Mr. Del Rosario, do you have their phone number?"

"Kyle!" Alejandro yelled.

That pulled me from my trance, and I grabbed my phone and called Derek's cell. I tried to focus on the call, but I couldn't miss the chaotic events around me. They happened everywhere. I doubted anyone was able to miss all this. Every car alarm on the street now blared, and some of the vehicles were rocking back and forth. That caused more yells and screams as people retreated. More than one kid had their ears covered and cried.

"Kyle." Hearing my name spoken pulled my attention.

"Derek, you and Mercedes need to get home, right now. The whole neighborhood is going crazy and we can't get to the kids."

I don't know if he responded or not, but by the time I focused on the building madness around me, another police car and an ambulance had pulled up. The occupants were as horrified as we were, but unlike us, after a moment, they all rushed into action. The paramedics were seeing to Mr. Patil and three officers now banged on the front door. "Get the hammer," one of them yelled, and Dannie's partner rushed to his vehicle, which had joined the others rocking back and forth with its lights and sirens going on and off.

As the officer opened the trunk, a bright flash of light blinded me and a boom so loud that I needed to cover my ears to block it out reverberated through my body as if being pricked by a million small needles. The pain was immense, and poof, the pain vanished. When I glanced at where the male officer should be, he was maybe five feet away, spread out on the ground. I reacted without much consideration. I ran toward him, as did a couple of neighbors, Mike Chen and Ken Martin. We tended to him as much as our abilities allowed. I moved over to his trunk and grabbed the big-ass door-busting 'hammer', they called it, and rushed to Dannie and the other officers.

"Where's Fernando?"

I shrugged in his direction where he lay.

"Jesus, Archangel Michael, help us in our moment of need," she called out. "Lord, give us strength. Get back. We're going to get those babies." Her words were filled with as much determination as I had rushing through every pore in my body. "Back off!" she shouted at me.

I did as I was told, moving to Alejandro, relegated to a spectator as we viewed our daughter and the two other children continue to bang on the glass window from the second floor.

The door burst open, and the officers were in the house. The light continued to go on and off, but the car alarms had stopped, and the cars no longer moved around like water on a hot, oiled pan.

Within seconds, the three adults and three children were out of the house on the grass. I pulled them all to me and held them as tight as possible. The moment the kids were free from the house, everything stopped. No bangs, no screams, and no more lights. No one uttered a word, only continuing to glance around our cul-de-sac in shock.

"Daddy, there were people in the house. They were crying and bunched up all over the house. We ran to the front door, but the lock wouldn't open. I ran to the back door but shadows blocked us. I pulled Jr. and Diane to the upstairs, and the people weren't up there. All the lights and the yelling. I wanted to call you, but I… I left my phone in the family room. We were safe upstairs, but the lights and the noise… I couldn't leave them."

I held my daughter and surveyed the officer. "You did great, baby. You did great."

"Officer Lancey, what the hell is going on?" Alejandro pointed. "This isn't normal. Three of us. Three grown ass men couldn't open that door." He shook his head. "How is that possible?" He continued to hold Jr. and Diane.

"The boy and girl were nice," Jr. voiced through his tears. "They are always nice. They play with us, but the dark man scared them off."

"But their mommies and daddies." Diane pulled into Alejandro. "They weren't so nice."

"Dannie." One of the other officers got her attention. "Fernando is conscious, and the paramedics are checking him out."

"Okay, let's get this secured. I want statements from everyone, all the neighbors. Get a call into PG&E and have them come out here. Now," she demanded of her team, glancing at Alejandro and me. "Officially, I have no clue what is going on."

We both frowned at her.

"Unofficially, the kind of help you need, the police and the paramedics aren't going to be able to assist you with."

"What?" I glanced at her, still holding Chloe. But I understood. We all did. This was beyond them. I had been down this road before. A long forgotten path I hoped to never travel down again.

"Then who?" Alejandro demanded. "Something or someone attacked these kids. You've seen what's happening here."

"Let's get this all sorted." Dannie noted all the terrified faces around her, some of them her own officers. "You still have my number, right?"

I reached for my pocket and my phone. "Yep."

"I'm off on Tuesday and Wednesday. Call me, and I'll swing by." Without another word, she was off, taking charge of the scene and moving folks and acquiring statements.

"Hey Jr., Diane, we made popcorn and are watching a movie. Why don't we get you in the house and taken care of until your folks get home, okay?"

"You won't leave us?" Jr. asked, squeezing Alejandro harder.

"Not for a minute, buddy," Alejandro reassured as he tussled the boy's hair.

"Take the kids to the house. I'm gonna check in with

Deepa and Hari." I regarded Chloe. "You did a great job."

She beamed up at me and took Alejandro's hand.

"Come on, gang." Alejandro pulled the three kids with him toward our house. I never grasped how loud the quiet could be. The birds, the insects, all the noises you pay no attention to until they're gone. And right now, there wasn't a sound. Even the summer bugs were too scared to make any noise.

By the time Derek and Mercedes got to our house, the paramedics were gone and only Dannie and one additional officer stayed to talk with the Johnsons, who, once they had their kids in hand, were no worse for wear. On the outside, at least, they appeared to have had the weight of the world lifted off them. The kids, for their part, were content to eat popcorn and watch the movie. Their ease of nature impressed me with how well these younger kids adapted to their environment. Maybe us parents needed to take a lesson from them. After all that happened that night, I couldn't sleep for two days. I was up and about most of the night, watching and waiting for something new to happen. But nothing seemed to happen at night, only during the day or early evening at the latest. It was like everything we'd seen in movies and on TV had been complete bullshit.

# ~ Chapter Eleven ~

Inhaling deeply and forcing my hands to stop trembling, I picked up my cell and called Officer Lancey. Three days had passed since the freak show our street put on for all the neighbors to see. And similarly to past events, all was quiet in the neighborhood, but unlike before, everyone was on edge. I scared the heck out of Mr. Chen when I greeted him as he walked Muffin. Dr. Hernandez almost gave Alejandro and I both heart attacks when he popped out of his garage, seeing who was in our driveway. And poor Mrs. Gill hit the curb with her car when she assumed she almost hit someone. Chloe said a bird swooped down to get a bug or something. If the activity in the neighborhood didn't kill us, our own fears and paranoia would. So I called.

The other end of the line rang. Finally, she said hello. I spoke, "Officer Lancey, hello. It's Kyle, Del Rosario. You said—"

"Kyle, Mr. Del Rosario. How are you?"

"That's right. Good, thanks, considering…. how's Officer Fernando?" I took another deep gulp of air, glad to hear she at least recognized my voice. I had to wonder how many people must call her.

"He's fine," Dannie stated. "How are things there?"

"None of us know what to do—"

"I'm sure," she reassured me, sighing through her words. "As I stated, officially, there isn't much the police can do. We can respond to an emergency and if there is a fire or medical need we will be there, but… I'm sorry."

I was about to lose my shit on her, but I closed my eyes and released my anger with my next breath. All wasn't lost. I still hadn't gotten a message from Reza, so there was hope.

"Can you tell me how have things been the past few days?" Lancey asked.

As I tried not to jump all over her comments and questions, it wasn't easy, but I had the feeling in my gut she wanted to help us, so I bit down my continued frustration. "It's been quiet. No new activity."

I glanced out my office window, not sure what I expected to see, but happy to see nothing out of the normal. Another bright, sunny, summer day with a couple of kids playing in the park. The ends of my lips pulled up at the sight.

"That's good." Dannie's voice filled with relief. "I'd like to come and speak with you all. Can we meet tomorrow?"

"But you told us there wasn't anything the police were able to do." I huffed. "I doubt a neighborhood watch will do us much good."

"I won't be coming as a representative from the San Jose Police Department."

"Okay."

"Will it be possible to meet tomorrow? I would hate to put you all off for another week," she added.

My head bobbed up and down. "Tomorrow night?" I finally responded. "Don't worry, I'll make sure we're available." We didn't have anything planned tomorrow, except for Chloe's therapy, but Alejandro and Chloe would be home by five.

"Do you think you can get the rest of your neighbors there as well?" she asked.

I sighed as I continued to peer out the window. "I can ask. I'm sure most of our neighbors will be eager to hear what you have to say, given what we've all been through."

"Good. I'll be there tomorrow at 7 p.m. if that works?"

Rustling on her end of the call broke the silence.

Relief rushed through my body as the knots in my shoulders lessened, as did the tightness in my stomach. "Thank you. We'll see you tomorrow at 7 p.m." I ended the call and put my cell on my desk. I would need to go and talk to the neighbors and see who we'd be able to get to come and speak with her. My plan at the moment: talk to everyone home this afternoon, and Alejandro and I would catch everyone else tonight when he and Chloe got home.

I want to say I was surprised, but given all the recent events, just like us, everyone managed to agree to meet at our house to talk with Officer Lancey. We all wanted to learn how to stop this, whatever this was, from getting worse. As ridiculous as this may sound, I worried about snacks and drinks for our meeting. I pulled out chips and made a dip. I offered wine and coffee as well as soda and I managed to pull together some fresh cookies that we had frozen in the freezer from one of our baking days. Not since our housewarming party had we had so many people in our home, and I wanted everyone to feel welcome.

With all the activity, sadly, none of Chloe's friends came to our house, so she would go out with them. And none of their parents came in anymore when they dropped Chloe off. Not even Sara or Carter, which hurt, because we were so close. I'm not sure if Chloe told them anything or not. She assured us she didn't say anything to anyone, not wanting to be bullied anymore. I couldn't blame her. Even Alejandro and I didn't say anything to anyone; we didn't want to risk our jobs or have people think we were crazy. Or worse, have them believe us and camp in our front yard—not that there was much room to camp. The idea of turning our home and our neighborhood into a circus... no thanks.

By 6:45 p.m. our family room, dining room, and kitchen

were filled. Everyone showed up, even the Chens and the Martins, and the space echoed with small talk. None of us wanted to put our kids through any more trauma, so we sent them over to the park to play. Vyan and Chloe and the other older kids offered to keep an eye on them. Every few minutes one of the adults would wander to my office, to what I assumed was to look out and make sure the kids were fine. We insisted they go no farther than the park and we ensured they all had their phones—well, those that had cells, which was most of them.

A knock at the door got all our attention and killed the conversations bouncing around the room. I glanced over at Alejandro who was chatting with Mr. Harris, who lived at the end of the cul-de-sac. I caught his gaze before I wandered over to the front door. I blinked several times before recognizing Officer Lancey. She stood before me, dressed in jeans and a short-sleeved shirt with her hair down. "Officer Lancey?" Her appearance stunned me with how different she came across outside of her uniform, almost like an elementary school teacher ready for a hectic day.

"Tonight, call me Dannie." She smiled and shook my hand.

I glanced out, seeing a black Ford Edge parked in front of our house. "Please, come in," I stepped aside. "Would you like something to drink? We have nibbles as well." We walked down the hall.

"Not right now, thank you." She beamed at me.

As we made our way to the family room, everyone grew quiet and scrutinized the officer as she moved in front of our family room windows so everyone had a view of her. "Good evening, everyone." She smiled. "Thank you for letting me come and talk to you."

There were mutters of welcome as all eyes were focused

on her.

"I know you're all worried and scared. However, tonight, I'm not here as an officer of the law." She took a breath and relaxed her shoulders. "I don't know what Kyle shared with you, but as I told him, there isn't a lot the police can do in situations like this… in an official capacity. I think you are all dealing with something that I, as an officer, can't help you with…"

There were mumbles and several glances around the room. Before anyone spoke, she held up a hand. "However, I, as a paranormal researcher, might be able to…"

"Seriously?" Mr. Harris instantly jumped in. If I had to guess, he waited for something like this, so he'd be able to laugh at us, or whatever. "We've had our lights going on and off and you all think it's ghosts. It was the power, nothing more." He sipped his glass of wine.

"Doug, how do you explain what happened at the Johnsons'? What about when you and Kathy were sick when we all moved in?" Deepa countered, holding a napkin in her hand. "And, Marsha, tell him what you witnessed in the park."

"Well… there were these Indian children watching me," Mrs. Martin, Marsha, pointed out the window. "And not in the park."

"And the tall dark man who's been banging around in our house." Lidia Hernandez winced. "Always with the banging." She hit her hand with her fist. "It's not the AC or the water heater, or the washer or dryer."

"We've seen him too," Derek mentioned, putting his glass of wine on the counter. "And a lot of other weird shit. Not Native American kids, but several people. Some of the men looked like warriors or hunters. About jumped right out of the shower when I noticed them in the mirror."

"There are no such things as ghosts," countered Dr. Chen,

Emily, sipping her coffee, her black hair flowing down her shoulders. "As a scientist, I can assure you…"

"We've all seen and heard things," someone countered.

"Show me the video," Dr. Chen asked, her voice calm as ever. "I wasn't here when everything happened the other night, so let me see the video. Surely someone has a video, we all have cellphones…"

She waited.

"My phone died." Marsha Martin frowned as the words dropped from her mouth. "The thing had a full charge…"

"Emily, I saw those things as well," Mike, Dr. Chen's husband, softly expressed . "And the dark man, and I hear the voices in Spanish…"

"Mike, I told you, it's all in your head." Emily pinched her lips before taking another sip of coffee. "As for the Spanish, you're hearing the Hernandez family. With as close as these homes are built, it's no wonder." She glanced around the room. "Anyone with any video?"

This shut Mike down. He frowned and focused on the oatmeal cookie in his hand, or possibly on the floor.

"I couldn't get a video either." Lidia held up her cell. New phone hasn't worked right since we moved in."

"As I assumed." Dr. Chen's tone was filled with condescension. "You too." Alejandro glanced at Lidia, ignoring Dr. Chen. "Cell service keeps going out and my phone and tablet don't hold a charge either."

"Not just the cell phones and the internet," Mrs. Harris added. "What about the nightmares? Our kids have been sleeping with us for weeks now." She glared at her husband as if to dare him to discount what was happening.

He sighed and bobbed his head in agreement.

"We've seen what looks like men in uniforms," Hari gestured with his hands to illustrate what they had seen. "But not modern, like what you would see now. They had swords and big hats." He raked a hand through his hair. "I swear I think they are Spanish Conquistadors, or something like that."

The Gills and the Walkers gave their agreement.

They're in the park too." Mr. Walker added.

"Yes." Mr. Gill agreed.

"I spotted something like that when I was out with Muffin. I don't like the park," Mr. Chen commented. "I thought they were—" He stopped talking when Dr. Chen glanced at him with a shake of her head.

"Anyone else fighting a lot with your family?" Lidia asked. Now there were several conversations going on and the noise made hearing and keeping track difficult. "We've had some doozies over nothing."

"We have." Alejandro raised his hand. "Stupid stuff too."

"I can't tell you how many times I wanted to walk out and never come back." Ken Martin disclosed. "I love my family, but I've been getting so angry… I mean really angry, scary angry."

There were several more frustrated glances of agreement from around the room.

"And don't forget those awful smells," Mercedes commented. The remarks and comments came faster, and I lost track of who spoke, despite my best efforts.

"God, the smells."

"Sewer gas," Dr. Chen countered. "You heard what the—"

"Please, everyone." Dannie held up her hands. "I get it." She continued to speak louder. "I don't… listen, please." Her voice rose and took on her police officer tone. "Folks. I'm only telling you what might be happening. Yes, I research the paranormal, but I'm a skeptic. I don't go and point to every dark shadow and call it an apparition. Now, please." Her voice echoed around our home.

That quieted our group down.

"Thank you." Dannie's tone came out more natural and relaxed. "I've reached out to a colleague of mine. His name is Dr. Anson Thomas, and he's the Lead Researcher and Investigator of the Silicon Valley Paranormal Research Society. I've asked if they would be willing to come and investigate what's happening here."

Everyone surveyed the room, not sure what to say, or even if they were allowed to speak at the moment.

The knots in my stomach pulled tighter, but still I raised my hand.

Dannie acknowledged me. "Kyle."

I took a sip of my glass of wine. "Would you be part of the investigation? I have a friend, Dr. Reza Zadeh-Ezra. He and his husband are researchers out on the East Coast. Their group is called, The Paranormal Institute of Clearwater (PICs for short), do you know them? Also, what does an investigation entail?"

"How much will it cost us?" someone asked.

"To answer your first question, yes, but I would have them come out first without me. I want them to investigate your homes and the neighborhood without my contamination. If they feel a continued investigation is warranted, they would come and spend time here exploring every possible explanation and figuring out a course of action. Since I'm requesting the team's help, a lot of the initial Q&A to verify your accounts is being skipped." She scanned the room. "Kyle, there are a lot of researchers out there, so I can't say I know your friend. As for the cost, there wouldn't be a fee."

Deepa raised her hand.

Dannie gestured at her. "Mrs. Patil."

"Can you tell us what you think might be happening?"

Dannie inhaled. "Well, from what I've seen and from what

you are all saying, it's possible you have a mix of things."

"A mix," Mrs. Walker, Janice, commented. "Sorry." She shook her head as several people scrutinized her. She and Tim lived at the end of the street next to the Martins. From what I've learned, they haven't experienced much, which had been good for them.

"The Native American people some of you are seeing," Dannie explained as she shifted her stance so she wasn't standing in front of the window, but more in the corner where the two walls meet. "They may simply be images from the past. Think of them like videos. They don't interact with you. Like a video playing on a loop, you can watch them and that's all, they do their thing as you do yours. This would be what we call a standard haunting—"

"But these…" Derek raised his hand. "Sorry, but some of them have been playing with our Diane. We assumed she had an imaginary friend, but we… we saw them."

"Excuse me, Officer Lancey," Dr. Hernandez waved a hand and cleared his throat.

Dannie signaled for him to continue. "Go on."

"I spoke with a friend of mine, William Marshall. He occasionally comes to my class and is a guest speaker on the local First Nation people who lived here and still do." Dr. Hernandez gestured as if giving a lecture to his students. "He's a member of the Muwekma Nation, and he stated this whole area was part of the Tamien Nation before the Spanish came and built their missions, killing or enslaving a lot of the Native people. A tragic mess, really. Could some of what is happening now be caused by what happened in the past?"

Dannie considered a moment. "It's possible, but remember, please, typically there is never any evil intent but an evil act. A tragedy might have happened here. See, what some of the people you've all seen might be apparitions or what you all think of as a classic ghost. They can change how they appear, they can pick an age they want to show you, they can also decide how they want to manifest themselves: ball of energy or a full figure."

"I've seen the ball of energy thing." Fatma, Mrs. Gill, pointed as she called out. She lived with her husband Nasir down in between the Walkers and Harris. "Driving right down to our house, poof, gone. I assumed I was seeing things, but it's happened several times during the day, and my husband and I have seen these energy things as we were heading out or coming home. Doesn't matter, day or night." She added.

Mercedes raised her hand.

Dannie gestured her way.

"Is this what caused the lights to go crazy, trapping the kids in our house, and setting the car alarms off? No one can figure it out. Would these apparitions be able to hurt Hari and your officer?"

Dannie shook her head. "No."

Everyone got quiet as several folks glanced at each other.

"What I witnessed the other night wasn't any apparition or haunting. I think what we experienced the other night was the work of a poltergeist."

"Well, we're talking about moving." Mr. Martin shook his head. "It's not worth it."

"Moving might not work." A frown on Dannie's face echoed in her voice. "There may be an attachment, in which case the spirits follow you."

"What?" I gasped.

"You've got to be kidding," Deepa countered.

"That's insane." Mercedes reached for Derek's hand.

There were several more mumbles and frowns from the assembled group.

"I'm sorry, Officer," Dr. Chen spoke up, cutting off anyone else from speaking. "I can come up with a million causes for what's been going on: electrical malfunctions, shoddy workmanship, ball lighting, mass hysteria, a localized earthquake, the Johnsons' home is backed onto Evergreen Creek, so the house settling caused the doors and windows to jam. There is a rational answer, and there are no such things as ghosts or poltergeists." She pushed her glasses up her nose, her coffee cup on our coffee table. "This isn't a Hollywood movie or one of those *over the top* paranormal shows on TV. I'm sorry we live in the real world with real explanations."

Dannie remained silent a moment, waiting for the mumbles of agreement and annoyance to pass. "And I hope you're right." Dannie's shoulders stiffened as she stood taller. "Nothing would make me happier to know everything happening here is bad luck and shoddy construction."

Janice Walker raised her hand, "I read—"

Cutting her off, the front door of our house burst open with a bang as a pair of feet pushed through. "There's a fire!" Vyan called as he reached the kitchen. "Our phones aren't working. There's a fire at the Martins'! Please, there's a fire!"

It was as if an explosion erupted through the walls and floors of our home. We were thrown into pandemonium. A hand or arm to my chest pushed me into our sliding door as Ken and Marsha blasted past me. Alejandro motioned to me to open up the sliding door, which I did and he, Dannie, and I raced out along with the Patils. Everyone headed toward the front of our house, but the red and orange glow from where the Martins' home stood filled our front windows. Within seconds, the whole block stood on the street in front of our house. I found Chloe. She, Cynthia, and the Harris boy had the children huddled around them. As the kids spotted their parents, they hurriedly ran to them. If I had time I would have been proud of Chloe and the other kids for how they handled themselves, making sure all the smaller kids were as safe as possible.

"Kyle, Call 9-1-1," Dannie instructed, pulling my focus off my daughter and into action. "Let me know what they say."

I did as she instructed, pulling out my phone as Chloe reached me and wrapped her arms around me. She was so small. "It's dead. My phone's dead." I held the useless device up.

"Mine's in the house," Alejandro called out.

"Like all ours." Chloe glanced up at me. "Daddy, our phones are all dead."

"Mine too," someone shouted.

"Me too," another voice called out.

"How can none of our phones work?" Dr. Chen glanced at her phone as she snatched her husband's phone that didn't appear to be working either.

"Our house!" Ken yelled, heading toward his home. "God, our house."

"Ken!" Marsha called out, Sammy holding onto her mother's hand.

"Get your garden hoses, aim low!" Dannie instructed everyone and pushed people to get them moving. She raced to her SUV and pulled out a radio, or perhaps a walkie-talkie.

People were scurrying around like an army of ants descending on a piece of dropped candy. As Dannie finished her call, the radio getting tossed to the passenger seat of her vehicle, leaving the door open. She hurried over to Marsha. "Mrs. Martin, is there anyone in the house?"

Marsha didn't speak, her gaze fixed on the fire and her husband.

"Mommy!" Sammy pulled her mother's hand.

"Marsha." Dannie shook the woman. "Is there anyone in your home?"

"No." Marsha's voice was now icy calm, much too serene given the amount of smoke, steam, and chaos filling our street. "The boys are with my parents before they start school. Sammy's here because of her illness. We figured it'd be safer." She licked her lips. "They're in New Jersey."

"Good." Dannie motioned to Deepa. "Stay with her," Dannie instructed.

Deepa wrapped an arm around Marsha's shoulder. Nodding. "It'll be fine, Marsha. We'll save your house."

"Keep those hoses low," Dannie barked as she moved over to the folks with hoses. "Ken! Not so close, back away and aim lower." She glanced over at the others. "Guys, if you can water down the roofs of the other homes." She pointed to Alejandro, Hari, and Lidia who all had hoses pointed at the Martin's home. "We don't want this to spread. Fire response is on the way."

Those that weren't helping with the fire were staying with the kids. Or rushing to their own homes to ensure that everyone was out of the house in case the fire got out of control. Fear and amazement pushed through my body, seeing the house almost fully engulfed in flames. "What happened to the sprinkler system? Why didn't it work?" I asked to anyone listening. No answer came. I moved myself and Chloe away as my skin warmed from the heat of the fire. Even from my new spot, the heat prickled my exposed skin. Sirens occupied the late afternoon sky, blocking out the dogs and birds in our community. With Dannie in charge, she insisted everyone clear off the streets and Ken and a few of the others moved their cars to ensure there was enough room for the emergency vehicles.

"Dad, why is this happening?" Chloe squeezed me tight,

peeking up toward my face. "Before the fire, a tall black figure ran into the garage door."

"What?"

"We saw … this thing, from the park, Vyan said he was gonna go after him, but when he vanished into the garage door we all watched, right after the house burst into flames," Chloe explained. "How'd that happen? Is our house going to burn down too?"

I shook my head. I didn't know. Perhaps it might be a ghost, or some kind of haunting, maybe this poltergeist that Dannie mentioned, or maybe this was something else, something worse terrorizing our street, something I was too afraid to even think about? Something completely different to what happened to Reza and I all those years ago. That activity had been almost comical by comparison.

The fireman took charge of the scene, clearing out those with their garden hoses. The fire crew replaced our neighbor volunteer group with professionals and Dannie stood, already informing the Captain on what had happened.

Hints of relief and hope crept into my body, removing the fear and worry. However, we all continued watching in horror and fascination as the fire unrelentingly devoured the Martin's home. They had the same style home as us, and if their house could go up so quickly, couldn't ours? I would be calling the builder in the morning to have them come and inspect our fire system. Given the faces of our neighbors, I doubted I would be the only one. I hoped with the professionals here and in charge, we had nothing more to worry about.

I couldn't have been more wrong.

Bellows and screams erupted from the Martins' home as the windows shattered. The shrieks threw an already chaotic situation into additional panic. Who was in the house? Another screech plowed through the cul-de-sac and, almost in sync with the roars, the flames burned brighter. My eyes refocused after blinking a few times, not wanting to believe what appeared before us; a burning figure burst from the front door.

Standing there.

Unbelievably, someone had been in the house. The fire fighters refocused and threw everything they had at the figure, but the person continued to burn with no end in sight. One of the firefighters ran to the engine as water continued to rain down on the burning figure. The burning man stood there screeching and roaring but not moving.

The pain they had to be in. I couldn't and wouldn't want to even imagine.

The firefighter at the truck rushed with some kind of blanket in their hands, ready to tackle the burning figure. With a rush of a murder of crows coming to their perch for the night, the burning figure sprinted at full speed toward the firefighter. As the figure moved, everyone in the area got hit by not only a ball of heat, but an overwhelming smell of human feces. I kept myself from heaving. The burning man hit the firefighter and vanished. I don't know how such a thing was possible, but there, in front of all of us, we perceived a person who had been on fire leave the Martins' home, rush a firefighter trying to help them, set her arms and fire blanket ablaze. Additional firefighters sprinted to her aid and, when I peered toward where the burning man should be, he was nowhere. As suddenly as he appeared, he vanished, only the smell of burning and shit left in their wake.

With the being's disappearance, the fire engine's lights and sirens began to blare out, followed by several of the cars in our immediate area joining the chorus. Once again, we had a light and siren show assaulting our already frayed nerves. I pulled Chloe close to me, kneeling down and wrapping my arms around her. Alejandro joined us.

"Daddy. Papa. Make it stop. Make it stop."

"We're trying." Alejandro's voice broke as he took in the scene, wrapping an arm around me and Chloe.

Our neighbors continued to call out for people to turn off their alarms as the shouting overlapped the noise and chaos afflicting our street. All at once, nothing. The night's activity stopped, like with the burning man from the house, the neighborhood fell silent. I stood up and glanced around. Alejandro and I made eye contact and I shook my head. Several other people were stunned into silence. The fire crackled and appeared to lessen. For a brief second, even the firefighters were taken aback. The firefighters refocused as they got the blaze under control as an ambulance turned down our street.

"Hey, Dr. Chen," Hari called out as he moved himself, Deepa, and Vyan to the sidewalk in front of their home. "How do you explain all this?" he barked, watching her. I couldn't blame him. She had basically been mocking us the whole night.

Dr. Chen said nothing as she, her husband, Lee, Marc, and Rose made their way to their home. Mr. Chen glanced over his shoulder at us and shook his head. I spotted the terror in his eyes, not for anything happening around us at the moment, but for his family.

Hari walked over to me, shaking his head. "You remember that damned face, right?"

Alejandro stood between us.

I inhaled as deeply as possible, filling my lungs with as much air as they would hold. "How can I forget? The housewarming."

Hari shivered.

"My mother wasn't exaggerating." He worked on his

fingernail with his teeth.

"The poor Martins." I rubbed my mouth, adjusting my glasses and bringing the scene into focus again.

"Hari, you shouldn't have said that to her." Deepa shook her head. "I think we're going to need everyone."

"He ran straight into the garage." The words were coming from Vyan. "He was gone. Mom. Dad. We can't stay here…" Vyan's eyes were huge dampness playing at the edges. "We need to move. We need to go."

"It'll be fine," Hari countered, trying to assure his son, but the certainty of his words didn't reach his eyes.

"We can go to Neil's." Vyan licked his lips as his voice shuddered. "We can go to grandma and grandpas. We can't stay here."

"Vyan, we're getting help." Deepa offered, her voice as calm as I'd ever heard it. "We'll be fine. It'll be fine."

I don't think I was the only one who didn't believe Deepa, but what were we supposed to do. Especially if Dannie was right about there being something that might move with us. We can't afflict this on anyone else. Could we?

The porch lights on the Chens' home turned off. We didn't see much of the Chens after that; they stayed to themselves for the most part. As for the Martins and their home, when all was said and done that night, they drove away in their car with the clothes they had on and nothing else. We never saw them again, not even during the fire inspection (*causes unknown* is what we were told), and not when the insurance company, or maybe the bank, put a fence up around their property.

I finally reached out to them on social media and learned they quit their jobs here and moved to New Jersey. Sammy and her brothers were all doing well and they were happy living with her parents until they found a new house. They told me they had no intentions of ever coming back to Golden Hills Court.

Since we first moved here in June, two families moved out. One by the terror our neighborhood subjected them to, and one by a mysterious fire. All I comprehended for sure was we needed to do something, and I was hopeful that Dannie and the researchers from the Silicon Valley Paranormal Research Society would be able to help. Especially since it sounded like moving wouldn't solve our problems.

# ~ Chapter Twelve ~

By Saturday, Dr. Anson Thomas sat on our couch holding a cup of coffee in his hands. His rich brown gaze danced around the room fixing on each of us for a moment before moving to the next set of eyes. His confidence held strong in his shoulders, giving him a more youthful appearance, countering the gray in his hair and goatee. He was every bit the researcher and lecturer I found out he was. The steam from his mug filled our family room with the warm, rich scent of roasted coffee beans. "Thank you for allowing us to invade your homes and your neighborhood." He sipped the coffee. Once satisfied, he returned the cup to the coffee table.

Alejandro's hand slipped into mine. "We appreciate you coming and helping us. All of us."

There were murmurs of agreement from everyone assembled.

Since the fire, our home and our street again returned to normal. Well, normal for us. Dr. Thomas's team came and spoke with several of our neighbors—those who agreed to speak with them. The Chens, Walkers, and Gills declined to engage with the investigators, but the rest of us were happy to share our stories. They interviewed us together and separately, asking us everything from what types of books we read, TV shows we watch, videos we enjoy, and if any of us have been treated for mental health issues.

We shared that Chloe had been in therapy for the abuse caused by her mother before we adopted her, after her mother's drug overdose. The team found this information so interesting that they asked to speak with her separately, and asked if we would provide the name of her doctor. I happily shared the information, as Marsha understood everything we were going through and continued to see Chloe and everything in her powers to help. Plus, there was no harm in giving them the information since Chloe's files were protected by HIPPA. Unless we gave Marsha written authorization, there wasn't a lot she would be authorized to say.

I also provided my journal of events for review, including the first names, dates and times of each event, so the researchers could follow up with the folks I mentioned in my notes. Zoe, one of Dr. Thomas's research assistants, chuckled when I handed over my notes. She eagerly took the files, mentioning having this information at the start would really help them along. As for other evidence, we weren't the only ones to provide photos. The Patils had video from their security cameras, as did the Johnsons. The Hernandezes didn't have any photos or videos, but some of their stories were as disturbing as ours. This afternoon, the team wanted to speak to us all together and review what they had learned.

"We've spent some time talking to everyone," Dr. Thomas commented again, making eye contact and beaming at the group. "And we believe the activity is mainly focused on your homes." He pointed to those sitting or standing around our kitchen and family room.

For today's gathering, we were joined by the Patils, Hernandezes, and Johnsons.

Ethan, the youngest member of the SVPRS group, couldn't be more than 20. Studying him, I didn't think I was ever that young, and to my eyes, he didn't seem much older than Chloe. But he was about the same age I was when I had my experiences with Reza, so Ethan only appeared young to my older eyes. He pulled out a large rolled-up paper. Derek and Mercedes moved their cups as he placed the map on the coffee table for us all to see. "This is your street. We've marked the locations of each of the events and the type of event. The circle represents where the focus has been." He tapped the map right where our homes sat.

"So not the Walkers, Gills, or Harrises," Derek commented, shaking his head. "Boggles the mind," he added.

"That would explain why they didn't want to have anything to do with the investigation," Deepa commented, tapping the side of her glass with her ring finger.

"They seem to be on the fringe, and even though they've had some experiences, they've either been in the park or on the street, except for the night you all got sick." Zoe brushed her purple bangs out of her eyes. "I find it hard to believe that the…" She pulled out her notepad. "The Chens haven't experienced anything."

"Oh, that reminds me." I dug into my pocket and pulled out a folded piece of paper. "Mr. Chen, Mike, slipped this to me today when he was out with Muffin." Alejandro raised his eyebrows at me. "He wanted me to give it to the SVPRS folks."

Zoe took the paper I offered her and reviewed what had been written, immediately making her own notes before handing the message to Dr. Thomas.

"So, they have seen things. Why won't they talk to us?" Dr. Thomas questioned, returning the paper to Zoe.

"His wife." Hari huffed and shook his head, annoyance at home on his face. "She won't have any of it. She thinks we're all crazy and making a big fuss out of nothing." He took a sip of his tea.

"She may not believe, but Mike definitely came across as scared and even depressed. Like he hadn't ever been happy." I shrugged. "You know, I don't think he's been sleeping either." I sipped my glass of water.

Dr. Thomas made a note, as did Michelle, and they shared a look. Michelle, the team's psychic or sensitive, struck me as a woo-woo. She did a lot of walking around and commenting on what she felt. She appeared nice, but if you asked me, she also struck me as haunted, like something or someone always hovered around her.

"I'm an engineer," Deepa broke me from my thoughts. "I live for numbers and science. A year ago I wouldn't have believed any of this, but with everything I've seen with my own eyes, my stubborn engineering streak can't deny what's happening as much as I'd love to."

"I agree." Mercedes pushed her braids off her shoulder. "Honestly, I want this to stop. Especially if we can't move, like Dannie suggested. When I was a kid, friends and I would joke about these things being white folks' problems—" She used air quotes around the words 'white folks'. "—that none of us strong black queens would deal with this BS. We'd be out of here, and yet here I am." She shook her head. "I want my normal life back."

Derek grasped out and took his wife's hand.

"If there is an attachment," Dr. Thomas leaned in closer to the assembled group. "Which there may be, so moving won't help. Leaving may make matters worse."

"And you don't believe any of this has to do with what happened to Kyle when he was younger?" Alejandro asked.

Dr. Thomas sighed. "It's hard to say."

"But we don't think so," Michelle countered. "I'm familiar enough with Dr. Zadeh-Ezra's work in the field."

"Wow, it's still hard for me to believe he's a doctor. I can't help but be happy and impressed, still I wish I'd heard back from him." I adjusted my glasses.

"I'll reach out to him as well," Michelle made a note.

123

"We aren't taking anything off the table…" Ethan added. "But since you didn't experience anything more, those events were undoubtedly a regular haunting."

Zoe examined Ethan as he spoke.

"When can we get our normal lives back?" Alejandro asked.

"The only way to get your normal lives back is to stop what's happening by figuring out what the apparitions need, or learn to live with the spirits and put your foot down."

I couldn't help but chuckle internally and wonder if any of us could return to our *normal* lives again. What did that even look like? With what happened before and what's happening now, did I even know what normal was for me?

"So maybe Dr. Chen's right," Hari bit at his upper lip. "Ignoring these things, I mean."

"No," Michelle countered, and the various necklaces and chains around her neck jingled with her movements. "What Dr. Chen's doing won't help and can make matters more dire for her and her family."

Several of us continued to focus on her, but she didn't say anything more.

"Well, Dr. Chen wasn't happy to see me out and about." Ethan frowned. "She told me to get off the sidewalk in front of her house as I took some pictures, not of their house, but the street and the park."

"They couldn't stop me from walking around. I steered clear of their yard." Michelle brushed her brownish red hair over her shoulder, adjusting her chains at the same time. "Everyone else seemed nice. Even the folks who didn't want to speak with us still let me walk around. Mr. and Mrs. Gill offered to let me come and walk through their home." She smiled. "Good people."

"And?" Alejandro asked with a raised hand.

Michelle shifted her stance. "There is definitely something here, a lot of pain and fear. There's also a lot of anger and energy. A lot of what you're experiencing is on a loop. I have the feeling that whatever happened occurred in the early morning, right at dawn or before. If I had to put my finger on the event, I would say there was some kind of raid or battle that happened here."

"Is that why things seem more active during the day?" Mercedes leaned in closer to Michelle.

"Activity can happen any time of day." Ethan pointed to the map. "As you can see, most of the events here happen during the day or early morning, but some big events have happened at night, which has been interesting."

"It's part of why we ask about the media you consume." Dr. Thomas added. "What we watch and read, as well as our culture and our background, affects how we perceive these happenings. However, something that is interesting is you are all from different backgrounds and cultures."

Juan crossed his arms over his chest. "Dr. Thomas, I appreciate what you're saying, but keep in mind we all share one common culture. We are all Americans, we all live in California, making us Californians, and we are all here in San Jose. That is a culture. If we go anywhere outside the U.S., we are spotted as Americans, no matter our ancestry. We often forget this as we insist upon segregating ourselves."

I bit back a smile, as did Derek. When I went with my parents to England as a kid, everyone pegged me for an American and I didn't even have to speak. They just knew.

"Agreed," Deepa seconded. "But why? What caused all this?" She glanced around the room, focusing on Dr. Thomas. "We've experienced a lot of things; hauntings, attachments, poltergeist...how did this happen?"

"We think things were fine until your subdivision was

constructed," Dr. Thomas began. "Ethan and Zoe talked to some of the other folks on your neighboring street and they've never had any issues here before, and still haven't. The family right behind the Martins had no idea the house even burned down until we came by asking them questions."

"How's that possible?" I asked, shaking my head. "All the screaming and sirens and noise."

"We think you might be in a psychic bubble. Whatever is happening here is focused here and doesn't seem to leak into the surroundings," Ethan gestured around the space. "But we still don't know the actual 'how'."

"We've seen things like this before," Dr. Thomas continued. "Granted, nothing of this magnitude, but still. It's like when you put your keys down, turning around only seconds later and they're gone, but after you look for them, you check again and there your keys sit. The apparition didn't want you to see the keys, so you didn't."

Alejandro and I shared a look.

"Those homes have been there for at least five years," Zoe shrugged. "And nothing."

"Perfect," I huffed. "This thing can mess with us both physically and mentally."

"Unfortunately." Michelle scanned the room, trying to speak with everyone. "Think of these events like a trick of memory or perception."

We all grew silent as many of us took sips of our drinks, letting what we've learned so far soak in. Images of what happened with Reza and me filled my mind. His clothes disappearing from the bedroom only to be found outside the cabin in the mud and rain, or my book being left on the side table, ending up in a closed container of cookies. How had I blocked so much of this from my mind?

"Did you get a chance to review the information I gave

you about the area and the Tamien Nation?" Juan spoke up, breaking the silence and our thoughts. "William Marshal would've liked to have been here, but something came up that he had to attend to. But if you need to call him, he said to feel free."

Michelle's posture changed as her shoulders stiffened. She glanced around the room, but focused on the conversation.

"No, but we'll be digging into those materials a lot more. See if there was a village around here, or a battle, or something like that. Try to see if we can tie it in with what Michelle sensed," Zoe glanced at Michelle. "Given the history of Santa Clara County and with San Jose being one of the first towns founded in the area only a few months after San Francisco in 1777, it wouldn't surprise me that there is a lot of pain and suffering caused by the Spanish to the local First Peoples."

"Events like that can really leave a mark on an area," Ethan commented.

Again, Michelle scanned the space, peeking at the corners of the walls.

"Michelle?" Thomas asked as he followed her eyes.

She shook her head.

Lidia's lips pinched tighter as she glanced toward Michelle. We all did, before she continued. "Our Spanish ancestors weren't kind to the people who were here first." A frown erased the pinch from her lips. "Given all the nasty things the Spanish did, I honestly can't blame the Native Americans for being pissed off."

"Well, we don't know for sure... yet." Ethan countered.

Sparing another peek over at Michelle, Dr. Thomas spoke up. "The purpose of this afternoon's meeting is to follow up on our basic review and findings. Unfortunately, these investigations take time. It helped that Dannie knows the case well. But we wanted to spend some time with all of you and evaluate your claims and see what we can pick up."

"I think something's here with us," Michelle eventually spoke, her eyes narrowing as she scrutinized the room, moving from corner to floor to ceiling.

"What?" Derek's head and gaze bounced around the room.

"Where?" Mercedes's voice shook as she peered around.

"It's the same thing I recognized outside, but now the energy is here." Michelle continued to focus on different parts of our family room and dining area. "And it's not happy."

"How can you tell? I don't see any equipment." Deepa put her glass on our coffee table.

The team chuckled, with the exception of Michelle, who walked around the space with her hand raised in front of her.

"Unlike what you see on TV and in movies," Dr. Thomas countered, unfazed by Michelle's movements. "There are no such things as ghost equipment. Most of that tech can be manipulated and, really, is just for TV." Dr. Thomas glanced over at Michelle. "Michelle will use some devices to assist her, and we'll use EMF meters and sometimes static electricity meters to help us form baselines and to ensure there are no environmental reasons for what is happening…."

"Is everything okay" I asked, unable to keep my eyes from Michelle's patrol of our home. A knot in my stomach grew and my shoulders and back squeezed with tension.

"Is there something we can do?" Deepa pinched the bridge of her nose.

"No," Michelle answered. "Continue… I don't think it likes that we're talking about this."

Dr. Thomas shook his head. "She'll let us know. However, if I'm honest, I've never seen anything like what's happening here in your neighborhood." He frowned and sat deeper in the chair. "But there is a lot we don't know in general."

"What do you mean?" Mercedes turned from Michelle

to the doctor.

"On the USS Hornet, for example, there are several apparitions. They interact with us and there is a hierarchy, if that makes sense, but they don't cause trouble, and if one of the apparitions gets out of hand, the Docent will tell the ghost of the commanding officer that is on the ship and the troublemaker will knock it off."

Hari laughed. "Seriously?"

Derek and I shared a look.

"I understand these details might be hard to believe, but that's how these occurrences work there," Dr. Thomas continued. "In other cases, like Dannie mentioned, events are more of a traditional haunting. You'll see things, hear things, smell things, but they won't interact with you." He chuckled, but something didn't feel natural about his mirth. "There was one case I went to, where at one point there had been a couple who were quite *amorous*. Well, their activity left an imprint on the bedroom they shared. The new owners weren't sure what to do. Once we told them, they decided to change rooms, not wanting to relive the couple's sex life."

"We've even seen pets," Zoe added, her voice higher as she said 'pets'.

There were a few smirks from all the assembled.

"But here…." Dr. Thomas paused. "You've got a lot of everything and that is something we don't often see, if ever…."

"But can you help?" I asked, the knots in my stomach getting tighter as my frustration grew, along with my voice. Alejandro rubbed his shoulder, a sure sign of stress. Lidia massaged her temples, and Derek's leg trembled. Something built up in our home, but I didn't know what. Maybe all the stress finally got to me. Got to us.

"We're going to do what we can," Dr. Thomas assured

the group. "Honestly, this is all quite interesting and I'm excited to see what we learn."

"There is something else." Michelle stopped her walk around the open space of our home. "You can all feel the energy, can't you?"

Everyone peeked around the room, ending up back at Michelle.

"I feel like I'm getting cramps." Mercedes rubbed her stomach.

"My head is throbbing." Hari massaged his temples.

"Anson won't agree with me, but I've detected something else, something darker, hiding not in any of your homes but around the street and in the park. But now the energy is here. This thing doesn't like that we're here, and this energy doesn't like that you're all together."

"My neck's twisted in knots," Alejandro commented as he continued to rub his neck.

"Michelle," Thomas warned, his tone sharp. "I don't want to add any more drama to an already stressful situation. We don't want to initiate any PK activity."

"Anson, I'm not feeling so good." Zoe wiped the beads of sweat from her forehead.

Dr. Thomas stood up. "This is what I was talking about." He gave a firm shake of his head.

Ethan shook his head. "Could it be—"

"Everyone, relax," Dr. Thomas commanded, his words tight. "There is no evil intent, only an evil former act." He tried to calm the growing tension in the room. "Really, this is all quite norm—"

"You're bleeding!" I pointed toward Anson, grabbing a couple of napkins from the dining table and moved to him. "Lean your head forward and hold this to your nose, pinching," I instructed.

He took the napkin and did as instructed, and continued to speak. "Michelle, what are you sensing?"

She was quiet.

"Doctor, is it possible this is a different type of attachment?" Ethan glanced around the room as he spoke, each of his words sharp and seemingly pinched together.

"A what?" several of us asked at once. My stomach and head throbbed and I wanted to vomit.

"Something attached to a person or to the land." Michelle continued to survey the space. "It's possible, or something else, but they keep moving. I can't pin them down." She adjusted her gaze as she continued to glance around the space, trying to find the location of whatever she noticed or felt.

"And you think we might have some kind of attachment?" Alejandro rubbed his head, his voice strained. "Why?" he demanded. "What did we do?"

"Maybe." Michelle rubbed her hands on her pants. "But I'll be honest, I've never experienced anything like the energy I'm sensing here."

"Are you talking about some kind of Demon or Demons?" Lidia continued to massage her temples. "Dios mi. You mean there might be Demons here in our homes, or neighborhood?"

"Let me be very clear." Dr. Thomas held up his head, the napkin still on his nose. The paper cloth had been white, but now was spotted red. "I do not believe in, nor have I ever seen anything that would come close to what any of you would claim to be a Demon or Demons. They simply do—"

As if on cue, the lights in the house began flickering. A howl and banging came from our upstairs. Ethan and Zoe rushed off to the hall and up the stairs. As they dashed off, everything on our coffee table—cups, map, cell phones, documents, napkins, cookies, and chips—crashed toward our fireplace in a thunderous blow. A blast of air whooshed by

131

everyone, causing shirts and hair to billow. The gust of wind carried a foul odor, the same smell of feces we all smelled the night of the fire.

Bile crawled out of my stomach and I rushed to the sink, coughing and spitting. I wasn't the only one, as I caught sight of Derek rushing to the powder room to do the same.

"Oh, god." Michelle waved her hand in front of her face, her necklaces clinking as she did so.

Alejandro moved to the sliding door, opening it and stepping outside. I spit the last of the bile in my mouth into the sink, turning the faucet on. Dr. Thomas and Lidia opened the windows in our family room to get fresh air into the house, and the hum of the fan in the kitchen added to the noises as Deepa and Mercedes opened the windows in our kitchen.

I pulled down several glasses and moved to the refrigerator, filling them with water for everyone, but the first one was for me. I had to get this foul taste out of my mouth.

"Alejandro, a little help." He hurried to my side and assisted passing out water.

As Derek returned from the powder room, we all focused on Dr. Thomas.

He moved to the window, blood-dotted napkin still at his nose. "Psycho-kinesis activity. Granted, the most I've seen in a while, but still PK." His tone wasn't as sure as before. "And it's no wonder with all the stress you've been under. You mentioned you have a twelve-year-old daughter. Where is she tonight?"

"In Campbell at a sleepover." I took an additional sip of water and swished the liquid around my mouth, spitting the contents of my mouth into the sink. "We figured the break from all this would be a good thing."

Michelle glanced at Dr. Thomas and he held up a hand.

"Maybe someone here," Dr. Thomas continued. "One of you?"

"We've never seen more then one living agent in a space. The odds—"

"Dr. Thomas!" Zoe called as hurried feet moved down the stairs. She helped Ethan down the stairs as we headed toward them.

"What is it?" Anson moved over to the hallway.

"Something attacked me." Ethan pulled up his shirt. There were five sets of three scratches all over his back and stomach and on his arms. Some were deep and bleeding. "Jesus, it's burning."

"Get the first aid kit," I instructed Alejandro as we helped Ethan to my office, putting him in my chair. "This is worse than what happened to Chloe." I shook my head.

"This happened before?" Dr. Thomas asked.

"To Chloe, but the scratches weren't this bad. And there were only a few. We took pictures. I think Zoe has them."

Alejandro returned with the first aid kit and we worked on Ethan's cuts.

"Anson, I've never seen a PK attack like this." Michelle focused on the doctor. "These cuts are deep."

Zoe pulled out her phone and snapped pictures.

"But we have seen them before. This is nothing out of the norm," Anson countered.

"Feels out of the norm for me," Ethan commented with a frown crossing his lips. He winced under our touch with the antiseptic.

"We were checking the upstairs for the noise." Zoe's eyes were as wide as saucers as she slipped her phone into her pocket.

"We don't know everything about the paranormal, Michelle." Dr. Thomas countered, ignoring his assistant.

"What happens in one location will not repeat in another. I'm guessing you have a couple of bullies here who—"

"I got some damp towels." Lidia pushed the damp towels at me, interrupting the doctor.

"No, we don't," Michelle fired off at Dr. Thomas, a strained glare of frustration following her words. "It might be a bully, or a couple of bullies, maybe the Spanish soldiers, but I'm not sensing them right now. Just several angry things that I don't believe were ever human."

"Let's get Ethan taken care of, and we can examine our notes and data and see what else we can learn while we do additional research into this location," Dr. Thomas announced.

We got Ethan cleaned up and, with some final words from Dr. Thomas saying that typically Poltergeist activity only lasts for six months to a year, our first meeting and investigation with the SVPRS was over. I'm not sure what we all got from the meeting, except for being more worried about the happenings here. Still, today had been the foundation. So perhaps that was a good thing.

As they made their way out of our home, Michelle pulled me aside. "I know Anson doesn't believe in Demons. However, not everything can be explained away as a poltergeist or an attachment, or even a bully spirit. I'm going to make a couple of calls on my own, and we'll be back. I'll definitely get in touch with Reza and his team. See what he has to say about your previous experience, but if you think of anything...."

I licked my lips.

"I promise we'll get this all sorted out." She took my hand and pulled me in for a hug. "Take care. Call us, any of us, if things get worse."

I hugged her tight, unsure what to say or even do at this moment.

Our neighbors and the team from the SVPRS slowly

vanish from our front porch. I glanced at Alejandro, but didn't say anything. After ten years, we understood each other. When they threw the 'Demon' word out, I was filled with a kind of terror I would never wish on anyone, and that frightened me more than these ghostly attacks. But nothing scared me more than what we were on a direct course to encounter.

# ~ Chapter Thirteen ~

Maybe an hour, perhaps two, passed after everyone left. We had finished cleaning up the house, and the mess left by our bully ghost. We had lit several candles to help neutralize the god-awful stench of shit in our house, but oddly, or luckily, the smell vanished almost as quickly as it had arrived. Both Alejandro and I were glad Chloe was hanging out with Jacky and Maggie over at Sara and Carter's. The farther she was from all this, the better. At least, as far as I was concerned.

Still, we missed her, especially now, when things were quiet and normal. That was one thing: given all we had been through these past several weeks, we were spending a lot more time together and a lot less time on our devices. I think our time bonding made us stronger and might be part of why we fared so well overall, but I can't say.

Alejandro and I were cuddled up on the sofa when red flashing lights announced the noise of an ambulance as the sounds echoed through the main hall of our house.

"God. Now what?" Alejandro hit pause on our show and placed the remote on the coffee table.

"I don't think I can take anymore, not tonight." I shifted and pulled myself up off the couch.

Alejandro and I made our way to the front door, flipping on the porch light. What new hell were we in for? I opened the front door and stepped out. The warm night air pushed over me as I made my way to the front of our porch. We weren't the only ones coming out. Several folks were on their front porches watching the ambulance. An inhalation of relief filled me seeing the paramedics weren't at the Hernandezes' home, or the Patils', or Johnsons'. That only left one.

The Chens'.

Dr. Chen rushed out of her home, hair mussed and something splattered on her face and her clothing. She ran a red hand through her hair, meeting the paramedics.

"Blood?" My eyes grew large and my stomach flipped with worry. That couldn't be what I observed. Maybe she was covered in chocolate or something that went poof in the kitchen. I spared a glance at Alejandro, and his expression confirmed my fear: blood.

The paramedics got their equipment together and, as a group, hurried into the single-story home. Deepa and Hari crossed the street, joining us on our porch. A patrol car pulled up and one officer rushed into the house as the other officer stood by the patrol car on his radio, watching us watch them.

The officer wasn't one that I recognized from the many who visited our neighborhood since we moved in. I had to wonder, and I made a mental note to ask Dannie, what the police and other emergency service providers thought of everything happening on our street or if this craziness was all part of what they signed on for. I couldn't imagine that being the case.

"What's happening?" Deepa asked as we continued to watch our neighbors' home.

"No clue."

"Did you see the blood?" Hari shook his head. "Now I feel bad for everything I said to her."

"I hope everyone's okay," I commented, thinking about the note Mr. Chen, Mike, gave me and how awful he looked today.

*I should have said something. I should have done more. God, I hope they are all okay.*

The summer night air hung still on our street. No birds, no bugs. The night was quiet, which was the worst possible noise there was these days. You don't realize how much ambient noise there is around you until it's gone. And tonight, nothing. That upset me, possibly because of everything transpiring with the paranormal team today and the talk of us potentially being here with something darker.

"How are you feeling about today?" Alejandro turned from the scene at the Chens'.

"I don't know," Hari spoke as he continued to watch the Chens' home. He stood in shorts and a tee-shirt. "I'm lucky I can get away from here for work. But I make sure none of us are home alone, and that's not easy with the restaurant." He rubbed his chin.

"We were talking with Vyan, before he went out. He really wants to move, and so does Neil…"

"I've considered moving," Alejandro admitted.

I played with the frame over my ear, ensuring my glasses were in place.

"But I don't like the idea of giving up and running." Alejandro smiled at me.

I nodded my agreement.

"That's how we feel." Deepa's voice was resolute. "This is our house, and we worked too hard to be chased off by something…" She waved her hand in the direction of the park. "Like this…"

"Honestly, I worry for Chloe and the rest of the kids in the neighborhood." I adjusted my glasses again. "They shouldn't have to deal with this."

"None of us should," Hari added.

"I hope the research team can help." Deepa pulled at her shirt. She stood in yoga pants and a long tee-shirt. None of us were dressed to be out of the house, but that mattered less

138

and less these days.

"I think they can." Alejandro scanned our group. "I have to believe they can."

"Lidia mentioned they might call the Catholic Diocese office downtown and see if they can help." Hari leaned against the rail on our porch.

"Do they even do things like that?" I asked. I wasn't raised Catholic. My parents were Church of England, but didn't go to church once they moved to California.

"Yep," Alejandro confirmed. "I considered the church too, after the housewarming. My mom wanted me to have a priest come and bless the house. I didn't think we needed to, but now…"

"I'm willing to try anything." Deepa fluttered her shirt to make a breeze of the still night air. "I've pondered about reaching out to the Sikh temple over off Quimby, but…."

"I didn't know you were Sikh." Alejandro faced them. "Hari, you don't have a beard or wear the head wrap… drape?"

"We aren't," Hari rubbed his smooth-shaven chin almost to emphasize the point. "Well, Deepa was raised—"

Conversation ended as the paramedics left the Chens' house. They were making their way with a body on their gurney and Dr. Chen followed with her kids in tow. She appeared to have cleaned herself off and changed what she wore.

"Emily. What happened?" Deepa called out. "Do you need us to watch the kids?"

Emily, Dr. Chen, glared over at us. "You did this!" she yelled. "Ming, my poor Ming."

*Ming…must be Mike's real name.*

She pointed at us, jabbing the air with her finger. Both anger and fear filled her expression. "All this crazy talk. You made him do it. He would never have done this… It's all your fault."

The officer walked up to Emily. "Mrs. Chen, you need to calm down, please. This won't help your husband."

"What?" Alejandro retorted, his voice and tone harsher than I would like to hope he meant. "You can't be serious."

"What happened?" Hari's tone filled with concern, but came across as the calmest amongst us. Or the guiltiest, after all he said to Dr. Chen.

"You and your nonsense about this neighborhood. Our neighborhood! Our home!" Emily shouted, shrugging off the police officer.

"Dr. Chen, we need to go," the paramedics called to her from their rig.

"I'll follow in my car," Emily hissed at them. "I'll meet you at the hospital. I'm not leaving my kids here." She pointed, saying something to her children in what I believed to be Mandarin, but I couldn't say for certain. She pointed at us. "I'm not trusting my children with any of them."

The paramedics went to work on getting Mike in the ambulance. As they were getting him secured, the officer continued to stand with Mrs. Chen, gently trying to usher her to a car, any car.

"All your ghost talk," Dr. Chen continued. "Craziness. You pushed him to do this. I blame all of you," she shouted and trained a finger on all of us, and the Johnsons, who were out on their porch trying to figure out what was happening. "Ming wouldn't do this on his own… it's all you."

"Emily, what happened?" Hari questioned again. She still hadn't spoken. "What did Mike do? Please, we want to help if we can." His offer was genuine and kind.

Mr. Patil was definitely a kinder person than I was at the moment, but given what happened, his words and actions made sense. If I spoke, my words would be filled with venom.

None of this was our fault. We were all victims, but we were at least willing to acknowledge what was going on, and we were planning on fighting. We were going to fight for our homes, our families, our neighborhood, and our friends.

"I didn't know what he was doing in the kitchen until Lee found him." She swiped at her eyes. "I did what I could to stop the bleeding…"

"And your actions saved his life," the officer reassured her.

Her gazed burned into us all. "All this is your fault," she yelled again, looking at her hands.

"Mrs. Chen, this isn't the time. Don't you want to be with your husband?" the officer tried.

"You and your crazy talk almost cost me my husband," Mrs. Chen continued. "I wish they'd arrest you for this…" She pointed again, at all of us.

"Mommy!" One of her kids got her attention; it sounded like Marc. He pointed to the ambulance.

The vehicle with Mike pulled away and headed off. The officer glanced at us and at Mrs. Chen.

"Come on." Emily pulled her kids into her car and she turned and pointed right at us one last time. "Your crazy talk caused him to take a knife and…" she stammered. I noted tears glisten down her cheeks. "I wish we never moved next to you crazy people."

She got into her car and sped away. The officers got into their vehicle and proceeded to leave. They stopped as we continued observing them. They had spotted something, or someone, at the park. They flashed their lights and turned on their spotlight, focusing on our park.

"I thought I saw someone over in the park, too." Deepa motioned in the park's direction.

"Undoubtedly some looky-loo out for a walk." Hari shook his head.

The officers moved the light back and forth several times, finally slowly pulling away. They turned on their flashers and drove away.

"God." Alejandro watched them pull away from our street.

"I wouldn't ever have expected Mike to do something like that." Hari crossed his arms over his chest. "Is she right? Did we cause him to do that?"

"No." Alejandro shook his head. "It's not us. It's all on Mike."

"Are we sure Mike was… okay…and not something else?" I licked my lips as I glanced at their home and the rest of our homes. My gaze stopped on the park where the police had been scanning with their searchlight. I would've sworn I saw someone standing watching the Chens' home, then watching all of us. I wanted to blame a trick of the light, but I knew better. Especially as the police had scanned the area and Deepa mentioned seeing someone as well.

But poof, they were gone. Like everything else; hit and run.

I rubbed a hand over my cheek and hair and glanced at the Patils and Alejandro. Why would Mike, Mr. Chen, try to take his own life? He did seem a bit depressed, but I… maybe I might have been able to stop him. No. How? I only saw him on his dog walks and I always treated him with kindness, but maybe I might have been able to do more. Perhaps we all might've done more. I didn't know, and in a way, that scared me. If something like that happened to him, what's to say something like that wouldn't happen to one of us, or one of our kids?

I pushed those dark thoughts from my head. I couldn't go down that road, not with everything else happening. That night I promised myself I would do a better job checking in with Alejandro, our daughter, our friends, and our neighbors.

That is the least I could do—show some kindness and let people know I was here for them and they weren't alone.

None of us were.

I also decided I needed to reach out to Reza again and see what help he would be able to provide. I know we had the local team, but he and I had seen something similar to this before. Nothing to this degree, and in a way, those events kind of pushed us together. This was something completely different, but still, he might be able to help as well.

After Mr. Chen's incident, the family didn't spend time at their home. Whether their continued absence had to do with Dr. Chen's work or Mike's recovering in the hospital from his suicide attempt, I couldn't say. On Sunday, the next day, Dr. Chen came home and picked up Muffin without a word to any of us. We all tried to reach out to them over the next few days, but Dr. Chen wouldn't have any of it, which worried me. Isolation wasn't a good idea. Based on what we found out from the paranormal group, isolation was the worst thing possible. Dr. Thomas mentioned that suicide rates can be abnormally high when dealing with an attachment or severe PK attacks, and we were definitely meeting those criteria. Dealing with the incidents together, showing your collective strength, was the best way to do battle with the paranormal, at least we all hoped.

# ~ Chapter Fourteen ~

In my office, I stared at my computer screen, drumming my fingers on my desk. I couldn't focus. Since the meeting with Dr. Thomas and the members of the SVPRS, concentrating on my actual work had been a challenge, not to mention what happened with Mr. Chen. He was still in the hospital, and we all hoped and prayed he would be okay. Dr. Chen hadn't softened her attitude toward us and, if anything, the Chens as a whole became more reclusive and I hardly ever saw them at home anymore.

I—we—wanted to reach out to them, but what do you say to people who either are too terrified to listen or refuse to believe what their own eyes see? I managed to check in with the Hernandezes and Johnsons. I even walked over to say hello to the other families on our street, just to check in. I didn't want to see anyone else suffer or feel like they had no one to talk to.

I couldn't say if things were better for my efforts, but doing the check ins helped my mental health and that was important too.

There was a ping on my messenger, and I clicked over. There was an active window from Reza asking if I was free to chat. I didn't waste any time, and I opened up a screen and on my monitor a familiar, if not older, face greeted me. His dark wavy hair peppered with grey and not nearly as long as he once kept it played well with his square jaw and high cheekbones, his skin not as youth full as it once was. However, his dark brown eyes were still able to catch your gaze and not let go. I inhaled and could almost smell his wonderful rosewood scent.

"Hey, handsome." He beamed at me through the screen.

"Hi." I waved, my heart skipping a beat and my stomach suddenly doing summersaults. I knew our relationship was long since over, and Alejandro was the one for me, however, seeing Reza after all these years filled me with so many wonderful memories.

"Sorry it's been a minute." He moved off screen then back again.

"I get it. I know how busy you are. How's the hubby?" I straightened how I sat so I wasn't slouching. "How're your folks? Your mom still making those wonderful cookies of hers?"

Reza laughed. "They're fine. They're still out in Milpitas. She doesn't bake as much as she used to, but whenever we go out, she has them ready for us." He beamed. "I think she's still trying to bribe me with her cooking, to get us back out there. They're not thrilled with what I'm doing. They don't think it's safe…"

*Well, they're not wrong.*

I decided not to say anything to that.

Reza continued. "Micah, he's good. We're trying to wrap up a few things up here." He rubbed his stubbled chin. "How's Alejandro?"

I cleared my throat. "He's good." Things hadn't worked out between Reza and I, but that was okay. We both ended up where we needed to be and from the sounds of things, we both landed some terrific men.

"You free to talk for a bit? Michelle reached out." Reza's tone changed to his professional psychology, or, I guess, parapsychology, manner.

I licked my lips. "I don't know what she told you…"

"Enough, but I wanted to hear the story from you."

I spent the next several minutes filling him in on what had been happening and what happened with Mr. Chen. Despite being with Alejandro for so many years, I won't lie; Reza still looked amazing, especially his welcoming smile. I was taken back to when we were together. Talking to him was like old times. He was so comfortable and we got on so well; I wondered what happened to us.

*Life.*

"Well, I have a different take on things than Anson does, but I will say Anson is a good guy and despite us disagreeing on the paranormal, I'm sure he'll be able to help you. Plus, Michelle is amazing, so you'll be in good hands."

"I don't suppose you can come out and check things out for us? We have a guest room all set up and there'd be plenty of room for you and Micah. I can't promise the cooking would be as good as your mothers, but Alejandro and I do alright."

He laughed. "I wish, but my team and I are heading to Europe for a couple months. We're filming a pilot for a TV show…"

"Wow, that's amazing…"

"But…" he continued, despite my interruption. "If they aren't able to help you, let me know and we'll be there. You have my word. I'm going to send you all my personal contact information, both here and in Europe."

"Thanks."

"Kyle." Reza's tone grew serious. "Did anything else happen to you or around you after our event at the cabin that weekend? I know we didn't talk much about it afterwards given what happened with my folks, but was there anything more?"

I pushed my lips together and shook my head, thinking. "No. Nothing. I almost forget all about what happened to us until things started up when we moved in."

"Hmm. Interesting." He raised his eyebrows as he spoke. "Why?"

Now he shook his head. "I thought… well, it doesn't matter." He peeked over his shoulder. "I need to go, but now you know how and where to reach me, so let me know what happens and if I can help I will, but I think you're in good hands."

"Thanks for reaching out, and sorry that I didn't do a better job keeping in touch."

Reza laughed. "We both got busy and life took us in different directions. You know how these things go."

I sighed my agreement.

"Tell Alejandro I said hello and let him know he better take good care of you." His grin filled his face. "Especially since I know how and where to track you both down."

I chuckled. "Tease."

"Always." He waved and closed the window.

I leaned forward and sighed. Seeing Reza filled me with a lot of memories and talking with him gave me hope that things would be okay.

Despite my lack of concentration and drifting in and out of memory lane, I managed to plug away at my job. My work gave me a great distraction from all the recent activity. However, unlike Alejandro, I was at home three days a week, which was good when Chloe was here, but with school starting this week and not wanting her to have to deal with our neighborhood, we let her spend as much time as she wanted with her friends in Campbell. As a thank you, we told Sara and Carter we would take them out for an adult only night.

If I was honest, I wished I could have been with Chloe or even heading to Europe with Reza, but bills needed to be paid and these reports wouldn't review themselves. Plus, I wasn't about to evict our renters so we'd have a place to run to. And despite the memories I had with Reza, my heart belonged to Alejandro and nothing would change that.

"Hey," Alejandro's voice called my attention to the doors of my office.

Facing him, a smile moved over my lips. "I didn't hear you come in."

He grinned at me, his dark hair shining in the hall light and his pale-yellow polo shirt fit snug at his shoulders, his gray khakis showing off his solid legs. He crossed the distance between us, and his soft, full lips pressed against mine. "Considering the volume of the music."

I shrugged. I didn't like having the house quiet. Too many noises made me jump. I figured at least with music, if something happened maybe I wouldn't catch it, or notice. I tapped my phone changing the volume of the music and selecting something softer and more peaceful.

"Oh, nice." Alejandro smiled. "Chloe over with Maggie and Jacky?" He stepped back, glancing at my desk. My regular glasses were sat next to my headphones, and my cell phone was located within reach. There were also folders, pens, and markers laying about. The space wasn't a mess, but not as neat as I normally kept it.

"Given school starts on Wednesday, I figured I'd let her spend these last few days of freedom with her friends. Get her away from all…" I waved my hand around the office.

He leaned against my desk, crossing his arms over his chest. "I haven't even asked. Is everything ready? Do we need to do anything?"

I picked up my phone and glanced at the time. "Between her and I, everything is taken care of. We were pretty much set by the time we moved in. Thank goodness." I placed my phone down, taking off my glasses, swapping them out for my normal glasses.

He laughed. "That seems like a lifetime ago." He peeked over at my screen. I had an excel spread sheet open with columns of numbers and words that I barely recognized. "Working on anything interesting?"

"Not really." I closed the file and opened up another file. "I've been digging into our street and the neighborhood, and Reza reached out to me."

"On company time?" He teased with a shake of his head. "Naughty, naughty."

"I don't want to hear it from you." I raised my eyebrows in his direction. "Anyway, I found out that, for whatever reason, this plot of land wasn't sold to the original builders when the bigger surrounding neighborhood was first built. The owner flat out refused to sell this land." I moved the pointer to an image, pulling up a map of the area.

"Was there a home on the land or something?" He leaned forward to better see what I showed him.

"No, that's the crazy part." I clicked over to the site map I got from the county. "Empty. Nothing here." I pointed to the screen. "See?" I clicked another image, this one more current, a map showing the homes and parks built around our street.

"What changed, I wonder?" Alejandro leaned in closer to the screen.

"Two years ago, the old man died." I pulled up another document.

"What a shame." Alejandro pulled away from the screen and stood up. He now stood behind me to see better. He rested his hands on my shoulder.

"And there was no family, so…"

"So, the builders swooped in and bought the land." The warmth of his exhale tickled my neck.

I trembled.

"And us foolish mortals bought a nice, new, shiny home right here in spook central." He huffed as his fingers rubbed my shoulders.

"Pretty much." I relaxed under his touch. I worked the mouse and keyboard. "I found this article about him and the property online. All farms, and a big section was once part of a winery. The area where the village shops are located, that was all vineyards in the 80s. They used to do a huge annual firework display on the Fourth of July." Seeing that must have been impressive for the people who lived here.

"But not where we are."

"Nope. This was all grazing or farm land for the longest time. The original neighborhood ended past Ruby Avenue. Fowler Road came to a dead end, but that all changed in the 90s and 2000s when the land became too valuable to sit around." I sighed, adjusting Alejandro to a more comfortable position.

"And instead of having farms, orchards, and vineyards, houses were dropped in." Alejandro tapped my shoulder. "No one thinking about what was once here, or who that might piss off."

"Our area was part of the city's master plan for years," I added. "Well, except for this plot of land." I tapped my desk.

"So, the city anticipated something might be wrong here?" He adjusted to look at me.

"I'm not sure." I sighed. "Maybe they recognized the owner and realized he wouldn't sell." I rubbed my temples.

"Do you think the land owner knew something everyone didn't?" He walked over to my bookcase as I studied him and his amazing form. He picked up a photo of our wedding day, running a hand over it. "Wasn't there that issue by Highway 87 and Automall Parkway, where the land was kept empty because that spot was a Native American burial site? And they found bones…"

"But forgot, or pretended to forget, and they built the solar farm there." I shook my head.

"At least the solar farm wasn't homes." He put our wedding photo down. "But still disrespectful."

"If I remember correctly, they did a Native American ceremony…" I wasn't sure what more to say. Maybe they should have done something like that here. But if they hid the information from us, wasn't that illegal? Couldn't we sue them? I didn't know, and I didn't even want to go down that path right now. Plus, the only people who won in lawsuits were the lawyers.

Alejandro huffed. "Are you going to send the info to the SVPRS team?"

"Maybe these details will help with the investigation."

"It can't hurt." Alejandro walked over and leaned against my desk. "And what did Dr. Reza have to say?"

I was so glad Alejandro wasn't jealous of my ex. Alejandro never made me feel like I had to hide anything, which I appreciated. I tried to afford him the same consideration. "Nothing really. He likes Michelle, doesn't agree with Anson, but thinks he'll be able to help us, and if not, he and his husband will jump on the first plane and come out to help us personally. Although he did ask me if anything else happened after our experience at the cabin, it was kind of weird."

"Really?"

"I don't know what he was getting at…" I shrugged.

"Hmm. Well, I guess it's good to have a back-up." Alejandro smiled. "For the paranormal group and for me."

"Ha ha."

He leaned in and kissed me. "You should send him the information as well."

"I'll get the docs all sent to them both in the morning." I turned to my computer, saved all my files, and glanced at my emails one last time. It was after five, and there wasn't much more I wanted or needed to do today, so I logged off for the day. "Do you think things will ever go back to being normal?"

Alejandro raked a hand through his hair. "Were they ever really normal? I mean, look at us, two dads raising an adopted black daughter. This wouldn't have been possible twenty years ago."

He wasn't wrong. A lot had changed, some of it good, and some of it not so good, but the key was to pick your battles. And right now, our battle was for our family, our home, and our neighborhood. Everything else had to fall to the background. What did Dr. Wilson call it? The hierarchy of needs. And we were stuck in safety and security. At least, that is what things felt like since we moved here.

He interlaced his fingers with mine. "Come on." He pulled me up from my chair.

"What?"

"Chloe's out of the house at least for a couple more hours, and I think we need some alone time. I don't know about you, but I need the release. Plus, I want to remind you why you're with me and not your ex." He kissed me, this time deeper and with more need.

"You have nothing to prove to me. And what about dinner?" I asked. "And I should go for my ride."

"Oh, I have a ride in mind, but it involves you and me naked upstairs in our bedroom. If you want to go for a bike ride after that, you can, but maybe wait until after dinner." He pulled me out of my office and up the stairs.

"You're so romantic." I laughed as I allowed him to lead me to our bedroom.

"Isn't that why you married me?" He pulled me close,

twirling me under his arms, and kissed me again.

"No, I married you for your looks and the beast housed between your legs."

"Now who's the romantic one?" He smirked again and pulled me closer, pressing his groin into mine. "You mean that beast?" He whispered into my ear. His growing excitement was impossible to miss.

We made our way into the bedroom, soft music continuing to greet us every step of the way. Once we reached the bed, Alejandro pulled me to him and kissed me again. His full arousal was now very much present against my body. "Someone's ready to go."

"You have no idea," Alejandro commented, kissing my neck and tugging at my shirt. "It's been like this all day."

"Well, let's see what we can do about it." After he tugged off my shirt, I pulled at his belt, unbuttoned his pants, and pulled down his zipper. We made our way onto the bed, clothes littering the floor behind us. I got him on the bed and took in the sight of him. He was sexy as hell; tanned skin, smooth chest and stomach, with a rock-hard cock not pointing to the sky like most dicks I've seen. Alejandro had what I referred to as a banana dick, and I loved it; even when hard, his cock hung over his balls. He joked that if he stretched enough he wouldn't have a boyfriend because he would be able to fuck himself. I called him on his boast once and instead of proving his point, he pounded me like a machine that night. Thinking about how he hit all my pleasure points that night still got me hard. Focusing on his current state only added to my own excitement, and I felt an ache in my groin as I grew harder, matching Alejandro's excitement.

"Like what you see?" he teased as he moved to the head of our bed, resting on a pillow and showing himself off to me. His hand moved over his stomach and squeezed his dick and balls.

"You know I do." I climbed on top of him and went to work. I slipped a finger in my mouth, getting my digit slicked up before taking him in my mouth. He tasted good on my lips. Within seconds I had him in my mouth, savoring him as my mouth slid up and down on him. With each motion of my tongue, soft moans escaped his lips, reaching my ears. I took my slicked-up finger and probed into him, wiggling my finger, feeling him bucking under me.

These moments when we were together, alone, nothing else mattered. I couldn't say if our sex life improved or worsened during the events in our neighborhood, but what I do know for certain is that these moments reminded us what we were fighting for. Not the sex, but that was part of it. We were struggling for our lives together and our love for each other. When you are this close and when you've been through so much, these moments of pleasure remind you that you are alive and there is love and other joyful things worth fighting for.

He pulled from my maw. "Your finger is magic, but I need you inside me." He pulled me close to him.

I was eager and willing to comply. Anything he wanted or needed I would have happily done. I believe this is the same for all couples and people who truly love each other. When you're with the one you love, anything they ask you to do, you'll happily provide. You want them to feel as good as they make you feel. Maybe this is why evil fights so hard to destroy families, why unhappy, miserable people, both living and dead, continue to make others feel as badly as they feel. If they can't be happy, fall in love, be loved, they don't want anyone else to feel those wonderful feelings either.

I shifted off my husband and nabbed what I needed from the night table and got myself situated for our encounter. In a flash, I slid in Alejandro and we both gasped. I found his mouth and kissed his beautiful lips again. We found our tempo and were joined together as one. Our rhythm continued as we lost ourselves in each other. My soul purpose was to give him as much pleasure as possible and in turn that was his only mission for me. Our bodies pulsated together. Our movements grew more frantic, as did our gasps for air.

He pulled away from my face. "Fuck, I'm so close, baby. Tell me you're there with me."

I couldn't speak. My body was now on autopilot as I thrusted harder into him as my left hand worked his cock, stroking him faster, trying to merge my hand movements with the actions of my hips. It wasn't too much longer before we both achieved climax. For that brief moment we were in complete bliss and wrapped in a warm blanket of love and safety. I stayed frozen inside of him for what I assumed might be hours, and finally shifted off him, but doing my level best to keep myself in him. Alejandro's eyes closed as he inhaled assisting in my movements ensuring we remained as one before he leaned over and kissed me again.

He chuckled and rested his head on the pillow. "Can we stay this way forever?"

"I'm always happy to be inside you for as long as you want me there, but at some point we'll want to get cleaned up."

"Spoil sport." He wiggled his back side and clenched almost daring me to leave him.

Despite wanting to stay like this and knowing that my dick would eventually soften and pop out of him. I chuckled.

He kissed me once again and then stretched his legs and arms before releasing me from him. "How about a shower?" He smirked at me.

After laying in our afterglow, we made our way to the shower and got cleaned up. Mentally I had no doubt we each wanted to make the other come again, especially with how much we focused on cleaning each other's private parts, but physically our bodies needed time to recharge. Still, it wasn't often that we got to shower together since we adopted Chloe, so we took full advantage of our shower time as well. We ensured that we were both nice and clean by the time Chloe got home later in the evening. I never did make it out for my bike ride, but the workout I had with Alejandro had been far better than any ride on my bike in the golden foothills of Evergreen.

# ~ Chapter Fifteen ~

"Do you have everything you need for school?" Alejandro moved from the toaster, pulling out the browned bread, dragging over the butter tray with his free hand. He put the toast on the plate and grabbed a knife from the drawer, so he could put butter on the heated slices. He slid the plate of toast next to the bowl of cereal on the counter.

"I think so." Chloe tugged at her peach shirt, sitting at the counter and pouring a glass of orange juice.

"Are you excited?" I asked, re-drying my hands from my visit to our powder room.

"Did you want me to drive you?" Alejandro offered as he poured himself a glass of OJ.

"I think I can walk, Papa." Chloe eyed him as she splashed milk into her cereal.

"If you're sure." He drank his juice.

"And I'll be home all day, in case you need anything," I sniffed, smelling the buttered toast and moving to the cabinet holding the honey.

"Dad," she tried speaking through a mouthful of cereal.

I raised my honey-free hand. "Fine." I crossed and sat down, picked up a piece of toast, adding honey to the slice before taking a bite.

"I packed your favorite." Alejandro finished off his OJ and nabbed a piece of toast for himself. "Pringles, turkey and cheese, carrots and an apple."

Chloe huffed. "Can't I buy lunch there? Like everyone else."

"No." Alejandro shook his head, wiping crumbs from his shirt. "I've seen what schools feed kids and I won't have you eating that..." He didn't continue; instead, he dusted off his shirt.

"Fine." Chloe took a spoonful of cereal.

I waited for Alejandro to turn away from us to put something in the sink. I hastily slipped Chloe a ten-dollar bill I had ready for her in my pocket. She smiled and pocketed the money as I raised a finger to my lips.

*Our secret... or so she assumed.*

"Finish up your breakfast." Alejandro turned around, rubbing his tongue over his teeth to ensure there was nothing caught in his smile. "I don't want you to be late, and we still need to take your picture."

"Seriously?" Chloe frowned, picking up her cereal bowl and slurping down the rest of her breakfast. She got up from the stool and rinsed out her dish and spoon, and put them in the dishwasher.

"We've taken a picture every year on your first day of school and I'm not stopping this year because you are becoming too cool." Alejandro glanced around the counter, craning his neck to look at the dining table. "Now, where did the board with the date and grade go?"

"On the side table by the front door... where you left it." I finished off my piece of honey toast. "And it's still there as of five minutes ago." I pushed a frown to my face knowing full well how objects magically vanished and disappeared by the time we all got to the front door.

As breakfast wrapped up and everyone did their last-minute dashing about, both Alejandro and I doubled-checked to make sure Chloe had everything: lunch, backpack, phone, keys, and everything else a twelve-year-old girl needed for her first day of school. Once we were all satisfied, our family unit made our way to the front porch.

"Hold this." Alejandro gave Chloe the plaque with the year and her new grade. We all stood on the porch as Alejandro fussed over Chloe, ensuring her peach top lay flat and her jeans weren't messed up. She looked perfect; even her braids had a fresh shine to them. "You look beautiful." He smiled at her.

"Papa," her upbeat tone and cheery eyes gave away her false annoyance.

"Alejandro, let's get the photo finished and send her off." I stood and let him fuss about our daughter. His family had the tradition of taking first day of school photos and he was insistent on doing the same with Chloe each year. I didn't mind and I don't think she did either, but being a cool pre-teen, she never acted like she enjoyed these things. Alejandro took a couple of pictures, moved Chloe for better lighting, and took a few more.

"Hi, Mr. and Mr. Del Rosario," Vyan called out from across the street, tossing his bag in his car.

"Morning, Vyan." I waved. "You off to school?"

"Yep…" he frowned. "Looking good, Chloe. Have a good day."

Chloe waved but didn't say anything and I noted the hints of color in her cheeks. I wanted to say something, but I understood how crushes worked and I didn't want to embarrass her any more than needed. I would save asking her about it for later when she got home tonight, assuming I remembered, and we were all alone. I pondered what her protective Papa would think.

I smiled at the notion of him freaking out. 'She's a baby and too young' is what I guessed he would say.

Alejandro luckily continued to focus on the photos he took, not saying anything or even noticing what was going on around him. "What do you think of this one?" He showed Chloe and I.

"Fine," I replied, understanding my opinion wasn't the one that mattered.

"Come on, Chloe," the Harris' son called out. I couldn't remember his name. "Hi, Mr. and Mr. Del Rosario," he added.

"Morning." I waved. "Enjoy your first day."

"Papa, the other kids…" She pointed to a few of the neighbor kids leaving for school.

"Alright," Alejandro relented, with a final tug at her collar. "You sure you don't want one of us to walk with you?"

She raised an eyebrow at us. I raised my hands and pointed to Alejandro.

"Wait for us," Cynthia and Miguel called out. They were the Hernandezes' kids, bursting off their porch and catching up with the Harris boy.

"Go on." I indicated to all the kids.

Chloe smiled and waved, rushing off. She stopped and ran over to us, giving us each a hug. "Bye." She hurried off, and we stood watching our daughter head off to school on her first day with the group of kids we had all gotten to become acquainted with since we moved in. Hearing some of the horror stories about kids being abducted and how easily kids can be taken, I shared Alejandro's worry for our daughter, but given what we all have been through, we needed to give her hints of normalcy, and Chloe was a smart kid. A wave of relief washed away my worry as there were kids Chloe's age here and they all got along. Hopefully, this would give her some built-in friends now that she wouldn't be seeing Maggie and Jacky every day.

"Chloe, text me when you get to school," I called. Despite my faith in our daughter, I didn't have a lot of faith in my fellow man.

She waved.

"Think she'll be alright?" Alejandro glanced up and down our street as we surveyed the kids on their march to school. He waved to Lidia, who monitored the kids as well a pensive expression hovering all over her face.

"She'll be at school. I'm the one that'll be here all day." I glanced at our front door, glimpsing my office window as well. I spared a glance toward our park and in the shadows, I'd have sworn I observed a couple of people in military uniforms. I took off my glasses and glanced a second time before putting my specs on.

"Everything okay?" Alejandro squeezed my hand.

"A trick of the light," I commented.

"Well, hopefully the *trick of the light* will stay in the park." He wrapped a hand around my waist. "Did you give her the ten?"

"Yep. Although you could've given the money to her, we didn't need to be all cloak and dagger."

"We all need our hero moments," he rubbed my side.

I peeked at my watch. "You need to hustle."

"I told my boss I'd be in late today," Alejandro commented with a look up the street, our daughter and the rest of the kids no longer in sight. "Still, I should head off."

We made our way into the house. Alejandro grabbed his keys and his own lunch. He checked his phone and, with a kiss, he headed off to work and I had the house all to myself. I made quick work of the rest of the breakfast dishes and made sure the kitchen sparkled. I pulled out the stuff for dinner tonight so we could cook once Alejandro got home. With a sigh, I made my way to my office. I opened my phone, found the music app, pushed a couple of buttons until music filled the house. I had a couple of meetings and I had a massive spreadsheet calling my name, but music was first on the list.

With a ding of my phone, Chloe sent me my requested message letting me know she was at school. And with that, my day progressed without incident, which wasn't a surprise. A lot of time between occurrences wasn't unusual. Things weren't happening on the daily, yes, we might see something or there might be a stray noise here and there, and occasionally some kind of pressure would build in the house, concluding with a pop of our ears, but most of the time nothing, which lulled us into a false sense of security thinking that maybe things were coming to an end. Then bang, something big would happen and we would all be on pins and needles again.

By the time Chloe came home, I was actually having a great day, and I got a lot done. I even managed to get out for a walk, and I strolled by Chloe's school around lunchtime, to perhaps get a peek of her. I didn't. Getting out had been nice and always helped my state of mind. The bright August sky, the warm weather, the light breeze, how could anything ever be wrong? As she walked in, I needed the break. "How was your day?" I turned from my computer screen to see my daughter standing there with a bright smile on her face.

Her grin was something akin to a wave of a magic wand. Seeing her happy, truly happy, made me relax, especially after all the trouble with her school last year. The days she would come home crying or depressed had put daggers in my heart and Alejandro's. Once she told us what was happening, we were in the Principal's office demanding some kind of action, but like in so many cases, the school did nothing. The bullying was up to us to deal with and we did what we needed to do for our daughter. Events got better, but the damage was done.

Chloe walked all the way into my office and dropped her bag by my office door on the floor with a thud. "It was good."

"Everyone nice?"

"I think so." Chloe glanced around my office. "I like my science teacher and I think P.E. will be fun. Oh, I'm gonna need to get a P.E. uniform."

"Okay."

"I'm glad P.E.'s at the end of the day so I can come home afterwards." She scrunched up her nose.

"I hated having P.E. first thing in the morning." I shuddered at the memory. "How was lunch?" I studied her, seeing if I could detect or see anything that set off my worry.

"Papa's sandwich was good, but I got a candy bar with the money you gave me." She smiled. "I hung around with Cynthia. Miguel came over and sat with us for a while before he and Jason took off. I split the candy with Cynthia."

*Ah, Jason, the Harris's son. Let's see if I remember.*

"Well, don't go crazy, the money has to last you," I reminded her. "If you want a snack, there are some apples in the fridge."

"I know." She leaned against the door and pulled out her phone. "Oh, Jason and I have math together. And there was another nice girl I met in English."

"Good. So, you have a few friends," I added, before she was lost in her phone.

She shrugged, and with that, I lost my daughter to social media and her virtual world. She walked off.

"Don't forget to do your homework," I called after her.

"Don't have any. First day," she called and rushed up the stairs to her room, laughing.

"That's so stupid."

She snickered again, tapping on her phone.

The door closed upstairs and, with a bit of a disappointed frown, I turned to my work, music still playing through the speakers. I would've loved to have a long conversation with my daughter, but that didn't happen often, more so than others had with their kids, I wanted to believe, but still the call of her screen clearly more interesting than anything I had to say. At least, that's how it felt when the kids' heads were buried in their phone. That's why I liked our vacation times. No phone... for any of us.

# ~ Chapter Sixteen ~

Being out of the house for dinner was a godsend. I felt normal—no, we felt normal. We dressed in our smart casual clothes and sat with our friends in a nice restaurant. Tonight was what the doctor ordered. The rushing of passersby, catching bits of conversations or the floral scent of perfume, and the warm mid-summer weather hit all the right cords. We needed to do this more often. I sipped my cocktail and inhaled the fruity sweet scent.

"How was Jacky's first day of school?" Alejandro asked through sips of his soda. Seeing as he drove, he didn't get to enjoy any booze tonight. I almost felt bad for him until I took an additional sip of my lemon drop.

*So good.*

"She misses Chloe." Sara placed the menu down next to her bread plate. "But I think she's had a good start. She's already mentioned a couple of boys she's keeping an eye on." She laughed.

"She's too young." Alejandro put his drink down.

"That's what I said." Carter agreed.

"Not that young." Sara smiled.

Both Carter and Alejandro shook their heads.

"I think that's the toughest part of all this." I placed my drink on our outdoor table.

"Boys?" Carter questioned.

"No." I smiled. I never did ask Chloe about Vyan and I didn't think to bring it up to Alejandro... darn old age. "Chloe misses Jacky and Maggie so much, but that school..."

"The principal wasn't back this year." Carter smiled with a firm nod of his head. "The rumor is she got sacked for how she handled things with Chloe and the other kids."

"Good." Alejandro frowned, finishing off his soda, putting the empty glass on the table. "She had no business running the school after everything those kids went through. How do people like her even get those kinds of jobs?"

"In all fairness, it wasn't only her; the district wasn't much help," Sara added, and held up a hand. "I'm not defending her or what she did. I'm saying there is a lot of blame to be passed around."

"I suppose." Alejandro let out a hefty exhale.

"I'm honestly glad we got Chloe out of there," I added. "Her new school has a zero tolerance policy on bullying and has a closed campus, both of which should keep problems from occurring."

"I know this might sound awful of me," Sara lowered her voice. "But I'm glad Jacky wasn't involved."

"You have nothing to worry about. I'm happy neither Jacky nor Maggie were involved." I made sure to face both Sara and Carter when I spoke so they would know I'm sincere and don't blame them for anything that happened.

"Not for not trying." Carter chuckled, leaning closer to us. "There were a few times I imagined we would be called in and yelled at because of Jacky doing something to protect Chloe."

"We have some tough kids." Alejandro relaxed into his seat, glancing up and down the sidewalk at the shoppers rushing about.

"I wish Jacky and Maggie's help would have made a difference." Sara sipped her red wine.

"These days you never know what's going to happen with bullies," Alejandro added as the conversation stalled.

"Okay, no more talk about our kids." I forced out a laugh. "We're here on an adult's night out. We have booze, and at some point, great food, plus wonderful fellowship and conversation. The kids are at the movies with Dan. We're free." I picked up my drink and took another sip, allowing the sweet and sour mixture to flow down my throat.

"How are things going with Dan?" Alejandro peeked at his empty soda glass.

"He enjoys spending time with Maggie, and I think he likes when Jacky and Chloe are there." Sara placed her glass of wine down. "I know he's going through a lot with the custody hearing. Man, I can't believe his ex…"

"Are you ready to order?" The waiter arrived at our table with another soda for Alejandro. We all scanned the menus again and placed our orders as the waiter took the empty glass, ensuring we were all happy with our current refreshments.

We ordered oysters for the table, which was a splurge, but why not? We deserved it. I ordered the lobster bisque and, keeping with the seafood theme, I asked for the seared Hokkaido scallops. Alejandro went with the baby wedge salad and six-ounce filet mignon. Both Sara and Carter went for the Tomahawk rib eye for two, and they each got Caesar salads. We also got a side of lobster and pork belly macaroni and cheese and brussels sprouts for the table to share. I didn't want to order too much as I eyed either the chocolate and butterscotch pudding or the chocolate molten cake for dessert.

Sitting and talking on the patio, enjoying a good meal with some great friends in the steakhouse on Santana Row in the middle of August, life doesn't get much better. And we enjoyed every bit of the people-watching, and our conversation. I loved being in a restaurant that allowed you to sit back and enjoy the experience. They didn't rush you through your meal, which was the main difference between a steakhouse like this, and some cheaper franchise joint. I couldn't remember the last time we had been out like this. Yes, Alejandro, Chloe, and I had been out to eat, but Alejandro and I out with friends... well, it'd been a minute, for sure.

Dipping my spoon into the chocolate and butterscotch pudding made my mouth water, and I was glad I didn't over-order or over-eat. My dessert was worth every calorie and the hour and a half I would be spending on my bike in the morning.

Sara glanced over at Carter. They were relishing the chocolate molten cake. "This dinner has been everything," Sara commented, wiping her mouth with her napkin. "I'm so glad we picked this place."

"Us too." Alejandro beamed. "We don't get down here near enough these days and that has to change."

"We, ah..." Carter cleared his throat as he began to speak. "We're sorry we haven't seen you guys much since the housewarming." He reached for his coffee.

"Trust me." I put my spoon down. "We get it."

"How are things?" Sara sipped her tea. "With the house?" She lowered her voice. "We're worried about you and Chloe."

Alejandro raked a hand through his hair and sighed.

I inhaled, forcing down the knot building in my stomach. I wasn't going to let talk of our house problems ruin a wonderful meal with our closest friends. I glanced at Alejandro.

"I'm not going to lie." Alejandro faced Sara and Carter, his gaze moving between them. "Some days are hard..." He glanced around; no one listened to us talk. "We've seen things and experienced things." He shook his head. "I never imagined anything like this was real or possible." He released a half chuckle-huff thing with another shake of his head. "But who does, right?"

"And not just us," I continued, taking off my glasses and massaging my temple. "Two of our neighbors have moved, or were chased off. And our next-door neighbor tried to kill himself." Sorrow bubbled up inside me. I still partially blamed myself for what happened; I should have seen the signs. I should have done something, but I honestly didn't know. That didn't help my guilt, though.

"Jesus." Sara examined us, a frown stretched across her lips. "We had no idea."

"Why don't you leave? Move?" Carter placed his fork down. "Get the hell out of there. Yes, it'll cost you, but is staying worth the risk?"

"And go where?" Alejandro shook his head, focusing down on our half-eaten dessert. "Make it someone else's problem. I can't... we can't do that. This is our mess and we need to fix it, or at least try."

"What about Chloe?" Sara licked her lips. "Hasn't she been through enough?"

"We ran once." I shook my head. "We picked up and moved. Our daughter was being terrorized and I can live with that choice. But this, we can't run away again. We want her to know that she can stand up and fight. And win."

"We will win," Alejandro added.

"But a bully is one thing..." Sara peeked around the restaurant and leaned in. "This is something else. You're playing with things no one fully understands. Things I don't think we are meant to understand." She bit her lower lip. "What if it hurts you or Chloe? Whatever you have there already made a bunch of you sick, and the fire. Is a home in Evergreen really worth all the struggle? Hell, is a home anywhere worth all that?"

I rested a hand on Alejandro's leg. I needed some support. They weren't wrong. "We talked about leaving, but it's not that easy…" A nervous chuckle escaped my lips. "I mean, it is, but we can't pack up and go. There is a chance this activity might move with us."

"What?" Carter sat taller and shook his head. "How?"

"That's what the SVPRS team mentioned." Alejandro continued patting my hand on his leg. "Moving might not work, depending on the type of haunting we're dealing with."

"There are different types?" Sara rubbed her forehead before fanning her face.

I shook my head. "Honestly, I never knew. I mean, okay, yes, I had that experience all those years ago and we watch the ghost hunting shows and we've all seen the movies or videos on social media, but…"

I wanted to add that those shows and movies were all BS. Okay, that wasn't fair, they weren't all BS, just sensationalized for mass consumption. Yes, some of it mirrored what we were experiencing, but almost all these events in the shows and movies were focused on a single family or home. There were a couple of programs that had these supernatural experiences happening in and around a whole town, but none of what they went through was like what we were experiencing.

"I don't think I'd be able to handle these things every day." Carter sipped his coffee, eyeing his fork and the cake again.

I glanced at my wonderful dessert. "That's the thing. These events don't happen all the time." I picked up my spoon and took another bite. This chocolate and butterscotch was the best thing I've had in my mouth… well, second-best thing. "We haven't had anything happen for about a week, and before that, ten days… I think."

"Still, that's a lot." Sara took another bite of her dessert. "What about getting a priest out there to bless the house and the neighborhood?"

"Our neighbors, the Hernandezes, have mentioned the

same thing." Alejandro took a sip of his soda. "And my mom said as much after the housewarming and the fire."

"Why not? What'd it hurt?" Carter picked at his molten cake again. "Who knows, maybe that's all that's needed, is a bad ass priest to come and kick some paranormal butt." He smirked as he brought another piece of the cake to his mouth to enjoy.

I glanced down at our dessert, trying to hide the heat raising in my neck and cheeks. My stomached flipped in knots. I didn't want to say anything about the idea and my feelings on the Catholic Church in general, so when Alejandro spoke, I was grateful.

"I don't believe the church would help us." Alejandro's tone was neutral, more than mine would have been.

"What do you mean?" Sara placed her fork on the side of her dessert plate. "The church is all about helping…"

"People like you." Alejandro gestured between Sara and Carter. "You know how most churches view us. Sure, you might find a priest who doesn't judge you, but the Catholic Church as a whole…" He shook his head.

"Then another church," Carter countered. "I'm sure the pastor from our church would offer to help."

"Maybe," I eventually spoke up. "Maybe not. We had a hard enough time finding a priest willing to officiate at our wedding, but with something like this, assuming they even believe you…" I shook my head. "Plus, the Catholics, at least as far as I know, are the only ones with an official documented process for these things. I think what we have in our neighborhood is going to take a lot more than a house blessing. Plus, what if doing a blessing makes it worse?"

Our table fell silent again, but only briefly. Enough time passed for our waiter to come over and top off our drinks.

"But surely the Catholic Church has to help." Sara's tone

came across more annoyed than worried. "If they got to know you…"

"I think how they choose to either support or oppose us depends on the Diocese and the Bishop, or at least the Priest… but I don't know." Alejandro frowned, rolling his soda between his hands. "I dug around when things first started happening, but given their stance on gay marriage and gays in general…" He sipped his soda, putting the glass down and poked at the last of our pudding.

"You really are going through it." Sara pushed her hair over her shoulder. "I'm sorry. I never even thought the whole gay thing would add another level of trauma to what you are going through."

"It's fine. It's not your fault." I changed the expression on my face to ensure I showed I wasn't angry. I wasn't upset at them—in fact, I was grateful, as they were offering solutions or potential options. What annoyed me was being in this position in the first place. If we were a straight family like the Hernandezes or the Patils there wouldn't have been an issue, but with Alejandro and I…

"Somedays it's difficult," Alejandro began. "But like the past couple of days, the events at our place and in our neighborhood feel like a nightmare or not real at all. Life is normal." He glanced at his place setting as our table fell silent. We finished our desserts and coffees, which I was glad for. I didn't like that our conversation ended the meal on a down note, but I appreciated our friends' worry. When the bill arrived, Carter snatched the tab up.

"Come on Carter, it's our turn." I reached for the dinner tab. "This was supposed to be our thank you for letting Chloe hang out with Jacky so much these last few weeks, as we sort all this craziness out."

"Yeah, come on guys, please." Alejandro pulled out his

wallet.

"Given all the hell you guys have been through, this is on us." Carter raised a hand. "Plus…" He peeked at Sara.

"I—well, we feel awful leaving you to deal with this on your own. We're your friends, we're supposed to be there for you and…" She shook her head.

"Honestly, I don't think there is anything for you guys to do. Kinda like Dr. Wilson, Chloe's therapist. There's nothing she can do but listen and support us, and that is a lot on its own."

"We should be doing more," Sara countered, her tone softer and gentler than typical for her. "But I was scared."

"We both were, especially for Jacky." Carter's voice grew quiet and gentle. "Our fear had us abandon you."

Alejandro and I glanced at each other. "Well, thank you." Their kindness warmed every part of me to the point where I felt hints of tears dancing at my eyes. "And you have helped, more than you know."

"You don't think we're insane." Alejandro glanced around the restaurant and shopping complex. "Knowing you believe us makes a world of difference. I don't know what we would've done if we were all alone trying to figure things out."

"Do you think this team will be able to help you?" Sara asked.

"God, I hope so." I adjusted in my chair, "But if not, Reza, my friend from a while back, mentioned he would come out and help." The notions of them failing never crossed my mind, and even having Reza and the members of PICs in our back pocket was a shot in the dark, because saying you'll help and actually helping are two different things. "The local team seems to know a lot about the subject and has helped several people."

"Well, maybe…" Carter pulled out his card and slipped it into the billfold for the waiter to pick up. "When things are all sorted, you can treat us and Jacky to a bar-b-que. We've missed your grilled salmon and roasted vegetables." He gestured to our waiter. "I can't seem to get them right."

"We would love that." I beamed from where I sat. This is what we needed. This is what we were missing. Our friends. Our connections. This was something no bully spirit or poltergeist or whatever negative energy thing was called from our neighborhood could take from us. Not if we had any say in the matter.

It took a while but, we finally made good on our promise to have Sara and Carter to our house for a bar-b-que, but getting to that point almost broke us; all of us.

# ~ Chapter Seventeen ~

Our house now appeared to be mission control for us and the paranormal research group. We tended to host the meetings and I don't know if us hosting was because we helped rally everyone together or if no one else wanted to risk making things worse at their homes. Reflecting back now, I think it was happenstance, but at the time I wasn't so sure. Either way, I didn't mind. Despite everything, I felt safe, or safe enough, in our home.

For our meeting, we pulled all the chairs from the dining table to the family room so everyone had a spot to sit, and we had provided our usual assortment of snacks and drinks. I figured, and Alejandro agreed, treats and drinks were the least we could do. Today our group shifted in dynamics from the last meeting. Hari had to work, so Deepa and Vyan were present and had helped us to get things organized and set up. Both Derek and Mercedes were in attendance. Today, however, only Juan was present from the Hernandez family, and Lidia stayed home with the kids. We suggested Chloe keep them occupied, but they declined. Chloe had become a knight in shining armor; she played upstairs with the Johnson kids, keeping them entertained, which was for the best. No need to worry them anymore than we were all worried.

"After our last meeting." Dr. Thomas glanced at the group. "We reviewed everything and we've done a deep dive into this area. We've also spoken with Mr. Marshal, who put us in contact with the representatives of the Tamien Nation here in San Jose."

"Good." Juan placed his glass of water on the coffee table.

"Indeed," Michelle responded with a polite nod of acknowledgement in his direction. Today she was sans necklaces, with the exception of a small gold cross. "I've also spoken with Dr. Zadeh-Ezra, Reza, and we caught each other up."

I continued to watch her, curious about what they spoke of, but didn't want to ask.

"There appears to be a lot more going on here than we assumed," Ethan shifted in his seat, placing his laptop on the wood floor next to him.

"And the information Kyle provided helped as well." Zoe beamed in my direction, her gaze meeting mine.

Alejandro squeezed my leg.

Honestly, hearing the updates pleased me and knowing the information I put together helped, because I had no idea what I was looking for. I was grasping at straws to find some kind of reason for our haunting.

"It seems," Dr. Thomas wiped a hand over his goatee, "several current and former members of the city council realized that there was something different about this particular parcel of land—"

"Of course they did. Bastards," Derek grumbled, cutting off Anson. He reached to the bowl of almonds we had out, grabbing a few and popping one into his mouth.

"What do you mean, they knew about this parcel of land?" Dr. Hernandez glanced around our family room as if there were answers to be held in our four walls.

"When the land was originally sold, Jeremy Fowler and his family insisted that this section, where your homes sit now, would, upon his death, be turned into a park in honor of the Tamien Nation and the slaughter of their people by the Spanish Conquistadors." Zoe leaned forward in her seat.

Ethan picked up his laptop, opening the device. "From what we found. The land has been in the Fowler family for as far back as the records go, and, we assume…" He tapped on the machine, turned the computer so we viewed what he pulled up. "The family learned some of the history prior to them getting here and passed the stories down."

"Which makes sense," Dannie continued. "There wasn't a lot here, farming and orchards mainly, and if they were one of the first pioneers, they would have seen a lot."

"And the city knew all this?" Mercedes shook her head.

"Those assholes." Alejandro rolled his eyes.

"No wonder everything here is angry." Deepa shook her head. "I would be too."

"I'm sorry." Vyan's gaze bounced around from face to face. "But if that was the case, why didn't anyone sue the city or the developers for not doing what they were supposed to?"

"What about the Tamien Nation representatives? Didn't they try and stop all this?" I asked. "And better yet, why wasn't any of this in the media?"

"Technically, the City argued that the park they put in met their obligation and the money from the development of the land was needed to build the park, and the taxes, your taxes, would help for the maintenance."

I shook my head as a disgusted chuckle broke from my lips. This reeked of backroom deals and all the shit that people hate about politics and big business.

"And the Tamien People?" Juan picked up his glass and took a sip of water.

"They got screwed over like every minority in this country," Mercedes clapped at the group. "And we have to pay the price."

I took off my glasses and rubbed my eyes. What were we going to do? How were we going to fix this? Can we fix this? "I don't even want to suggest this, but can we sue them? Not the Tamien Nation, but the city or the builder?"

"I'm not a lawyer." Dr. Thomas began crossing his right leg over his left. "But given what we found, I don't see how."

Dannie scanned our group. She rested her hands on her lap as a thin line took over her lips. "Oh, I'm sure there's a lawyer out there willing to take the case, but..."

"The only people who win in a lawsuit are the lawyers." I sighed, placing my glasses on my face.

"Okay, so let me see if I understand," Alejandro started, his voice harder than I recognized it to be. "Mr. Fowler wanted this land for a park. The city agreed, but only did that park up the street. At one time there was a massacre of the native peoples who lived here in this area. And they are drifting around wondering what the heck happened to their lands and their families. Meanwhile, as an added bonus, we have some of the Spanish who died here during the battle as well, reliving the battle every day. Oh, and let's not forget we potentially have poltergeist activity going on..."

"And..." Michelle cleared her throat, calling all our attention. "I want to address Chloe." She faced Alejandro and I.

My heart sank as heat rose in my neck, and a swarm of butterflies filled my gut. "What about her?" I asked.

"We believe..." She paused and spared a peek at Anson and Dannie. "We feel she may be the cause of the poltergeist activity."

"What?" Alejandro scoffed, but fire burned in his eyes and that one word was much harder and harsher than any that had come before.

We were hitting a lot of firsts today.

"She's becoming an adult and has had a difficult childhood," Michelle pulled out her tablet and scanned her information.

"She's in therapy due to the abuse caused by her mother when she was a baby." I added to protect my daughter. This couldn't be happening. I refused to believe Chloe was the source of any of this.

"And the bullying she experienced last year," Dannie added, glancing toward both Alejandro and I.

I huffed and crossed my arms over my chest.

"We find that, in a lot of poltergeist events, teenage girls are typically a big magnet, because of their emotions and hormones," Michelle promptly added, "But it's not always teen girls. It can be anyone with some psychokinesis abilities, but we think in this case, Chloe is the living agent."

"So, this is our fault?" Alejandro scowled at the paranormal team. "We're the cause of this whole mess."

"No." Dr. Thomas shook his head. "You misunderstand us, please."

"Well, that's what everyone here's gonna think." Alejandro's frown grew larger on his face. "Chloe's not been around for everything. There was the figure we witnessed when we moved in. And what about everyone else?"

"That's true," Deepa nodded her agreement. "We've seen a lot at our house. The pressure changes, the temperature shifts, the smells. Chloe was nowhere in sight. And I would never think this is Chloe." She smiled at us, but the brightness didn't reach her eyes.

Was she saying what we wanted to hear, or what she truly believed?

"This isn't about Chloe." Mercedes stretched out a hand to us. "The Martins' home didn't burn down because of Chloe. And the older couple didn't move out because of Chloe. It's about all of us. Maybe all the BS with the land and the native people brought this up."

Michelle sighed. "That's exactly what caused these

179

disturbances. All the underlying stress and trauma of the events that happened here potentially activated this inside her. Think of how stressed you've all been, and now think about her."

"We all want this to end and no one is blaming you or your daughter." Juan sat taller.

"Alejandro, please." I reached for his hand.

"Let me ask you all this," Dr. Thomas spoke up, sitting taller on our sofa. "Have you been in a situation where you're angry, stressed out, rushing around, and all that?"

Everyone confirmed his question with various gestures.

"And have you all, in those same moments, had your phone, computer, tablet, TV, coffeemaker, whatever, act up for no reason?" He surveyed everyone. "Getting you even more flustered?"

"Happens more than I care to admit." Derek shook his head. "Annoying."

"And why do you think, when you're upset, these things go wrong?"

"The universe is trying to piss us off even more," I shrugged with a tilt of my head.

Dannie smiled.

"Maybe," Dr. Thomas stated. "But we find, typically, these events are related. See, we all have a small amount of PK, and when we are in a heightened state, angry, stressed, whatever, these events manifest."

"We even have a name for it: JOTT," Dannie smiled, holding off her chuckle.

"What's that stand for?" Vyan leaned in.

She smiled. "Just one of those things: JOTT. We see it a lot."

"Poltergeist activity requires a living agent and, based on everything that has happened here, that we've documented,

Chloe appears to be the focus," Zoe explained. "But some of these smaller events can be caused by you."

"You're all going through so much, experiences that would have never registered with you before—"

"Now do." Alejandro sighed.

"She's a little girl." My own frustration and annoyance were building, but I needed to keep my emotions together. Still, I wanted to kick everyone out of our house. I wanted to end the meeting, but what if they were right? How do we stop all this, and how do we help our daughter? "Hasn't she been through enough?"

"We're going to help. All of you," Michelle reassured us. "She's sensitive, which has left her open to such events."

I forced down my exasperation before saying anything.

"But you said all this with Chloe is only part of the problem here." Alejandro gave my leg another squeeze.

Dannie and Michelle shared a look, peeking over to Dr. Thomas, who huffed but waved Michelle on. He crossed his arms over his chest and sat, stony-faced and silent.

"I know Anson doesn't agree with me," Michelle continued, ignoring the doctor. "But you also have either a pissed off apparitional attachment to one or several of you, or a horde of Demons."

"That's it. We're so out of here." Derek stood up and Mercedes pulled him down into his seat with a thud.

"Mom, let's leave." Vyan had grown pale and pulled at his mother's arm. "We can move down with Neil."

I reached over and took Alejandro's hand. His eyes were as wide as saucers, but neither of us spoke. *Demons*. Can they be causing all this? Can they be hurting Chloe? The cuts on her rushed to my mind, hearing her scream and us unable to reach her, her bedroom door stuck—or was it being held shut by something evil?

"And go where? Do what?" Mercedes shook her head, not letting go of Derek's hand. "Everything we have is tied up in our home."

"We can move in with your parents," Derek countered, fear and anger filling his words.

"And watch you kill each other." Mercedes shook her head, ignoring the cross talk. "Boy, you better get that nonsense out of your head."

"Lidia and I can't afford to move, either." Dr. Hernandez's voice was low as he glanced around our family room. "All her family's in Columbia and my parents moved to Arizona during the pandemic."

"Everyone, please," Dannie tried to call order. "Please," she repeated.

"And this is why I discourage all this Demon talk." Dr. Thomas gestured around at the group, everyone talking over each other and no one listening.

"Please, everyone." Michelle held up her hands. "Please."

Ultimately, everyone stopped and Michelle continued. "Like we've told you, moving may not solve your trouble, especially if there's an attachment. All you'll do is take the apparition with you, which will make things a lot worse." She held up a hand. "But we have a plan."

"Yeah, well, so do I." Dr. Hernandez's voice grew stronger. "We called the San Jose Diocese and are going to have the exorcist come out. Fr. Lloyd Flynn will be here tomorrow to bless our house and rebaptize my whole family."

"Fr. Flynn." Dr. Thomas raised his hands and dropped them on his lap. "Wonderful." His tone was exasperated.

"Come on, Anson." Dannie faced him, her lips pinching together. "He's a good man."

"Every shadow that man sees is a Demon." Anson wiggled his fingers. "Every case he has ends up with someone being 'possessed' and needing months of 'treatment' at the church. He's a joke, and this is why people don't take parapsychology seriously. If the Catholic Church says boo, we don't all have to jump. We aren't in the dark ages anymore."

"And what about the families and the people we can't help?" Michelle added, eyes shooting daggers at Dr. Thomas. "Where do you think they go?"

"The people we can't help don't want our help or won't listen to us. They want there to be Demons... so there are Demons." Anson's words flew like venom spat by a viper. "Tell me, how many people does he help? Truly?"

"Hundreds," Michelle countered. "And you would know that if you didn't brush off all his good work."

"He has a similar process to yours," Dannie added. "As we do."

"I've seen their—"

"Please, everyone!" My voice came out louder than I think it needed to be, but the room fell silent. "If the Hernandezes called this Fr. Flynn and they believe he'll help. I'm happy for them, but what about the rest of us?" I stood up. "I doubt the Catholic Church will help us; one, I'm not Catholic, and two, Alejandro and I are gay... so."

"And I'm not sure they would help us either," Deepa spoke in a voice softer than mine. "We're not even Christian." She glanced at Vyan with apologies running around along the lines in her face like a train on a track.

"He doesn't only help people who are Catholic." Dannie's tone softened. "There's a family in Piedmont, over in the East Bay, who are Mormon. He helped them, without question."

"Mormon's are Christians..." Vyan seemed to find his voice, however weak.

"So, what do the rest of us do? Who aren't straight or Christian?" I scanned Dr. Thomas, Dannie, and Michelle, my arms firmly crossed over my chest.

The space grew silent as everyone focused on me.

"How do we help the spirits that're trapped here and get rid of the pissed off attachment or attachments, or whatever we call them, and make this a safe place for our families... all our families?" I licked my lips. I wanted to ask how we help Chloe, but I understood I had to think of the whole and not only us, as much as I wanted to.

My aggravation pulled us all together and quieted everyone down, except for my pounding head and heart. As a whole, we spent the next couple of hours going over different solutions from house cleansing to crossing the spirits over that wanted and were willing to be crossed over. We also talked about putting up barriers around our homes. One of our more generous discussions was about offering to pay for and installing a monument for the Tamien Nation in our park. It was my hope, our hope, that all these things would bring an end to this shared nightmare in our neighborhood. One of the best pieces of news Alejandro and I got from Michelle had to do with Chloe being in therapy. Her having a place to focus and work through her worry and anxiety would lessen the poltergeist activity. Michelle offered to work with Chloe personally to ensure she understood her potential for psychokinesis, which was a huge relief for us, or should have been, if we lived in a better world and comprehended what we were actually dealing with.

# ~ Chapter Eighteen ~

After the events of the day, I lay on our bed, the beating in my head familiar to the beat of one of the nightclubs downtown I would go to in my younger years with Reza or our friends. For the first time in a long time, I felt every bit of my thirty-plus years. My eyes were closed as I focused on pushing everything from my mind, trying to encourage some kind of peace to find me.

"Dad, the people from the paranormal group are going to be here soon." Chloe's voice was soft, like brushed cotton on my ears.

I opened my eyes and pushed the hair from my forehead off my face. "Thanks. I'll be down in a couple of minutes."

Instead of leaving, Chloe moved over to the bed and cuddled next to me, resting her head on my shoulder. I had images of her in this position when we got her seven years ago. She had picked me as her comforter, I don't know why, but she had and I didn't mind. I relished being the one. Because of her and my closeness when we first got her, Alejandro did everything possible to build their relationship, something that came easier for her and I.

"Are you scared?" she whispered to me.

I didn't want to admit that I was, but I also didn't want to lie to my daughter. "I'm worried," I stated. "But I know we'll be alright."

"How do you know?" she asked as she inhaled.

"Good always beats Evil." I exhaled.

"Not always." The frown in her voice tore at my heart.

"Yes, always." I turned to face her. "If it didn't, our world would be a far worse place; you, your papa, and I wouldn't be here." I believed this to my core. Yes, people did shitty things. Yes, there was pure evil in this world and people died every day because of it, but overall, good always won. It might take a while, but good had to win.

*It has too. God and his angels wouldn't have it any other way.*

"The kids who bullied me…" She didn't say anymore.

"Those kids were punished, and will live awful miserable lives due to what they did to you."

"How do you know?"

"They have ugly hateful souls and people with ugly, hurtful souls are never happy. That is how they are punished, and maybe someday, they'll realize what they did and feel guilt for it and change their lives, becoming better people."

"Do you believe that?" Her gaze bore into me.

I kissed the top of her head. "With all my heart."

"I'm still scared."

"I know you are, but we're going to be fine." I swallowed and pushed this belief throughout my body. I was not going to let any of this paranormal activity win. And I sure as hell wasn't going to let my beautiful daughter be afraid anymore. "Come on." I sat up, bringing Chloe with me and hugging her.

*****

Today, only the three of us met alone with Michelle, Dr. Thomas, and Dannie, so we all sat comfortably around our dining table. The sun's rays from the patio door filled the space with bright light, but the house always came across as dark and cast in shadows no matter how open the curtains were or where the sun shined through. I hadn't noticed until the

SVPRS team mentioned the darkness and shadow to us, and now the difference was all I ever observed anymore.

Dannie coughed, pulling my attention to the conversation. She picked up her glass of water and took a sip. "Sorry," she uttered after swallowing.

I smiled as Alejandro and I observed as Michelle spoke with Chloe, explaining ways for her to deal with all the scary events and how to control her burgeoning abilities. Dr. Thomas chimed in and provided an account of his own experience and how it's taken years for him to develop the slightest bit of PK for himself.

"So, I'll be able to move things with my brain?" Chloe asked, a grin creeping over her face.

"Maybe," Dr. Thomas answered his expression as deadpan as one would imagine, however, I would have sworn there was a bit of a twinkle in his eyes when he spoke.

"But that isn't the goal." Michelle rested a hand on Chloe's. "The goal is for you to control your emotions, work through them with Dr. Wilson, and live a happy and healthy life."

"Still, I can move things?" Chloe asked again.

I chuckled. "Remember, whatever you break comes out of your babysitting money."

"Oh." Chloe frowned.

Dannie coughed again. Her cough sounded raspy, or maybe phlegmy, like something was caught in her throat. She sipped her water again.

"Are you alright?" I asked.

"I've got some decongestants," Alejandro offered.

"Allergies." Dannie glanced around the room.

Michelle faced her, her gaze narrowing. "Are you sure you're okay?"

Dannie ran a hand over her forehead and grinned.

The look set my spine to shiver.

Before anyone spoke, a knock on the front door called all of our attentions.

Alejandro glanced at his phone. "It's the Hernandezes and some other folks."

"Excuse me." I got up and headed to the entry and pulled open the front door. "Lidia, hi." I greeted offering her as large a smile as I could. "Is everything okay?"

Lidia stepped aside. "We all thought, that maybe, you'd want to meet Fr. Flynn."

An older man stepped forward. His gray hair framed his face neatly, his cheeks held a few freckles, and his blue eyes sparkled. In his youth, I had no doubt, he had red hair. He was donned in his priest uniform, but he also wore an embroidered white tunic alongside a purple stole.

"Good afternoon, Father," I greeted.

"Mr. Del Rosario." He smiled at me. "This is Deacon Huy and Deacon Sebastian, as well as the rest of my team: Roberto, Pam, and Teresa. I understand from your neighbors you've been having spiritual problems and I'm here to offer a house blessing and a blessing for your family."

I rubbed my head as heat rushed up my neck, finding a home in my cheeks. I had forgotten, or chosen to forget, that Juan had mentioned the Catholic Church would be out today. "I, ah…"

The Priest held up a hand. "It would be my pleasure to offer a blessing to you, your husband, and your daughter. It isn't my place to judge, as we are all children of God, and are created in his image. Therefore, we are all worthy of his love."

Something in his words or his gaze filled me with emotion. When all you hear your whole life is how you are damned, to have a man, a Priest, standing in front of you, dressed in all his religious paraphernalia finally telling you you're worthy of God's love—there is something powerful in that.

And with that realization, I swelled with a fire of hope and joy. It was everything. And at that moment, the whole thing went bad.

At once, my ears popped and the vile smell of decay and feces burst through every part of our house. From behind me, there was a crash and several calls of Dannie's name. A burst of cold air pushed me forward, somehow pulling me back. A chill of terror ran down my spine. I forced myself to rush to our dining room, pushing the foul scents out of my mind. Alejandro held Chloe as Michelle and Anson held Dannie down. She was having a seizure.

"What's happening?" I shouted.

"Papa, the lights," Chloe cried out.

"After you left the table, she coughed again," Michelle struggled to speak. "I felt them…"

"She coughed up puss or mucus or something." Alejandro stood away, his grip tight on Chloe. "Her eyes…" He shook his head. "And her face…"

"Anson, hold her," Michelle called out, trying to keep a grip on Dannie's arm.

"She's fighting me," he responded. "I can't…"

"What's that?" I pointed to our fireplace, where a shadow of a beast stood watching Michelle, shifting its dark gaze to the rest of us. I can only describe the creature as a beast, because I have no other words. The creature was a shadow with burning eyes. The monster sprinted toward Dannie and vanished inside of her. Her seizure escalated and a snarl burst from her. The sound was deep and guttural, unlike any I had heard before.

"Saint Michael the Archangel," Fr. Flynn's voice boomed over our house, and his Irish inclinations filled his words. "Defend us in battle. Be our protection against the wickedness and snares of the devil; May God rebuke him, we humbly pray; And do thou, O Prince of the Heavenly Host, by the power of God, thrust into hell Satan and all evil spirits who wander through the world for the ruin of souls. Amen."

"Amen," responded several voices at once.

"We need to call 9-1-1," Lidia called somewhere behind me as the lights above the dining table and over the breakfast bar swayed, flashing on and off as they moved. Above the fireplace, our TV kicked on and flicked through the channels.

"No," Fr. Flynn countered. "They can't help." He glanced toward two of his people, his voice calm. "Deacon Huy and Sebastian, assist Dr. Thomas and Michelle." He pointed to Dannie and the others. "Roberto, Mr. and Mr. Del Rosario, please move the table and chairs. Be careful of the lights," he instructed. "Lidia, please see to the young woman, Chloe. I understand." He beamed at her. "It'll be okay."

Lidia rushed to Chloe and pulled her out of harm's way.

We all did as instructed by the Priest. I don't know why we listened to him, but given the stench in the air and everything going crazy, he projected certainty, so we complied. By the time we moved everything out of the dining room, Dannie lay out on our throw rug we had protecting our hardwood floors. Four grown men, Roberto had replaced Michelle, now held Dannie down, barely, as she continued to convulse on our floor.

"Dr. Thomas, what do we do?" Alejandro asked, getting close to Dannie. When she jerked, he backed away.

"I…" He shook his head, finally glancing at the Priest as he focused on holding Dannie in place. "You and your ilk…"

"Anson!" Fr. Flynn's tone was firm. However, his voice remained calm. "I'm quite aware of your opinion of me and the Church. We can argue later, but right now we have bigger concerns."

"Agreed," Anson relented.

"Saint Michael the Archangel." Fr. Flynn kneeled next to Dannie. "We call on you to help us in our hour of need. Restrain this child of God so we may cast out the wickedness that beseeches her."

Similarly to how the cold and pressure engulfed us, an energy filled the space. I couldn't see this new force, but something had joined us. Maybe St. Michael, or perhaps—wishful thinking. But as I observed Dannie on the floor, her body stopped thrashing about as if restrained by several hands. Hands more powerful than the men currently struggling to hold her in place.

"My God," Alejandro spoke.

"This is my territory," Dannie snarled in a voice not her own.

"Dannie, fight," Dr. Thomas shouted. "You can push this thing out."

"Aren't you the optimist?" Dannie's words came out, but I didn't understand them. It wasn't until later that I was told Dannie had been speaking Latin, Aramaic, and Tagalog, depending on who she spoke to at the time.

"What is she saying?" Dr. Thomas asked.

Alejandro stuttered, "She said you're an optimist."

Dannie faced Alejandro and snarled at him. Her face wasn't hers, but the same face we observed in the fire at our housewarming and when the Martin's home caught fire.

"What language was that?" Fr. Flynn repeated.

Alejandro stood there, not speaking at all, color draining from his face and neck.

Dannie laughed, or snarled. It's hard to say.

"Mr. Del Rosario, what language?"

"Alejandro…please call me Alejandro, Father." The words came slow and low out of Alejandro.

I reached over and took his hand, giving it a squeeze.

"Alejandro, take a breath." Fr. Flynn instructed, still keeping his voice calm and level. "What language did Dannie speak?"

"Tagalog."

"Does she know Tagalog?" Flynn asked the group assembled.

"No," Michelle exclaimed. "I don't think so… Spanish and some Vietnamese." She continued to watch as things progressed.

Dannie laughed again. "You have no power here, priest. This is our land! Our territory! Be gone! Go hide in his house."

"Latin," Fr. Flynn shouted.

"Who speaks Latin?" I asked.

"My Lord, you are all-powerful, you are God, you are Father," Fr. Flynn raised his hand to make the sign of the cross. "We beg you through the intercession and help of the archangels Michael, Raphael, and Gabriel for the deliverance of our brothers and sisters who are enslaved by the evil one. All saints of heaven, come to our aid. Amen."

"Amen," responded the chorus of voices from all over the room. I even found myself joining in.

Dannie snarled at the priest.

"Pam, my case, please," Fr. Flynn instructed as he continued to pray, not taking his eyes off Dannie.

Transfixed, I couldn't keep my eyes off of what was happening. My understanding was that he spoke in Latin for much of his deliverance of Dannie. But with all the various languages being tossed about, I honestly couldn't say. I was startled when Lidia moved closer to us, Chloe slipping her hand in mine.

The woman, Pam, returned with a case and handed it over to Fr. Flynn, who promptly opened the satchel and pulled out his various tools. I spotted a cross and something that must be holy water or oil, which was in a plastic bottle, and those wafer bread things they use at mass. There were a few other items I didn't quite see. As the priest recited the Lord's Prayer, which I recognized from school, he also recited Hail Mary, and what I found out later was an Athanasian Creed, which he recited in Latin.

More laughter crawled out of Dannie's mouth. "Not all are believers in your false god, Priest." She glared at Anson, now speaking English. "Isn't that right, boy?"

Anson remained quiet.

"Come on, Anny." The voice from Dannie changed. The tones were more female but not Dannie's. "Let me hear you cry. I love when you cry. It makes it so much better when I do that thing to you. The thing that Daddies and Mommies do when good boys are sleeping."

"Shut up!" Anson shouted. "Shut up!"

"The Demons lie." Fr. Flynn's tone measured but loud enough for us all to hear as he recited his prayers again.

"But I'm not lying, am I, Anny?" Dannie's voice mocked the Priest and Dr. Thomas.

"You're dead!" Anson shouted, moving away from Dannie. "We buried you." He stood up.

"Alejandro, we need your assistance, please," Fr. Flynn called.

Alejandro moved over to Anson. "I got this," Alejandro got down on the ground and held Dannie in place.

"A good Catholic boy," Dannie mocked as she spoke in Tagalog for Alejandro to hear. "Except when you're sucking him off and letting him stick it in you. And oh, how you love when he's in you, we've seen what you do to each other and we can't wait to do that same thing to you. We can't wait to be inside of you like him, and we are so much bigger then him. We know how you long to have something really big inside you, not like him." Dannie laughed.

"Ignore it," Fr. Flynn instructed Alejandro. "They are afraid of us."

Michelle pulled Anson over out of the way.

"She's dead," Anson stammered. "She died twenty years ago. I was at her funeral. I saw her body." He shook his head. "I never told anyone what she did to me. I never told. How did Dannie know? How?" Anson shook his head.

"I'm going to take him to your office," Michelle pointed in the direction of my office.

Unable to move, my eyes fixed on Dannie and now Alejandro in the line of fire of the Demons inhabiting Dannie.

Fr. Flynn and his group continued to recite their prayers and Dannie would continue to throw out insults in various languages, mocking everyone and telling us how we were all going to suffer and how nothing we did would get rid of them. Fr. Flynn went through his rites of Exorcism, continuing to pray. As his words filled our house, the day grew quiet. Dannie grew quiet, and I assumed the attack, or whatever, was over, until I heard her speak, but no one recognized the words except for Fr. Flynn. He leaned away only slightly, eyes narrowing as he continued his prayers with greater passion.

"What is your name, Demon?" Fr. Flynn demanded.

Dannie laughed.

"My Lord, you are all-powerful, you are God, you are Father," Fr. Flynn continued. "Require this beast to reveal itself to us, so I may cast it out of this child of God," He commanded.

The air in the house became deathly still. No sound came through the window or sliding door despite them being open. I peeked down at Chloe, sparing a brief glance at Lidia.

Fr. Flynn lowered himself and faced Dannie, glancing in her eyes, offering another blessing and blowing in her face. I wasn't sure what he was doing, but his action didn't make Dannie—or whatever was in Dannie—happy and she snarled at him, blowing or spitting into his face. Fr. Flynn pushed away and wiped his face. He bent down, facing Dannie.

I glanced over at Alejandro and made eye contact with many others in our dining room, but no one appeared concerned.

As Fr. Flynn continued to demand the Demon's name, all time stopped and, with a roar, Dannie shouted, "Leraje."

The house erupted as the lights began swinging again, and the TV did its channel thing, and all the lights—at least on the first floor—began to do their crazy light show. Fr. Flynn and his ministry continued to work with the assistance of Alejandro and finally, with a scream, we witnessed a black shadow vacate Dannie and rush out the sliding glass door. I don't know why, but I ran over and slammed the door. Locking the glass barrier. I had no delusion this wouldn't stop ghosts or Demons from returning, but at the time, my actions made me feel like I had power.

It took another half hour, maybe forty-five minutes, for the situation to return to normal in our house. Fr. Flynn and his group prayed over each of us, our house, and provided all of us communion. Despite not being Catholic, I took the offering in the spirit which it had been given. We all did.

For Dannie's part, she didn't remember much after her coughing fit. What she told us was parts of her experience had fogged over her brain like a bad dream, one she couldn't wake from, but now that the experience had ended, the memories of the nightmare faded.

As we all sat around the table, I glanced over at Fr. Flynn. "What happens now? Is it over?"

He shook his head. "I'm afraid not."

"You mean that thing can return?" Alejandro asked.

"This is its territory. Leraje is a warrior, so something invited them here. Opened a door and they took up residency."

"The battle with the Tamien people and the Spanish," Dr. Thomas disclosed. He had returned to his normal self again.

"Perhaps," Fr. Flynn acknowledged.

"But you blessed our home, and this didn't happen," Lidia commented.

"I think we chased the beast out of the other homes," Deacon Huy met each gaze he could.

"When we came here..." Teresa added.

"It followed us," Lidia finished.

"But for right now, it's gone," Michelle exhaled with a stiff bob of her head. "I don't detect anything else and, if I didn't know better, I would say your house is clean."

"Hiding again." Dannie shook her head. "Waiting... but... why me?" She was massaging her temples.

Fr. Flynn glanced over at her. "You're a warrior, and if they showed they were able to take you, there would be no hope for anyone else."

"Fr. Flynn, what do we do now?" Alejandro glanced around our house. "Is our home safe? Is our daughter safe? Should we move? Leave? Go to a hotel?"

"You've all taken communion and I've blessed your home. My group and I will walk around the house one more time and we'll walk around the street offering another round of blessing. We've expelled the Demon for now, but that is only the first step. I wasn't fully prepared to do battle with a Demon today, so we'll need to plan and prepare..."

"But is our house safe?" I demanded.

"I believe so," Fr. Flynn's words eventually touched all our ears, providing us the words we needed to hear.

"Our home as well?" Lidia asked.

"Yes."

Relief washed over me in a single wave.

Lidia sat deeper in her chair; her relief matching mine. She peeked at her watch. "Lord, I need to head home, I left Juan with the kids." She shook her head. "And that's never a good thing." She gave me a weak, but warm, smile.

I glanced at the clock on the oven. Our entire afternoon was gone, but at the same time, it only felt like minutes had passed. "Before you leave, what do we do now?"

"I'd like to meet with everyone, but not here. At a neutral location. My Parish office is an option, but it might not be big enough."

"Our neighbor Hari has a restaurant." I suggested, not knowing if he would even allow us to use his space, but at this point, anything would be better than meeting here in our neighborhood. "I'll talk to them and message you all if we can meet there."

There were nods from the group. We had our next course of action and I felt good. A bit scared... well, more like terrified, given what we witnessed today, but at least given all these events, we had a plan and with the additional help and support, I trusted we'd get through this haunting. Like I told Chloe, good always defeats evil, and today I observed good win firsthand and so did she. As everyone vacated our home, after one more walkthrough by Fr. Flynn and his team, for the first time, in a long time I believed there was hope for all of us. No matter how small.

# ~ Chapter Nineteen ~

My nerves had been frayed all day—well, the last couple of days. Since the attack on Dannie. It didn't help that Alejandro told me what Dannie, or the thing in Dannie said to him. I know Fr. Flynn said they lie, but still part of me wondered if there wasn't some truth in their lies. I had hoped that getting out of the house would have helped, but walking into Hari's restaurant didn't offer any reprieve.

Hari's Indian restaurant was in Milpitas, right off Calaveras Boulevard, in a hole-in-the-wall strip mall with several other restaurants and a couple of shops. The location was nothing you would think twice about. Connected to his restaurant was a sweet shop that he ran. Since we had moved to our home in Evergreen, we had only come out this way a couple of times to have dinner. The food, and Hari, were always wonderful and Alejandro and I would comment that we needed to come here more. Tonight, we were in his back room, typically used for events. I'd not been in the banquet space before, however, noting the deep green walls with crown molding around the tray ceiling were similar to the main restaurant. The darker wood floors creaked under my steps, signifying the need for a refresh. Finding a seat, I ran a hand over the solid wood table and, given the cush in my seat, these were higher quality; not only designed for their appearance, but for their durability. A blank screen from the large mounted TV caught my attention, and I deliberated what they would play on the screen. Indian music filled all our ears with an enjoyable rhythm.

When I messaged Hari, he was happy to offer us the location and, since we were going to meet on a Tuesday night, the room wouldn't be used. He even suggested he would provide a light offering of food. Glancing at the buffet, Hari had a different version of light offering: the self-serve buffet stations had been filled with everything from two different types of naan, various pakoras, green salad, kachumber salad, two different versions of rice, several different chicken, lamb, vegetable, and goat curries, and at the end of the buffet, he provided tandoori chicken. If we weren't going to be stuffed from his main offerings, he provided a selection of his more popular traditional Indian desserts. His hospitality surpassed anything we required, but I, for one, was grateful. And the smells dancing all around me made my stomach rumble.

Alejandro raised his eyebrow at me.

I shrugged. It was my tummy, not me; plus, I skipped lunch to give my aching head and nerves a bit of a rest with a short lie down during my meal break. I would have called out and taken the day if it wasn't for these freaking reports I needed to finish.

The large room burst with glorious aromas of spice and meats, and the rush of new aromas pushed my aching head and raw nerves down, forcing me to acknowledge how hungry I was.

"I hope this is okay." Hari moved his head in the direction of the spread by way of greeting.

"This is more than enough." Alejandro smiled as they shook hands.

"Hi, Mr. and Mr. Del Rosario." Vyan brought in a stack of plates.

I bit back my amusement at hearing him say those words with ease, but said nothing. Chloe appeared disappointed when we told her she couldn't come with us tonight, and I questioned if she realized Vyan would be here. Given what she witnessed on Saturday, Alejandro and I didn't think we needed to add to her trauma anymore. Thankfully, Sara and Carter were happy to have her over for the evening. We would pick her up on the way home.

"I can't believe all this." He shook his head, calling my attention. "We'd have Vyan go stay with his brother, but he has school and I love having him here…"

"Well, after what Dannie went through…" I shook my head.

"Do you think this thing was a…" he lowered his voice. "A Demon?"

I peeked at Alejandro. I understood what we observed. That was why I was in my current state, but I didn't want to say the word out loud or even think about it. I didn't know how these things worked and I didn't want to give the being any kind of power over me.

"I don't care what *it* is. I want these things gone and our house and neighborhood to be normal." Deepa joined us. She had been checking the food and ensuring everything was set up.

The lights in the banquet room flashed a couple of times and there was a call from the kitchen. "Excuse me." Hari rushed to the kitchen.

"I'm sure they tripped a breaker again. Still, I better check as well, don't want anyone getting zapped." Deepa added, following her husband.

"Hi, guys." Lidia waved. "Doesn't this all smell wonderful?" She and Juan approached us.

"I'm not a big fan of Indian food." Juan's voice was hushed. "But man, this all smells so good. I can't wait to dig in."

"I know, right?" I patted my stomach, forcing myself to focus on the food and not the reason we were all here.

"I hope the others get here soon." Lidia glanced at her watch.

"Sorry we're late." Mercedes rushed in, Derek by her side. She stopped. "Oh, good. We're not late."

"680 was a nightmare." Derek glanced around the space. "Man, that all smells great."

"I got a text from Anson saying they'll be here shortly." I pinched the bridge of my nose, trying not to let on that I had a blossoming headache pounding at the edges of my skull.

"We didn't bring Chloe either." Alejandro gestured to the lack of kids with them.

"No. Definitely not. The kids are with my folks. Part of why we're late." Mercedes pushed her braids over her shoulder. "After what Lidia and you guys told us…"

"We took our kids to some neighbors where we used to live." Lidia wrung her hands together. "The kids were happy, but I don't know what we're going to do. We can't keep this up; it's exhausting."

"Tell me about it." I, one hundred percent, felt Lidia's comment to my core.

"We hope that, between the SVPRS and the church, they'll be able to help us," Derek finished.

"Well, I will say, things have been peaceful the past couple of days." I cleared all the worry and fear from my mind as I spoke.

"And we know how long that lasts," Deepa countered, rejoining our group. "Welcome to Hari's pride and joy, faulty wiring and all." She waved a hand around the large space.

Our polite conversation continued, but we were all awash with a mix of worry and concern. Despite the wonderful scents, tension hung over the room and all of us. As I glanced around the space, forcing myself to focus on the aromas, I deliberated how any of us had these kinds of problems. In a location like this, with all the great food and friendly people, how could anyone have any issues? This is what life was supposed to be like, not dealing with the paranormal. That was so far out of our range of normal at times, that even now, I still had a hard time believing any of what we had been through in the short time we had lived on Golden Hills Court.

We continued to make small talk as we waited for the rest of the group to arrive. At one point or another we all found our way over to the food to take in the sight and the fragrances. Fr. Flynn and Deacon Huy arrived, apologizing for their tardiness; they had been stuck on 680. Fr. Flynn worked his way around the group, greeting everyone and introducing himself to those he hadn't already met. Finally, Anson, Dannie, and Michelle arrived. Ethan and Zoe weren't too far behind. With our party complete, Hari took a moment to welcome us all here and, to my surprise, he invited Fr. Flynn to say a prayer for us all, the food, and his place of business.

Fr. Flynn again greeted everyone and offered his blessing to us all. I've never been much into religion and faith, but given recent events, I found that with Fr. Flynn's blessing over the food and our gathering, I felt better.

We made our way through dinner before we got into the business of talking about spirits and the paranormal. My stomach wasn't disappointed with the meal; everything had been incredible. As I peeked at my empty plate, I wanted to get up and help myself to thirds, but my stomach wasn't going to have any of it, no matter how much my brain and eyes pleaded.

"Thank you, everyone, for agreeing to be here." Anson stood up. "Thank you, Hari and Deepa, for the wonderful meal. And Vyan." He smiled at our hosts. "Before we get going, I'd like Dannie to let us know how she's doing."

I sipped my water, trying to clear my mind so I could focus as Dannie stood up.

"Thank you so much, Mr. Patil, for your wonderful hospitality today." Dannie glanced around the dining hall. "I wanted to thank you all for your concern for me and, with the help of Fr. Flynn and Michelle, I'm doing well, and honestly I'm slightly worried, but I've had a few days to recover. It's not over, but I know what I need to do. I'm lucky it was only trying to attach to me and between all of us, I was able to fight it off." She smiled at Fr. Flynn. "Fr. Flynn will be happy to hear I've been keeping with my daily prayers and Sunday was my first time at confession in…well, quite a while." She pulled out a St. Michael medallion and showed us. "And I'm feeling good. Ready to kick some butt."

I laughed along with a few others, despite the nagging tension behind my eyes, as she took her seat.

Anson stood. "We have reports for you all from Ethan and Zoe. It's all about what they found out about the Tamien Nation and all the information they put together regarding the county and city, and how this area was developed."

Michelle and Dannie walked around and gave everyone copies of the reports. I wasn't sure what we would end up doing with the information, but I was coming to fully understand that in cases like this, knowledge was power.

"Also," Dr. Thomas continued. "I would like to apologize for my reaction Saturday. To say I was taken aback by what happened is an understatement. Without getting into too many details, as you can imagine, past events were quite painful for me and somehow the attachment to Dannie recognized the buttons to push." He cleared his throat, reaching for his glass of soda to take a sip. "When I was young, there was an incident with a teacher at my Catholic School. No one believed me, and when she passed away I buried it… but…"

"Unfortunately, Demons know how to trigger us," Deacon Huy stated.

"Yes, well…" Anson shook his head.

"We all have trauma in our past," I acknowledged. "You don't owe us any apology or explanation. Just know we won't judge you."

"That's right," Juan added.

"No judgements from us," Mercedes joined in the acceptance of Anson's apology and explanation.

"We appreciate all you've done for us, Dr. Thomas," Deepa added.

"I appreciate that," Dr. Thomas nodded however his gaze remained lower. "Still, I wanted to offer an apology."

"The thing with Demons," Deacon Huy's words gentle. "If I may?" He paused.

Anson gestured him to continue.

"They're classic bullies," Deacon Huy continued, ensuring to make eye contact with everyone. "They exist to cause as much chaos as possible. These creatures will do everything they can to beat you down. They will make up things and if you give them the slightest acknowledgement that they are on the right path they will dig in." He shook his head. "And, like bullies, they have a gang they travel in, but they also follow a hierarchy and have territories they *rule* over."

Some of this information was similar to what Fr. Flynn had told us. Still, hearing how open they were talking about these things twisted my stomach into knots and I couldn't keep my legs from shaking. Alejandro reached over and rested a hand on my leg, but that didn't help.

"This *thing*," Lidia paused, unable to say the 'd' word. "Has control over how much of our area? Just our neighborhood, or all of San Jose, the county, the state… what?"

"Well, there isn't a map," Deacon Huy continued. "But what we've found is there are some Demons we continue to run into a lot here…"

"You've dealt with this one before?" Mercedes shook her head.

"Why can't you get rid of the monster once and for all?" Alejandro piped up, leaning forward. "If you know the name, cast it out."

"Knowing its name is important, and that's how we're able to vanquish it. Having the Demon's name, we can call it to the light, and Demons don't like being in the light; that is where God is most powerful."

"Okay, so why do they keep reappearing?" Derek asked.

"People invite them," Deacon Huy glanced around the gathering. "We may close one door, but they find another."

"Wait." Juan held up a hand. "You mean, we can kick this thing out of our homes and neighborhoods, but someone might intentionally or unintentionally invite it back?"

"That's why…" Fr. Flynn stood up. "When we sever the attachment, we must ensure that all attachments are cut and that none of you do anything to invoke a return."

"Jesus." Derek cried. "Sorry, Father."

Fr. Flynn waved off his apology.

"One of the biggest doorways is sexual abuse or assault," Fr. Flynn grimaced as he spoke. There were looks from the assembled. "But that isn't all; items of the occult, addiction, abuse, mental health issues, etc. all can bring back the Demon," Fr. Flynn continued.

"Don't take this the wrong way, Father," I stated. "But if you can't completely get rid of this thing… what help is all this? Why won't a cleansing like Michelle has offered be enough?" My heart pounded in my head and I would have one hell of a headache when we got home.

"No offense taken." Fr. Flynn smiled toward me. "That is a fair question. Deacon Huy and I are trying to fully explain the situation to you. We've spoken with Michelle and we don't feel a cleansing will be enough. Our plan is to do a full exorcism of your land, which is different from an exorcism of a person. Still, what gives us hope is that the rite of exorcism goes to the sixteenth century and is a regimented authoritative ritual." He stood taller. "And the Demons hate it."

"Why would they even care?" Deepa asked. "Why would they even listen to you? Or us?"

Fr. Flynn's lips raised a knowing thoughtful expression filled his face. "There are rules—"

"Rules?" several of us cut the priest off.

"Yes, rules, but…" Fr. Flynn rubbed his chin and peeked around the space. "Demons are litigious and you have to say the prayers exactly right, or they don't have to leave."

Michelle spoke up. "Think of it like this…" Everyone focused on her. "The universe has rules; gravity, for one."

Deepa's head bobbed up and down in agreement as did Juan and Alejandro, as I massaged my temples. I got what they were talking about, but I was getting overwhelmed.

"When you exert force on a ball, it continues on its course until some new force is exerted on it, right?"

There were several bows of agreement.

"That's what we need to do in your neighborhood," Michelle added.

"And you think you'll be able to stop this, change its current course?" Mercedes asked.

"That's our hope," Michelle added.

"Oh, we'll get rid of it." Fr. Flynn beamed at us. "In all my time as an exorcist, I've done hundreds of deliverances, like I did with Dannie, and twelve exorcisms, with good success."

"But we'll need to monitor your homes and your

neighborhood," Deacon Huy added. "Ensuring there are no more manifestations, and we'll do a couple of clean-up sessions once a month for the next several months."

"Are you okay?" Alejandro leaned in next to me.

I met his gaze. "It's a lot and I'm losing my battle with the headache I've been fighting all day."

He squeezed my leg. "We'll get through this."

"One can hope." I focused on the conversation, despite the louder banging in my head.

"What about the other spirits?" Lidia glanced around the table. "The children, the Tamien families, and the soldiers? The ones we've all seen."

"We'll encourage them to move on," Michelle offered, glancing over at me. "I think they all want to move on, but the evil is keeping them here. Even the Spanish soldiers want to move on."

"We'll call on the Blessed Mother to take them for their judgment," Fr. Flynn added. "The Spanish soldiers should go easily enough with her, and that should help with anyone who is lingering."

"And what about Chloe?" I asked, my voice louder than it needed to be, but as positive as all the conversation was, my head and nerves weren't having any of it. "Sorry, I've got a bit of a headache," I offered by way of apology.

"There is no attachment to her." Fr. Flynn smiled. "She seems perfectly healthy and normal with two loving parents. I think with time she'll be fine."

"I'll work with her…" Michelle focused on me. "Are you okay?"

I shook my head. "I'm fine. Worried. Overwhelmed. Like everyone."

I grasped for my glass of water as it shot across the room and shattered, missing Juan by inches. In tandem with the glass crashing, my vision was cast in darkness and light again, not allowing me to focus.

"What the hell!" someone called out.

"Is it here?" another person spoke.

"Remain calm," someone, either Dr. Thomas or Fr. Flynn, called.

What I assumed was my vision ended up being a light show like before. The lights continued to flicker. Smooth skin wrapped around my hand. It wasn't Alejandro's, his hands had calluses; these were smooth and soft. "I need you to relax and take a deep breath for me."

I couldn't focus. My head pounded and my vision was blurred at the moment.

"Kyle," the soothing voice whispered to me. "Inhale and close your eyes."

I did as I was instructed.

"Now count to ten with me, push everything else out of your mind, and focus on my voice." The hand wrapped around mine squeezed hard enough to get me to only focus on the voice. "One."

"One." I took a deep breath.

"Good," the female voice replied. "Two."

I took as much air into my lungs as possible. "Two," I uttered with my exhale.

We proceeded counting until I reached ten, then I opened my eyes. My headache faded, and the room came into focus. Michelle sat next to me, smiling.

"How do you feel?"

"Better. I think my headache is clearing up." I managed to peek around and I noticed everyone watching me. "Sorry about that. Normally, I don't get headaches like that. The occasional migraine now and again, but nothing like this... sorry."

"But you've had them before?" Michelle asked.

"In school." I huffed. "Happened a lot when I got bullied for being... well, being me. And one weekend with Reza, when we went through our own experience with the paranormal, but it was nothing like this. Then nothing not for years. Well, not since we moved to the neighborhood."

"He's like Chloe," Dr. Thomas declared. "I've never seen two Living Agents together, the odds..." He shook his head.

"No. I'm not like Chloe... it's a headache."

"Hon." Alejandro kneeled next to me. "The lights. Your glass. The table."

"The table?"

"You about knocked over the whole table," Hari replied. "I've not seen anything bounce like that since the firetruck and cars."

"It's a lot to take in." Michelle smiled squeezing my hand. "But it's okay. You'll be fine. I bet you have a lot of electronic issues, don't you?"

"I guess. I mean, our TV went out a lot, my computer never kept a charge, and cell phones were always an issue, but that's all normal... isn't it?" I asked. "I mean that's what Dr. Thomas said, we all have things like this happen on the daily."

"For a sensitive..." She pointed her head at me. "I think all the stress you've been under caused a new manifestation."

"Well, despite what Anson may think..." Fr. Flynn smirked at Dr. Thomas. "I agree with Michelle. This is nothing on my end of the paranormal."

"Still, two PK Agents in one neighborhood, let alone the same house." Dannie shook her head. "What are the odds?"

"I couldn't even begin to fathom a guess," Anson rubbed his chin.

"Can we do anything?" Deepa asked. "Do you need something stronger?" she pointed to my half empty glass of soda.

"I've got some great Indian wines," Hari offered.

I shook my head. I had a lot to process and think about. I didn't think my youth was unusual and nothing like what happened at home happened when I was a kid. One thing was certain: I would be having a long conversation with my folks when we got home. Even with Reza, nothing this big had happened.

"I'm sorry, everyone," I forced my gaze to the floor, unable to meet anyone's eyes. "I hope everyone's okay."

"We're fine," Derek answered. "Glad the activity was only you and not anything else."

"We can deal with you." Mercedes smiled.

"We will deal with everything. We have the power of Christ on our side." Fr. Flynn's words held absolute certainty and finality. "This Saturday."

Alejandro took my hand and helped me up. "I think I'm going to get him home, unless there is more we need to talk about."

"No, I think we have the answer to something that had been picking at my brain for weeks. And ties in with Reza's suspicions." Michelle hugged me. "Don't worry and, if you get stressed, focus on your breathing and count to ten. That should help. We'll work on more techniques with you and Chloe."

Saying our goodbyes and making our excuses were a blur to me, but if everyone was to be believed and I had no reason to doubt them, Chloe and I shared more than a last name. We both had some kind of psychokinesis abilities that we would need to learn to control and deal with. As strange as the night had been, and despite my lessening headache, I was feeling pretty good about what was coming, like we actually had hope and a better future coming our way. But we still had to get through Saturday and that would determine all of our futures.

# ~ Chapter Twenty ~

"Are you sure you're okay?" Alejandro asked, glancing over at me from the driver's seat of our car. I wasn't sure how we made it out of the restaurant, let alone the shopping plaza, but when I pulled myself out of my thoughts and replayed the night's events, we were almost at 680.

I wrapped my arms around my chest as the vehicle's seat absorbed all my weight. Images of the glass flying from my hand, the dishes, and the table all coming to life in my mind's eye, but not only those images, past events also pushed from the deep recesses of my memories: TVs going on and off, our cable going out all the time, power surges, everything I pushed aside as non-issues had me now questioning everything I assumed I understood. I focused on my conversation with Michelle before we left, and having to promise her that I would speak with her in the morning and set up a time for her to talk with both Chloe and me. She guaranteed me she'd help us… help me control this…power.

"Kyle, please talk to me," Alejandro pleaded as we merged onto the freeway. He always drove when we went out, and I appreciated not having to deal with traffic. He loved to drive… or he preferred his driving over mine. Either way, I like being able to zone out, or in this case obsess, as he drove.

I continued to stare out the window, not seeing what lay before me, but instead the faces of our neighbors held my gaze as they hovered over me. A mixture of fear and anxiety pouring from each of their faces. Yes, they said all the right things; Deepa and Hari wouldn't let us pay for any of the broken glasses or any of the food. Lidia, when she hugged me, whispered she would continue to pray for all of us, and not to worry; everything would be fine. And Derek tried to joke about how now no one should stress me out or cross me, but his joke fell flat on my ears. Dr. Thomas and Dannie assured me everything would be fine and to not worry. And Fr. Flynn offered spiritual council should we want his help, he also told me he would continue to pray for us.

"I've caused this." The words dropped from my mouth and I shifted my feet over each other as I sat in the passenger seat, watching the normal world fly past us.

"No." Alejandro nabbed my hand. "No one thinks that, and more importantly, I don't believe that."

"You're right." I huffed, unable to face my husband. "Chloe and I caused all this."

"Again. No," Alejandro countered, squeezing my hand. "We never had this issue in Campbell and look what we went through there." His tone was firm and resolute to my ears. "The stress, the apparitions, and the evil entity all came together and caused this perfect storm, releasing your PK abilities. Fr. Flynn and Dr. Thomas are correct; this isn't on you and no one blames you. All this shit would have happened with or without the psychokinesis abilities." He continued to focus on the road before us as he spoke. Still, somehow, our car found every bump on the road as we zoomed along.

"But why didn't you tell me about this happening to you before?" he asked after a long pause.

I faced Alejandro, a lump growing in my throat and tears threatening to fall from my eyes. "I didn't know." My voice cracked. I regressed to being a scared kid in school again. My leg trembled and my stomach battled the swarm of butterflies taking up residence there. "I never imagined … I mean… I was a kid and weird shit happened. I never gave the weirdness any thought. Plus, my goal at the time was trying to survive Junior High. And with Reza and I, these events weren't anything..." I huffed. "They were kind of fun and funny... at the time." I shook my head, my hand rubbing my stomach in hopes of settling things.

I opened the center console and pulled out a mint from the tin, popped the candy in my mouth. "Want one?" I offered.

"Sure." Alejandro opened his mouth and I dropped a mint on his tongue. He closed his mouth around the mint. "Nothing big, like what we've experienced, has happened before?" he questioned, and the mint shifted in his mouth as he spoke.

"If anything like what happened at our home or at the restaurant tonight had happened to me before, don't you think I would've said something?" I retorted, trying not to sound nasty or mean, but failing. My head sank into the headrest, meeting the typical heavily padded resistance. I wanted to put this night behind me, behind us. I longed for our life in Campbell. Even dealing with the BS of Chloe's bully was a better option than all this paranormal activity.

"Hon, I'm not accusing you, I'm trying to understand." Alejandro's words washed over me like a gentle wave on the shore of a lake. For a brief moment, I was splashing my feet in Lake Tahoe with Chloe playing in the water and Alejandro next to me, the sun warm and the chill of the water refreshing on our feet.

The tension melted slightly from my neck and shoulders as I exhaled. "I know. I'm sorry," I said. "I'm still trying to decompress and understand all this." I turned my head and stared out my window, watching the houses and trees race by. We needed to head over and pick up Chloe, but I wanted to retreat to our home and crawl into bed. "There are things now, looking back, that make a lot more sense, but we weren't as connected when we were kids and we were all facing a lot more shit: 9/11, the war in Afghanistan and Iraq…" I huffed again. "Not that our world has gotten any better, but no. The internet connection never working right, our cable going out, my PlayStation having to be replaced a couple of times…" I shook my head.

"And George and Diana?"

I laughed. I loved my parents, but they weren't the most perceptive, and since I was an only child, they focused more on making sure I was happy and not getting into trouble, so the small things… I doubted even registered with them. They had no idea I was bullied until we told them about Chloe and I told them about my experience. Anyway, I planned on finding out, and I should reach out to Reza again.

*No. Just my parents, for now. I don't want to drag him into this anymore than he already is.*

"No glasses flying across the room? No tables trying to levitate?" Alejandro smiled, peeking my way. "No amazing sexual encounters with your next-door neighbor? Or Reza?"

I laughed at that. "No. Nothing that exciting… sorry."

"Well, at least you're not alone."

"Thanks."

"And you'll have Chloe as well. The two of you will learn to deal with this. Maybe you should go to therapy too." He tapped his fingers on the steering wheel. "Can't hurt, and Michelle and Anson have some recommendations."

I massaged my temples again. Who could foresee what would actually help? I inhaled deeply and faced Alejandro. "You know there was this one time in school, before Reza and I…" The images flashed into my mind. "This older kid, a real jerk, cornered me in the bathroom during our morning break. I finished peeing and in he walks. I couldn't get past him, but I prayed if I ignored him, he would let me wash my hands and leave…" I sighed.

The anxiety from my past experience rushed into my body like a river following a long dried out stream, knowing exactly where to head.

"You weren't that lucky?" Alejandro asked.

"Nope." I rotated my neck as stress points popped. "He came up to me and grabbed me. He tried to push my face into the metal mirror thing they have in school bathrooms… you know what I'm talking about, right?"

"The ones that aren't glass and get all scratched to hell. Yep, I remember."

"He called me the usual slurs he was fond of throwing at me." My lips pinched together. "I asked him to please leave me alone, but he laughed and pushed harder. I fought back. I didn't let him push my face into the mirror. I don't know where the strength came from—this kid outweighed me by, hell, I don't know, forty pounds. But he flew against the metal stall door, maybe five feet away." I licked my lips and peeked down at my hands. I imagined they were shaking like that day, but they weren't.

"And you don't think that push was all you?" Alejandro asked. "You think maybe something helped you shove him away?"

"At the time, I believed it was all me." I faced Alejandro. "He was so scared. I yelled at him to leave me alone and not to ever touch me again. I think the lights might have even flashed, but that might not be accurate… a false memory or embellishment." I ran my tongue over my lips. "He sat there on the floor, terrified, not moving… maybe unable to move." I peeked up at the ceiling of our car. "After a couple of seconds of my staring at him, god, I got such a headache after that. Anyway, he eventually got up and ran out the bathroom door."

"You think you pinned him there with this PK ability?"

I shrugged. "I don't know. I didn't think that at the time, but now... he was so petrified and I think he tried to move but couldn't. Geez." I turned to Alejandro. "He never bothered me again, not the rest of that year, or even in high school. I think whatever happened that day in the bathroom scared him so much that he left everyone alone." I laughed. "I'm not sure what happened to him after school."

"Wow," Alejandro exclaimed.

"Now, I feel bad for him."

"What?" Alejandro glanced at me before facing the road again. "He was a bully and got what he deserved. Imagine what would have happened if you didn't... I don't know... zap him..."

"But think about the fear, and who could he talk to? Who would believe him? Everyone recognized him as a bully, even the teachers. He was all alone..." I grumbled. "Just like me in my youth, and Chloe last year."

"I suppose," Alejandro responded, his tone softer. "Still, I bet what happened to him that day changed his life for the better. Maybe the experience made him a better person?"

"Perhaps." I wasn't sure I believed that, but maybe. "Speaking of Chloe, what are we going to tell her?"

"That she takes after her dad and she got her gifts from you." Alejandro smiled. I appreciated how hard he was working at calming me down and helping me to relax.

I chuckled at the ridiculousness of his comment. "I think our daughter is smarter than that."

"True." Alejandro beamed. "But now she won't be alone and you can talk to her and share your experience, like you did when you talked to her about being bullied."

"You know you suck." I hated when he was right, and I especially hated when he would use logic and sincerity to get me out of my moods.

"And I'm damn good at it, too." He smirked as we passed a freight truck that had decided that the third lane was a perfectly fine spot to go under the speed limit as we approached our exit.

"That's not the point." I had a difficult time hiding my grin from him. "Anyway, how lucky were you to never have been bullied or had to deal with any of this craziness? I mean, come on. Everyone loved you in school."

"But I didn't love myself." Alejandro frowned as he continued to merge onto Highway 17, heading toward Santa Cruz. "It was hard being in the closet. I know what I went through doesn't compare to dealing with bullies, but in a way, I was my own bully."

"I suppose." Alejandro turned the wheel as he got into the exit lane for Hamilton Avenue. "I'm fine with talking to Chloe about this, but let's not tell anyone else for the time being. I don't want to feel anymore under the microscope than I already do."

"What about your folks?" Alejandro asked. "What about Reza? Sounds like he already realized, or at least had a suspicion."

I glanced out the car window. "I don't want to bug Reza, and I'll feel my folks out when I ask them questions about when I was a kid. If worse comes to worst, I'll wait until things settle down, and I understand better what Chloe and I are going through and how we can control it."

"I'll support whatever you want to do." He smiled over at me. "Promise me."

"What?"

"That you won't whammy me with your abilities. We both know you got a temper." The smirk on his face grew. "Although having you pin me down with your mind…"

"No promises." I peeked out the window, wondering what all this would come to. What this ability would mean for Chloe and me in the future. How we were going to control this gift and what our lives would now look like. And I was curious if our PK abilities would continue after we got rid of our unwanted guests, or if the powers would go away like they did when I was a kid.

*****

I took Wednesday off as a sick day to pull myself together and get my head straight. But I wasn't sitting around watching YouTube all day. I made my call to Michelle and set up a meeting with her at the coffee shop in our neighborhood village the next afternoon when Chloe got home. I spent an hour on the phone with my mother, poking and prodding, trying to learn what I could about my childhood. Unfortunately, they didn't know much, and since I didn't want to get into the nitty-gritty, I didn't push too hard.

The good thing I learned from my call with my mom was since she couldn't think of anything 'odd' happening when I was young, meant whatever happened in my youth was so minor, those events weren't on her radar. Which pleased me.

Instead of sitting in the house, which I didn't enjoy doing alone, I went for a bike ride to clear my mind. When I got home, Chloe was due to come home, and I needed to start dinner. Luckily, the rest of the night ended up being quiet and restful, which is what I needed.

The next afternoon, Chloe and I sat at The Village House Coffee, which had good hot chocolate and teas, way better than the stuff you would get at the chain places, and I happily preferred supporting a local business over a chain any day of the week. And they were quite the location and destination for several people in our community, which I appreciated.

"Are you scared?" Chloe asked me.

The day was warm, but not too warm, so we sat on the patio in the shade created by the second floor above us. I glanced out at the square with folks walking their dogs or out and about.

*How could anyone be scared on a day like today?*

I smiled at her. "No." I tapped the side of my drink. "I wouldn't say scared… worried, I think." I focused on her. "You can be scared. It's okay, but we'll sort all this out."

She picked at her pastry.

"Hi," Michelle called as she dashed across the street. "Let me grab a coffee." She pointed to the shop.

"Sounds good," I responded, peeking at Chloe. "We've got this. Honest."

She smiled at me. "I'm glad you're here."

"Me too," I replied.

After a few minutes, Michelle appeared with coffee in hand. I stood up and greeted her as she reached our table. "What a great day." She smiled.

"It really is."

She took a seat, dropping her satchel on the chair next to her. She took a sip of her coffee, sighing before putting the hot drink down on the table. "Typically, I like to do this in a more private place with fewer distractions, but given the situation…"

"We didn't want to meet at the house," I articulated.

"Understandable," Michelle nodded as she dug into her satchel and pulled out a folder. She was back to wearing several necklaces. I noted all the different ones as they flopped out of her shirt. "Here's information for you and Chloe. There are also a couple of counselors who we've worked with before and I think will be able to help a lot."

I took the folder and flipped through the documents.

"I know Chloe is working with Dr. Wilson, and I think she's quite good and understanding."

Chloe beamed. "I like her a lot."

"Good." Michelle smiled and leaned deeper in her chair. "I know there is a lot going on and we have a big weekend ahead of us, so I don't want either of you to get overwhelmed…"

Chloe and I shared a look. If I was honest, this meet-up felt more like Chloe and I were the same age and we were speaking with an adult. Silly, I know, but that's what the conversation felt like.

"Again, I don't want to dive too deep today. We'll work on more of this later, but for now there are five things I need you both to do, every day, and I promise it'll help."

"And what's that?" I asked.

"First, I want you both to either pray or meditate. Find a quiet spot, wear comfy clothes, and breathe. It's important for you to attend to your thoughts as you control your breathing. Either focus on your prayers or focus on the blue sky or something equally peaceful."

"Sure." I forced the words to flow from my lips.

"The goal is to be mindful. Most people focus on hundreds of inconsequential things every moment, so taking this time for yourself helps."

"I can do that," Chloe declared. "Hopefully, I don't fall asleep."

"If you do, it's fine." Michelle smiled.

Chloe laughed.

"Next," Michelle continued. "I want you both to journal."

"Journal?" I raised my eyebrows at the idea.

"I do that for Dr. Wilson." Chloe sat taller in her seat.

"Excellent." Michelle beamed. "Kyle, it's a way to process your feelings and your mood. You don't have to spend hours writing. Write down how your day went, what bothered you, how you handled difficult situations, etc." She chuckled. "What you had for lunch."

"Okay."

"It's another way to help with your mindfulness and helps get rid of the clutter in your mind."

"Journaling seems…"

"Oh, Dad…" Chloe shook her head.

I raised my hands in surrender. "I shall endeavor to journal every day. Starting tonight."

"Now, Kyle, I know you bike ride and walk."

"Yep."

"Good, cause you both need to do this every day," Michelle continued with a glance to the bright day beyond the shadows. "You don't have to spend hours, but maybe the three of you can go for a nightly walk as a family. We underestimate the power of fresh air and nature."

"Does P.E. count?" Chloe asked.

"'fraid not, Chloe."

"Hmpft." She crossed her arms over her chest.

"This is both a way for all of you to reconnect and, again, we're trying to work out all your extra energy and frustration you may have." Michelle sipped her coffee. "Now," she returned her cup to the table. "When you get flustered or scared or angry or any negative emotion, I need you to force yourself to breathe, recognize your feelings, but then release them."

"What?" I said.

"I don't want you to suppress your feelings. You need to allow yourself to feel them, but more importantly, release them…" She paused. "Let's say someone says something hurtful to you."

"Like Carter…" Chloe frowned.

"Like them," Michelle answered. "Instead of focusing on what they said, recognize the hurt, take a breath, hold it for a count of four, lastly release the words and the hurt over a count of eight."

"That's hard." Chloe worked her jaw as she spoke.

And I agreed.

"Yes, doing this takes a lot of practice, but with that practice, it'll get easier," Michelle promised.

"This all sounds a lot like stress reduction exercises," I summarized.

"Pretty much." Michelle smiled.

"Okay, so that's four. What's the fifth one?" I asked.

"When something happens…" Michelle glanced around. "When something happens that doesn't have an explanation, I want you to address it."

"What?" My voice rose and Chloe glanced at me, biting her lower lip.

"You take a second to focus and to breathe and you say, 'stop it' or 'this is my house, don't do this' or 'you don't have my permission to do this' or 'I'm in control, not you, and you need to stop.' Something like that. Remember, you hold all the power and the control. You can't give into fear. That's what it wants."

"But they can be scary." Chloe's voice was meek. "Especially the dark man or the fireman."

"I know." Michelle reached over and took Chloe's hand and held out her hand for mine. I placed my hand in hers as she squeezed. "But I know you both are strong and powerful, and there is nothing, and I mean nothing, that you can't handle, so when something happens, you don't run and hide. You don't cry. You stand up to it. Remember, like any bully, the minute you confront them, they lose all their power." She smiled. "Chloe, do you think you can do that? Do you think you can stand up to these bullies?"

Chloe bit at her lips faster than I had seen since we adopted her. I was about to speak, but Michelle cut me to the chase.

"You can still be scared, you can still want to run and hide, but the same time you are feeling all these things, you can be strong and brave and you tell it, 'you can't do this and I'm telling you to stop. Stop right now.'" Michelle leaned closer. "Can you do that?"

Chloe's gaze met mine. "I think so."

"Chloe, you're gonna need to do better than that for me. What if your papa or dad need your help? Are you going to help them or only think about it?"

She sat taller. "I'm gonna help them."

"See, there is no thinking. You just do it." Michelle gave our hands another squeeze.

"And it's okay to be scared?" Chloe asked through bitten lips.

"Oh, yes. Being brave doesn't mean you aren't scared. It means you're not going to let the fear control you."

"Okay." Chloe's voice grew in strength. "I'll tell those things to go away and leave me alone."

"Good." Michelle turned to me. "What about you, 'dad'? Cause we're going to need all the strength and power we can muster."

"If Chloe can do it, so can I."

Michelle adjusted in her seat, releasing our hands. "I know it seems like a lot, but doing these five things is going to make a big difference, not only in your home, but in your lives."

"Well, it'll be a lot better than being worried and concerned," I offered.

I don't know if I can say I felt loads better after our meeting with Michelle, but Chloe relaxed and I liked the idea of us holding all the power. Keeping our power was a common thread throughout this trial. In a way, I looked forward to being bossy and telling this thing off and taking the power over my life. We'd allowed things to get out of control and now was our time to regain our authority, and I had no doubt we would do just that.

# ~ Chapter Twenty-One ~

Saturday came much too rapidly for my liking and, with as quiet as things had been, I questioned if we needed to do what we were planning. I don't know if what happened next was caused by my thinking about the lack of activity, or if what I witnessed had been the sun casting a shadow through the window. However, as I finished getting ready, I noticed a dark shadow move across the floor and wall that didn't belong to me. I took this is an omen to not question our plans again. I forced myself to take a breath, and with my exhale, I pushed out my fear and worry as I spoke. "I don't give you permission to be here. You need to leave." My tone was level, but forceful.

Since our meeting with Michelle, I had been putting into practice everything she said we needed to do. Despite only a couple of days passing, this was the most in control of our lives that I felt.

Checking the room and the bathroom, I didn't see anything else, so I moved to the bathroom and I peeked in the mirror, inspecting my reflection. Last night, I had a good night's sleep, and today, any puffiness or dark circles that had plagued my eyes were gone, and I didn't even mind how my hair continued to slowly give up on my head. I put on my glasses and headed out of our room, ready to take on the world.

*Well, at least the supernatural world.*

"There you are." Alejandro met me on the landing of our stairwell. No matter what happened during this adventure, he always greeted me with warmth, easing any tension or worry I may have had. "I was coming up to check on you."

"I had to use the bathroom, and I wanted to do my breathing and recite the prayers that Fr. Flynn gave me." I stretched out and ran a hand through his beautiful hair. The hair I was jealous of and wished I had.

"Ah, very good." Alejandro gave me a kiss. "Did you want something to eat? Chloe and I did PB&Js."

"I'm good." We reached the foyer of our home, the hardwood flood solid under my feet. "What time are we starting?"

"Everyone said they would be here by 1 p.m." Alejandro pointed to the front door and we headed to my study.

I glanced at my watch. "We have a couple of minutes."

He leaned against the doorjamb, scanning our surroundings.

I examined our home. Were these four walls all going to be worth everything we went through? Would this cleansing even work? Doubt and questions occupied every corner of my body. Dr. Thomas informed us they had never done anything this big, so he would be curious to follow the outcome. Fr. Flynn, despite his confidence, came across as more worried than I considered he should, but again, this whole paranormal world was new to me, so what did I know?

"Do you think all the neighbors will be there?" I asked, finding my shoes and sitting on my office chair. I peeked out the window as I slipped on my sneakers. There were a couple of folks already out and about. I noted the kids over at the park.

*At least they are enjoying themselves.*

"I think so…" Alejandro sneaked a quick look at his watch again, frowning. "Except for the Chens, but they're home. Mercedes spotted them getting home last night and Muffin barked a few times already today."

"I wish they would participate."

"I hope she doesn't give us any grief." He shrugged and scanned my bookcase and our photos. "We'll have to make do, like we do every day."

"I wonder what it would be like to have a normal family life, not having to continue to fight for our civil rights and, in some places, our very existence? I always feel like an outsider looking into a world that doesn't want us." I tried not to frown at the state of our world and our country. "Let alone deal with all this paranormal stuff."

Alejandro laughed. "We wouldn't know what to do with ourselves."

"Probably not."

"Still, the idea would be nice."

"Agreed. Where's Chloe?" I didn't hear her or see her, but that didn't mean she wasn't in the family room on her phone. Maybe she was doing her own breathing exercises before today's event.

Alejandro grinned. "She's out rounding up the other kids."

"Really?"

"She said that she wanted to make sure they weren't scared or worried. She told Lidia that she would be sure nothing happened to them." He beamed. "Our daughter is turning into a local superhero."

"We'll have to get her a special costume to ensure her identity is protected."

A knocking from upstairs called both our attention.

Alejandro closed his eyes.

"Stop it," I demanded, keeping my voice calm. "If you can't play nice, you have to leave."

The knocking stopped.

After a moment, Alejandro sighed. "I'll be glad when

that stops."

"It will." I had complete faith that these events would come to an end. I had to keep that mindset, if not for our family, for my own sake.

"Anyway." Alejandro pulled my focus to our conversation. "I think Chloe's attitude was boosted when Vyan came by."

I laughed as warmth filled my stomach and body with joy. "Ah, young love."

Alejandro's eyes narrowed. "If she has a crush, it's fine, but he's too old for her. And sometimes I think he knows she likes him and enjoys the attention."

"Yes, papa." I smiled, standing, giving him a kiss on the cheek. "I think the crush is sweet and I doubt anything will come of it. Deepa mentioned he has a girlfriend."

"Anyway." Alejandro changed the topic. "I see Fr. Flynn and the troops, so we should go out." He pointed.

With a deep inhalation, I moved to the front door. I walked out, letting Alejandro close things up. Taking a mental stock, I believed I was as centered as I would be today. The sun warmed my face and forced me to squint until my eyes adjusted. If I didn't know better, our court came across like we were having a block party. Everyone was out chatting and enjoying the bright sunny afternoon; a welcome sight. The noise of the kids running around playing filled my ears, but under this view of a perfect suburban neighborhood, I caught glimpses of people's worry; not only in their gestures, but in their conversations. I honed in on words like: *worried, can't wait for this to end, will it end, can they really help us, what do we do if this doesn't work.* With my eyes adjusting to the light, I noted Vyan jump into his car and pull away from the curb. He moved out of our court and vanished. He wasn't the only one; a couple of other folks, Derek, Juan, and Mr. Gill all did the same.

"Hey," Dannie greeted by way of a wave.

"Where's everyone going?" I asked, seeing Juan pass us.

"Oh, we're having folks move some of the cars off the street." She pointed. "Keeping the street clear makes movement around the neighborhood easier and keeps obstruction to a minimum."

The street had been cleared of cars, which took me aback. Typically, we kept our cars in the garage. Alejandro believed you used the garage for cars, not for storage, and I agreed. "Just in case?" I asked with my eyebrows raised and my hand moving up and down.

She inhaled deep. "You never know, anything might happen." She pulled out an envelope. "I arranged to have the street closed today for a 'block party'."

I laughed.

"All we need are the grills, chicken and veggies, and a bounce house," Alejandro chuckled with a smile, sniffing the air as if he'd smelled the food cooking.

"That sounds good. You'll have to invite me over some time." She beamed.

"When we get through this, you bet." Alejandro grinned.

"How are you feeling?" I asked Dannie. She appeared fine, but as I understood all too well, just because you looked good on the outside, didn't mean you were well on the inside.

"It's a strange thing." Dannie adjusted her brown-patterned short-sleeve shirt. "But honestly, I'm fine. Not tired. Not sick. Overall, I'm good," Dannie pulled at her short sleeves. "Not like what happened to Fr. Flynn."

"What happened to Fr. Flynn?" Alejandro moved closer to us.

"When he was working on me." The warmth and color drained from her face. "I guess the thing whammied him. He was doing a wedding on Sunday and started to not feel well,

229

he ended up in the hospital–"

"What?" Alejandro and I said together.

"He's fine now." She shook her head. "When he blew the Holy Spirit into me, the Demon blew something at him."

"Oh…right, he wiped his face."

A shudder ran across her shoulders.

"And he didn't say a thing the other night."

"He's better. The doctor figured maybe he had the flu, but they couldn't explain how the virus came on so quickly…"

"Geez." I shook my head.

"Well, I'm glad he's okay and nothing worse happened to him." Alejandro pointed. "Here come the guys."

Vyan, Derek, Juan, and Mr. Gill were at the park, chatting, as they returned to our street.

"I'm gonna go and talk to Juan a sec." Alejandro squeezed my side. "I want to ask him about the Tamien Nation, see if he heard from them about today. See if any of them are going to be here."

"Okay." I observed him scurrying off, falling into my own worried stupor.

"You good?" Dannie asked.

"What?" I turned to face her. "Oh. Yeah, I'm good, bummed about Fr. Flynn."

"I think that's why he didn't say anything. He's been doing this a while."

"True."

"I'll talk to you later. I'm gonna go check on Mercedes and Derek; they've been stressed. I guess a lot has been happening at their house this week."

"Really?"

"Yep." And with that, she headed off. I forgot that ours wasn't the only home, and we weren't the only family affected by these things. Still, right now, I assumed what we were experiencing was the calm before the storm or the battle. Despite a few knocks and shadows, everything appeared normal and nothing was out of the ordinary. How was any of this happening or even possible? And yet here we all were, dealing with our own fears and worries for our families.

"You ready for this?" Deepa glanced around, a nervousness crossing her lips, waving to Vyan.

I glanced at the golden hills our road faced, at the top of the hills Lick Observatory. The fields that were across Yerba Buena, lying at the threshold of the foothills reminding me of what once had been all around here. The beautiful view was part of the reason we moved here. We felt so far away from the city, but we were only minutes from everything. I noticed a guy on his bike peddle by, oblivious to our dilemma. There was a whole world maybe two hundred feet away that knew nothing about what plagued us. This made my head pound with anger and jealousy. I allowed myself to feel those emotions for a moment, and exhaled, releasing them into the world. "Hardly feels believable."

"I keep thinking the same thing." Deepa extended out and took my hand. "How are you? Really?"

I met her gaze. Her dark eyes held the worry of a mother and a friend. I took a moment, wiggling my toes in my shoes, stretching the fingers in my free hand. Finally, my heart rate slowed. "I'm okay," I ultimately replied. "The whole experience has been a lot. Who would have assumed in February that we would all be here today?"

"Well, on the plus side, we got to meet folks and become friends." Deepa's white, toothy grin filled her face, washing away her concern.

"True." I beamed at her, and warmth filled my chest, pushing away my worry. This allowed my cheeks to pull up into a smile. "Do you think we would have all become as friendly without all…" I waved my hand around.

"Maybe. Who can say?" Deepa glanced up at the sky. "It might have taken a bit more time, but I like to think so. We got lucky in some ways. Everyone here is kind and generous, not like a lot of places we've lived."

"Hey, y'all," Mercedes greeted, leaving Derek to continue his conversation with Dannie.

"Hiya." I waved.

"What a week, right?" She smiled, but the cheer didn't reach her eyes. "I'm glad Dannie and Michelle have been so willing to work with us… and to… listen.

"I'll be glad when we get through this," Deepa added. "I'm sorry you've had such a rough few days."

Mercedes shook her head. "I don't think Derek has helped matters. He's been confrontational with… this thing, and that didn't go over well."

"Well, it'll–"

"Good afternoon, everyone," Fr. Flynn called all our attention. He was standing near the park, the sun shining down on him and giving him a heavenly glow. "Thank you all for being here today. I know this all seems out of the ordinary, but each of you being here will make a difference. Confronting this entity head on, all together, is the only way to move forward." He pointed to Dr. Thomas. "For those of you who don't remember, this is Dr. Anson Thomas and the members of his team."

Dr. Thomas raised a hand, smiling. Ethan and Zoe waved as well. Michelle and Dannie shifted how they stood, but managed relaxed appearances to the group.

"Between us, we'll be giving you directions today, and he and his team will be monitoring the situation. Especially Michelle." He scanned the group and our court. "We are going to be relying on each of us, so keep checking in with each other and, with the grace of God, we'll get through this." He motioned to his team. "Briefly, I want to introduce you to my team. This is Deacon Huy and Deacon Sebastian." The two men wore gray shirts with a white collar, which was a contrast to Fr. Flynn's black shirt and white collar. "This is Roberto, Pam, Teresa, Ruben, and Dan." He pointed to each in order. "They will all be assisting me and are what I refer to as prayer warriors, so you can look to them if you aren't sure what to say or do, or if you need assistance."

There were greetings from all of us.

Alejandro made his way to my side, and we stood together. Chloe waved at us, still keeping a watchful eye on all the littles, but remained close enough to us that we didn't need to worry.

"Before we commence." Fr. Flynn raised his hands. "I would like to call us in together for a blessing." His gaze moved around the group, making eye contact with as many folks as possible. "I understand not all of you are Catholic, or even Christian. If you feel moved, you may join in or bow your heads.

"Heavenly Father, thank you for your glory and for bringing us together on this beautiful day in this, the valley of the blessed Saint Clare. We are moved by the love you have for your son, Jesus, and for the love you show to each of us. We ask that you bless this gathering and send your angels to watch over us as we proceed to bring peace to this land and to your children who live here. Amen."

My ears were greeted by a round of "Amens.", which I found myself joining.

Fr. Flynn continued speaking to our gathering. "Now. We are going to be doing a series of blessings and we'll be walking throughout the—"

"What's going on here?" Dr. Chen's sour voice called all

our attention as she moved from her porch to her driveway. "What do you think you're doing?"

"Dr. Chen." Fr. Flynn smiled, facing her and reaching out his hand. "I'm Fr. Flynn. We're going to—"

"More of this craziness," she barked with a shake of her head. Her black hair was cut short and her glasses were heavy on her face. "Haven't we been through enough? You need to stay off our property and not block the street or I'll be calling the police."

"Dr. Chen. Hi," Dannie called with a wave. "I don't know if you remember me or not, but I'm Officer Danielle Lancey." She pulled out her badge and the envelope. "This is a permit from the City of San Jose, allowing your neighbors to have this block party, which everyone is welcome to attend, including you and your family. Now I'm not here in any official capacity, but as a guest, and I can assure you that when the police arrive, they won't be happy you wasted their time."

Dr. Chen crossed her arms, and a frown crawled over her face. "I don't believe this."

I wanted to laugh, but I didn't. I now understood why Dannie did that. She had used her police senses and figured there may be an issue, and preempted any challenge.

"We would love to have you join us." Lidia smiled, reaching out her hand. "I'm so happy to see Mike doing better. We prayed for him and your family every day. Won't you please join us?"

"Absolutely not. We—"

"Emily. Enough!" Mike barked from their porch. "We've been through hell and you're not going to stop these people, our neighbors, from trying to stop these... Demons, Evil Spirits, or whatever is plaguing this place. This thing almost made me take my life..."

"Mike." Dr. Chen's face paled as she faced her husband

and moved toward him.

"What if it was Lee? Or Marc? Or Rose?" Mike snapped. "No." He shook his head.

"It's all nonsense…" Dr. Chen's voice dropped off as her argument deflated, and we all stood bearing witness to their drama.

"No!" he shouted, coming forward into the sunlight. "I almost died because of what's happening here and you will not stop them, not anymore." He marched into the full sunlight, despite the dark circles under his eyes and the bandages still on his arms. A strength filled his movements and his words that none of us missed. "In fact, we're all going to participate." He glanced at Fr. Flynn. "Assuming, Father, a family of non-Christians is welcome."

"We are all children of God and everyone is welcome," Fr. Flynn offered, the professionalism not leaving his face.

"You're most welcome. We can use your strength and conviction—both of your strength." Michelle's face filled with the warmth of the summer day.

Alejandro tapped me on my ribs and we shared a knowing expression with each other as we continued to watch.

"Good." Mike pointed to their home, speaking to Emily in Mandarin. His words ended any argument, and she vanished into their house. He moved from his driveway into the street. "I'm sorry," he added. "I'm sorry I didn't stand up to her sooner. You have no idea the hell we've been living through."

"I can assure you," I cracked my neck. "We all know."

"Knowing I'm not crazy…we're not crazy…" He swiped at the tears in his eyes. "I would never hurt my family. I would never do what those voices wanted. That's why…"

"It's okay," Alejandro declared. "We all know."

Deepa moved over to hug him. "You're among friends. You don't need to explain or apologize."

"Thank you." Mike's voice cracked, returning her hug.

Dr. Chen appeared with their three children in tow. Mike pointed toward Chloe. "Chloe, can you?"

Chloe called Lee, Marc, and Rose over to stand with her and the other kids.

Mike took Emily's hand. "Emily… I love you, you know I do, but we're doing this. As a family. And you won't stop us, or there will be more than this *nonsense* for you to worry about." His expression was hard, as the words he spoke were in English for us all to hear.

She bit her lip. "Father, what do we need to do?" Her voice was barely above a whisper.

"We're getting to that…" Fr. Flynn started his explanation, which I'll admit I only half-listened to. Since we moved in, I never noticed Mike as forceful as he was when he stood up to Emily. He always struck me as the Beta to Emily's Alpha. However, seeing how he confronted her and how he was willing to risk their marriage to save not only us, but his family…his children, impressed me. From the few snippets he had shared, he had been through it with the spirits and had his fill, and flat out wasn't going to take it anymore.

Something about having the Chens here with us filled me with more hope than I had at the outset of the day. Anson, Michelle, and even Fr. Flynn told us cleansing our homes and our neighborhood would require all of us, a united front, and now here we were. All of us together, for the first time since we moved to Golden Hills Court. If Mike's strength was an indication of the fortitude all these people had, there was nothing and no Demon we couldn't stand up to. We were all ready to fight to save our community.

# ~ Chapter Twenty-Two ~

Fr. Flynn and his team pulled everyone into their family units, offering each family a blessing and anointing each of us with holy oil. Michelle, Dr. Thomas, and the rest of the SVPRS passed out white candles and provided support and words of encouragement to everyone. They also received blessings and were anointed. I glanced up and down the street on what should be a bright sunny day, but a shadow crawled over the street and our homes. I peered up at the cloudless sky and deliberated on where this darkness came from. Was it possible that the shadows normally cast were able to grow and fill all the lit spaces around us? I wasn't sure, but given the muddiness I experienced in my mind and with my thoughts, I figured anything could be possible.

"Dad." Chloe squeezed my hand.

*She's feeling it too.*

I spared a peek at Alejandro as he inhaled, unease filling his face.

Forcing my lips to raise in what I hoped to be a strong smile, I spoke. "We've got this." The words came out less determined than I hoped.

"Can you feel it?" Chloe whispered up to me.

I wouldn't lie to her, but I didn't want to agree with her and scare her more than she—well, we already were. The pressure on my chest and in my ears had been impossible to ignore. Everything sounded a bit dulled, as if I swam underwater in a pool while trying to hear a conversation on the decking. I kneeled down. "Remember, we are in control.

There is nothing that these things can do to us. We can't give into our fear. Look at everyone here."

She peeked around.

"They won't let anything hurt us."

"Okay." She smiled at me, but the warmth didn't reach her eyes. Something echoed in my own eyes.

"Hey," Alejandro's voice broke through the pressure and the thickness of our neighborhood. "You guys going to be okay? We don't have to stay. We can get in our car right now and leave." He pointed to our garage, which, at the moment, seemed miles away from us.

"No, Papa, we have to do this." Chloe's eyes were large, but the set jaw and firm lips showed how certain she had become.

I felt so proud of my daughter's strength.

*She's so brave. I wish I felt half as brave as she came across.*

Dannie came over to us flicking her lighter, igniting each of our white candles. According to Deacon Sebastian, they, along with everything we would be using today, had been blessed. "It's getting heavy. You can feel the tension all around us." She peeked around at the others and shook her head. "You guys okay?"

"Is this normal?" Alejandro asked as his candle lit.

She huffed. "Honestly, nothing about what's been happening here has been normal. I know we may act like we know what we're doing and in a way we do, but a lot of this is way outside of our experience. We'll pull through. Stay strong and remember, as a group, we can overcome anything." The confidence crossed her lips as she moved over to the Patils.

Deepa waved to us, lifting her candle as Dannie moved away.

I bit at my lip as my stomach did all kinds of acrobatics.

"Afternoon, everyone," Dr. Thomas greeted, calling us

all to attention. "Before we get going, you're going to see us doing different things. While Father Flynn goes through the rights of Exorcism, Michelle, Zoe, and Ethan will be walking around, trying to call out all the lost spirits who are in need of deliverance." He pointed to Michelle and her team. "We spoke with Fr. Flynn to ensure our actions won't affect his efforts, and we believe we can work in tandem."

There were, happily, no questions.

Fr. Flynn stepped forward. "Deacon Huy and Sebastian will be walking around with their censers; it's the vessel used to burn incense," he added to clarify. "This smoke will help to draw out any negativity. Michelle and the others will be using smudge sticks, which is used in a similar manner."

I tapped Chloe on the shoulder and pointed over to the two Deacons as they got their censer things ready.

She peeked up at me.

"Once the prayers are started, we will not stop until we finish. I may need to change our prayers as we go along, but each grouping of prayers will be finished…"

I frowned, not fully understanding.

"It'll make sense once we get going," Fr. Flynn added.

I wasn't the only one confused, but glad something about this would make sense.

"Shall we begin?" Fr. Flynn called our attention. His tone changed, filling with an authority and energy I didn't recognize in him, "Most glorious Prince of the Heavenly Armies, Saint Michael the Archangel, defend us in our battle against principalities and powers, against the rulers of this world of darkness, against the spirits of wickedness in the high places. Come to the assistance of men whom God has created to His likeness and whom He has redeemed at a great price from the tyranny of the devil…"

As Fr. Flynn continued his prayer, he began walking to

the Chens' home. We walked—no, marched, not only as a family, but as a community. There was a power growing around us as we moved together with one purpose. I can't put my finger on the sensation exactly, but if you have ever been part of something bigger than yourself, you'll know this feeling. We reached the Chens' house and moved to the corner where their backyard met Yerba Buena Road. Fr. Flynn continued his prayer as a shadow or darkness continued to grow, swallowing all the light around us. As Fr. Flynn ran holy oil over the fence and deposited a medallion of Saint Michael, a scream cut through the air and a gust of wind pushed past Hari, Deepa, and Vyan. Vyan dropped to his knees, but Dannie and Hari were there in seconds to help him up.

"We've got its attention," Michelle said.

"Listen," Mercedes exclaimed. "You hear that?"

"Crying," Kathy Harris replied. "But all the kids…"

Fr. Flynn continued his prayers as we whispered and tried to figure out where the crying was coming from.

"It's them." Juan waved his hand, trying to point in a direction, but unable to pin one down. "But I don't see them."

The crying echoed all around us, or at least in the direction of our street.

"The ones slaughtered." Michelle gestured her head, moving closer to the street where our houses sat. "How many are there?" she asked to no one. To everyone.

Fr. Flynn acknowledged what we said with a bow of his head, but continuing his prayer. "…Deign, O Lord, to grant us Thy powerful protection and to keep us safe and sound. We beseech Thee through Jesus Christ, Our Lord. Amen."

Fr. Flynn raised his hands. That was our cue. "From the snares of the devil."

I glanced at the card we held and along with everyone

else I spoke our response. "Deliver us, O Lord."

We continued walking and Fr. Flynn called as the crying and moaning grew louder. "That Thy Church may serve Thee in peace and liberty."

Again, we all responded. "We beseech Thee to hear us."

We made our way down the street. Fr. Flynn sprinkled holy water as he stepped, his Deacons behind him, filling our path with smoke. The prayer Fr. Flynn recited was a long loop that, once finished, he would repeat over again. I assumed during these breaks he'd change the prayer, should he need to. We followed him and we would recite our parts in unison. We moved to the second corner of our cursed land, the farthest corner, the Walkers' home. I didn't know how we would all fit into the backyard, but we did. Fr. Flynn continued his blessing and placed a medallion of Saint Michael on the fence, anointing the fence with holy oil and sprinkling holy water as he walked.

"In the Name of Jesus Christ." Fr. Flynn spoke with the authority only a man of faith had: clear and powerful, unwavering. "Our God and Lord, strengthened by the intercession of the Immaculate Virgin Mary, Mother of God, of Blessed Michael the Archangel, of the Blessed Apostles Peter and Paul and all the Saints and powerful in the holy authority of our ministry, we confidently undertake to repulse the attacks and deceits of the devil."

We continued our procession, moving toward the backyard of the Harrises' home. Again, Fr. Flynn blessed the farthest corner of their lot and placed another blessed marker as he continued his prayers. We each repeated our parts as we continued on. I had lost sight of Michelle, Ethan, and Zoe, but assumed they were doing what they needed to do, so I didn't worry too much about them. I took a breath and frowned. The air smelled different. Stale. Despite the musty, still air surrounding us and the growing pressure in my ears and chest, a wind kicked up as we moved up the street. Growls and more cries filled my ears. The snarling grew the closer we got to the park, but these sounds were unlike the rumbles of any animal I'd heard before.

"Look." Lidia pointed in the direction of the park.

"What's that?" Derek called, pulling his kids closer to him.

There were mumbles from several people in our group, too many for me to pinpoint, as I focused on the inky black shadows moving in the trees by the park and the creek. What I witnessed made no sense. A being. But they had wings connected to an upper body of what I assumed to be that of an angel. Connected to the body, a head of a lion, and there was something odd about its legs and feet. I wasn't sure what, but they were thin like a duck or some kind of bird. The shadow presence absorbed all of the light and somehow expanded the darkness of the trees in the park all the way down the street toward us.

*How is any of this possible? What is that… thing?*

More crying pierced the afternoon air as well as pleas for help, but the sounds didn't come from us or anyone in our group—at least, that I noticed.

"What is your name, beast?" Fr. Flynn demanded. We finished our next round of prayers.

Nothing.

The creature paced back and forth, watching us as more shadows filled the area.

Fr. Flynn squared off his shoulders and started his prayer again. We stood there, watching and waiting for something to happen, but again the creature paced back and forth, doing nothing.

*What does the thing want? What is it doing?*

I reached for Alejandro's free hand. Taking his warm,

damp hand in mine, I was happy for the closeness and the added security as we continued the prayers.

"In the Name of Jesus Christ, our God and Lord, strengthened by the intercession of the Immaculate Virgin Mary, Mother of God, of Blessed Michael the Archangel, of the Blessed Apostles Peter and Paul and all the Saints. and powerful in the holy authority of our ministry, we confidently undertake to repulse the attacks and deceits of the devil…"

Wind yowled all around us but the air continued to be still, and there were hints of warmth and brightness glowing from sections of our block but nothing compared to the darkness that all but engulfed us.

"God arises; His enemies are scattered and those who hate Him flee before Him," Fr. Flynn continued. "As smoke is driven away, so are they driven; as wax melts before the fire, so the wicked perish at the presence of God."

Deacon Huy and Sebastian held their incense burners as smoke flowed, surrounding us and spreading out over the street. They were joined by Michelle, Ethan, Zoe, and Dannie walking around with smudge sticks. There was a battle of scents and smoke filling the area. The smells weren't unpleasant, but they weren't my favorite either.

Fr. Flynn held up a cross. "Behold the Cross of the Lord, flee bands of enemies."

Alejandro pointed to the card. Chloe, Alejandro, and I spoke. "The Lion of the tribe of Juda, the offspring of David, hath conquered."

Fr. Flynn stated, "May Thy mercy, Lord, descend upon us."

"As great as our hope in Thee," we all responded.

A mix of a growl and laughter filled our ears and the area surrounding us. These new sounds blocked out that of the cries, or maybe silenced them. I couldn't be sure.

Fr. Flynn's voice grew louder as he continued his rites. We matched his tone and his passion as we made our way through the rest of the prayer cycle.

"Who's that?" Dr. Chen pointed down the street.

Several of us turned and, behind us, a dark shadow of an archer, but it was unlike any human archer I had ever seen. Standing behind this new creature were several soldiers with fancy hats, shields, and long coats.

*They can't be.*

I shook my head, blinking my eyes.

"It's the bad men," Chloe called and pointed.

"That's what we saw in our house," Alejandro added.

"Us too." Mike Chen moved closer to his children. The color was all but gone from Dr. Chen's face. She may not have believed before, but now there was no doubting what we all witnessed.

"Don't give in to your fear," Dr. Thomas reminded us. "These things feed on fear. Don't feed it." His voice was matching in strength to Fr. Flynn.

"They have us surrounded," Ethan countered, holding his smudge stick like a shield or blade for protection.

"Look at our homes," Deepa called out. "They've been hiding in our homes."

Sure enough, there were men, women, children standing in our homes. They were on the porches or in the windows. God in heaven, what happened here? What did the Spaniards do to them? "We have to help them," I declared. "They need us. Please, Fr. Flynn, we have to help save them."

"Blessed Mother, come and take these lost souls," Fr. Flynn called. This wasn't part of his prayer. This was something new. "Mary, Mother of our Lord Jesus, come help these souls to their judgment, free them from the clutches of evil. Amen."

He raised his hands as the words continued to flow from

him. His helpers followed suit. "Holy Mary, help those in need, give strength to the weak, comfort the sorrowful…" Where what happened next came from I couldn't say, but light and a warm puff of air passed between Chloe, Alejandro, and I. This gust of air was the first hint of crisp air we had since the praying commenced. The energy moved through us all and slowly stretched out to each of our homes. One by one, the spirits vanished.

The harder and louder Fr. Flynn prayed, slowly joined by everyone of us. As our voices called out the stronger the white light got and the warmth grew. There was no smell of roses like I had imagined there would be, but the air smelled fresh and clean, like we would get when we hiked in Yosemite or up in Tahoe.

A scream of pain surrounded us, but the crying and wailing ceased as the brightness faded and the warm and fresh air vanished along with it.

"They've gone," Michelle proclaimed. "We freed them."

"Thank God." Alejandro beamed and squeezed my hand.

"Now, to deal with them." Fr. Flynn faced the Demons, one on either side of the street.

"Most glorious Prince of the Heavenly Armies," Fr. Flynn glanced to the heavens. We returned to the Exorcism Prayer. "Saint Michael the Archangel, defend us in our battle against principalities and powers, against the rulers of this world of darkness, against the spirits of wickedness in the high places. Come to the assistance of men whom God has created to His likeness and whom He has redeemed at a great price from the tyranny of the devil.

The Holy Church venerates you as her guardian and protector; to you, the Lord has entrusted the souls of the redeemed to be led into heaven. Pray…"

A scream and growl erupted on either side of us, and the

beasts at either end of the street charged. Fr. Flynn and his prayer warriors stood their ground, but several of us moved swiftly to get out of their path. I pulled Chloe toward me as Alejandro and I tried to get out of the way. As I reached the curb and glanced over my shoulder, the entities were gone.

Fr. Flynn and his team continued to pray, and I kneeled down to check on Chloe.

"Are you okay?" I asked.

She laughed.

"Chloe."

She continued to laugh, and I pulled her face to me. What I witnessed was no longer my daughter. It was a beast.

"Give me a kiss, Daddy." The voice coming from Chloe was hers, but not hers.

I stepped away and stretched my hand for Alejandro's hand. "Fr. Flynn!" I shouted.

"Oh, the Preacher can't help you now, Kyle." Alejandro snarled at me.

"God in Heaven." I jumped away.

"We're sorry, the number you are trying to reach has been disconnected," Alejandro growled at me.

I shook my head. My husband and daughter stood in front of me, but they weren't them, they were gone. What faced me now were those Demons. I wanted to vomit. I wanted to scream. I wanted to pull them to me and run. The hands on my shoulder didn't register until they pulled me out of the way. Everyone was around us—well, not everyone, but both the priest and his team, as well as Dr. Thomas and Michelle. I wondered where Dannie, Ethan, and Zoe were, but my question was answered when Dannie snapped her fingers in front of my eyes.

"Kyle," she demanded. "Kyle!" she shouted.

"Chloe." The words were only a whisper out of my

mouth. "Alejandro." I blinked.

"Fr. Flynn will help them," Dannie exclaimed.

I stood there. Peeking over my shoulder. Ethan and Zoe, as well as some members of Fr. Flynn's team, were with the others, keeping them away and helping those that must have tripped or fallen in the rampage.

"Dannie we need you." Someone shouted. She nodded at me and rushed off.

I wasn't sure what was happening around me anymore. I licked my lips. My family was in danger and I stood here, doing nothing. That wasn't right. I needed to help them. I needed to help save them.

"Saint Michael," I whispered. "I don't know if you'll listen to someone like me, but please come to my aid. I beg you. My family. My daughter. If you need a life, take mine, but spare theirs. Mary, Mother of Jesus, you lost your son; you understand the pain of losing a child, even if it is to save the world. Please don't let me lose my daughter. Please help me. Please help me help them." The words blared out of me. I must have been screaming, because I couldn't hear anything else going on around me. "Blessed Mary. Saint Michael, please come to my aid. Please hear me. I need you, not for me, but for them," I called out.

A tickle and warmth found my toes and moved up my legs, slowly filling my whole body. I didn't notice anything out of the range of normal. Well, considering what had happened, I understand normal is subjective. Still, a bright white light like a million suns filled everything around me. I noted all our homes, our friends, and our neighbors. Deepa, Hari, and Vyan were speaking, but their words were lost on me. Mercedes, Derek, and their kids were huddled together, holding their candles in trembling hands, words spilling from their mouths. Lidia and Juan held their children and pointed toward me, their candles laying burned out by their feet.

Their energy pushed toward me. All the families in our court were together, all speaking as a single voice. The more they spoke, the more the white light grew. I turned toward my family. A darkness, or shadow, connected Alejandro and Chloe and surrounded them. I couldn't allow this attack any longer; these events needed to end. I walked over to Alejandro and Chloe. A grin pulled at my cheeks as I surveyed Fr. Flynn and his warriors. They continued to call out, as everyone did, even Dr. Thomas, Michelle, Dannie, all of them. Each of their words finding their way to me. But now was the time for me to go to battle. With a deep inhale and standing tall, I moved the others out of my way. I no longer required their assistance. I waved a hand and the people holding my family down moved with ease. I glanced at the man and child lying before me. They were innocent and weren't given a choice in any of this.

*Innocent. And innocents will not be harmed. Not today. Not here.*

"It's time for you to go." A voice that was mine, but wasn't mine, addressed both Alejandro and Chloe.

"No," the creature in Alejandro shouted, snarling and baring its teeth. "We like it here. This is our land, and they moved here of their own free will. We've claimed them."

"They did not invite you," I countered, the words softly flowing from my lips. "You do not get to claim what isn't yours."

"Liar," the thing in Chloe growled at me. A beautiful child lay on the ground before me; now they tortured her for sport.

"I don't lie, Leraje," I corrected, somehow knowing the thing inside Chloe. It was the same thing that had tried to occupy Danielle. "Take your legions and vacate this child."

"Make us," Chloe hissed, her eyes blazing fire and

brimstone in my direction. "We're going to kill her and feed on her soul."

"I won't allow that, and you know it." My voice filled with a certainty and a calmness I had never known in my life. The words continued to be mine, but were they? I peeked over my shoulder at all the faces. So many people. So many voices, all doing battle against an evil they don't fully understand, but willing to fight for each other. This is how it should be; this is the world at its best.

I returned my gaze to my husband and daughter on the ground. "And these people will not stop fighting." I gestured at the crowd behind me.

*So many voices.*

"You have no power here..." Alejandro glowered at me. His eyes burned with a power of hate and anger so common in them. So much sorrow filled me when I dealt with them. Today wasn't the first, and our dealings today wouldn't be our last.

"I have all the power." Careful not to push too hard, however, I needed for them to fully realize who was in charge. I had my own army and, with the voices of all these people, my power only grew stronger. "It is you, Ipos, who has no power, only the power given to you by your master." I addressed the thing in Alejandro.

My husband and daughter glanced at each other and snarled once more in my direction, trying to break from those that held them down, a pointless endeavor on their part. My army was here and assisting me. They had lost, but they hadn't accepted that fact yet.

*Soon enough.*

I raised a hand to the sky. "She will come. He has called out to her and pleaded for his family, wanting nothing but their safety. As with all these other voices, they all have found her, wanting nothing but for these two souls to be free." I peered at the two on the ground. "Do you want her to come? Shall we wait for her to cast you out and banish you, or shall you leave now?"

"This is our land. These are our bodies," Alejandro shouted, and a rumble of earth radiated from where he lay.

"They are ours!" Chloe demanded, continuing to fight and struggle.

"No longer," I commanded, my voice filled with all the authority I possessed. "And your claim to this land is revoked. This land is now under my protection… and." I glanced to the heavens. "Hers."

An energy, a power, or maybe the same warmth I had been surrounded by started like a seed in my stomach and grew into a mighty redwood, exploding from my body and filling every corner of our neighborhood. The light didn't bother my eyes, and the warmth wasn't overpowering, despite this energy being more than the sun on its brightest days.

"Her," Alejandro hissed, his tongue flicking in snake-like movements around his mouth. "She comes." It squinted and struggled even harder under the influx of power.

"No!" Chloe yelled, shutting her eyes, her head shaking back and forth in protest.

"I warned you she would come. Now is your last opportunity to go." I peeked to the light in the sky before returning my gaze back down on them. She was close, and her power continued to expand. The nearer she got, the stronger the voices around me grew in prayer.

*So much strength for so few beings.*

Alejandro and Chloe shared a malice-filled glance, the darkness hovering around them vanished. The inky blackness burst into the sky, retreating to the shadows.

I bowed my head.

*They are gone.*

"Thank you, brothers and sisters," the white energy holding Alejandro and Chloe down moved away, returning to where it had come. I held out my hands to my husband and daughter to assist them off the ground, and they moved with ease. "Your lives and those of your neighbors will be blessed from now until you come home. Should you need us, we will always be here for you. Maybe not in a way you'll see, but we'll be watching…" I stopped, turned, and beamed up at the sky. "And so will she."

I noted as if spoken the questions in both Alejandro and Chloe.

"Leraje and Ipos, and their legions, are gone." I waved off their worry. I caressed Chloe's head and smiled. "There are rules and they, like all of us, must follow them. They try and find ways around our laws, but not this time." The warmth in my body swelled as I touched my husband's face. "They will not return to this place, nor will any of their brethren. Fr. Flynn has marked this location, as have I. You have no more to fear from them. As for the souls trapped here, she came and collected them as promised. They're home now." I stepped away and bowed my head in understanding. I examined the younger soul in front of me. "Your gifts are nothing to be afraid of. They were given to you like all the other gifts each of you have. Don't worry, you will grow to understand them." I extended out my hand and touched her cheek.

I raised my hand from her and laid my hand on him. "Your love for your family is strong, stronger than many. Never lose that. They are your joy; your bliss. Nurture them and they will cherish you in return." I stepped to the side and glanced around this blessed land. "I can't wait to see what becomes of you…" I spared a glance at the crowd of people

251

still praying and watching. I glanced around the assembled. "All of you," I added. "Now be at peace, Alejandro and Chloe, and know you are loved and perfect as you are."

The energy filling me pulled away, and nothing remained but peace and love.

# ~ Chapter Twenty-Three ~

I blinked several times, the warmth fading from my body and the light of the million suns withdrawing from around me. I stood, holding Alejandro and Chloe in my arms, their warmth and love replacing the growing void. We were together and they were safe. We all were. My mind was covered in a fog from the encounter. As the world returned around me, the noises of birds, insects, all the creatures who typically hid from this place, our home, returned. Voices continued to pull me out of my fog, calling for my attention. It wasn't until Fr. Flynn pulled me away from Alejandro and Chloe that I fully took in the world again. Anson and Fr. Flynn studied me, their gaze dancing all over my face.

"What?" I needed to understand the worry and the fear slowly leaving their expressions. "Is everything okay? Are they gone?"

"You…" Anson pointed, no more words came out as he scrutinized me. He raked a hand through his hair.

"Your glasses." Michelle handed my spectacles to me. I hadn't noticed her join our small group.

I didn't even notice I missed them. I absently put them on my face, the world coming into focus.

"In all my time as a priest…" Fr. Flynn began, wiping his face with trembling hands. "I've never seen such a thing," Fr. Flynn noted, not elaborating any further.

"What language were you using?" Michelle asked, her gaze bouncing from Fr. Flynn to Dr. Thomas.

"English," I declared, confused, my own gaze narrowing

on them. I didn't wholly understand what was happening around me. I glanced over to Alejandro and Chloe, who were as confused as me. I wanted to move to them and wrap them both in my arms, but we all stood as stone statues, jumbled in various thoughts, all reaching for some kind of understanding that wasn't being provided.

"That wasn't English," Ethan countered, reaching us.

"I've never heard anything like it," Dannie spoke, shaking her head, her eyes as wide as saucers.

"I think it was Aramaic," Zoe commented, moving closer to us. She and Ethan had been checking on the others, along with the members of Fr. Flynn's team. None of them were having any of whatever they were saying. They pointed toward us. Hari shook his head, and Derek pushed past them, heading our way.

Zoe's words registered in my mind, as they must have with Fr. Flynn, as we both considered Zoe. Things continued to settle, or became more animated, as the case may have been, with everyone rushing our way. It was pandemonium, but a good kind of chaos.

"Are you all okay? You went into a daze and..." Deepa asked, waving a hand toward me and my family. "I've never prayed so hard in my life. I couldn't even say who I prayed to exactly; God, of course, but I've never seen anything like this before."

"I've never been this terrified," Derek added. "It was like all the air got sucked right out of everything around us... then..."

"I would... my God," Dr. Chen shook her head. "How's any of this even possible? This whole affair has been terrifying, but at the same time, I've never experienced such peace and so much love."

"Something..." Lidia faltered, muttering something in

Spanish.

I missed what Lidia said as I shared a quick moment of silence with Alejandro, both of us peeking at Chloe. I mouthed the words "I love you so much" to her and she beamed at me.

"Juan, the kids, and I," Lidia continued. "We all experienced something here. Not the bad things, but something... I don't know... something akin to love and strength. I can't explain it. But the sensation touched my soul..."

"When we watched Alejandro and Chloe fall." Juan shook his head. "So much hate and anger, then... boom." He gestured his hand to mimic an explosion.

Alejandro caught my eye and peeked at our home as he took Chloe's hand in his. I met his gaze. I understood his need to retreat into our house, but at the moment, given the situation and the questions still needing to be answered, our withdrawal to our sanctuary would have to wait.

"Everyone, please." Dannie's voice rose above all the comments and questions that were being fired in our direction. I paid no attention to any of them. All that mattered at this moment was my family. A family that we would grow as we had planned. A family that had been on the brink of disaster, but now had been given a gift. A gift of peace and love.

I moved to Alejandro and Chloe, pushing out all the other voices. "Are you okay?" My hand traced the edges of his face.

"What happened?" Chloe asked, peeking around, squeezed tight against Alejandro. "I remember seeing the dark thing come toward me, and now..."

"That's all I remember as well. But there was something. A light. A force." Alejandro stretched out and touched my hair. "What happened to your hair?"

"It must be a mess." I ran a hand through my hair. I honestly didn't care about my appearance at the moment. All

I wanted to do was take my family home, and maybe take a shower and clean up.

*Priorities.*

"No." He shook his head, his gaze fixated on my hair as his free hand moved through my thinning mop. "It's all platinum." He beamed. "I've never seen anything like it…"

"It's so pretty, Dad." Chloe beamed up at me. "Like the angels."

Now I was curious. I needed to see a mirror. I moved up the driveway of the Johnsons' home and scanned my reflection in the window. "I…" My hair was now a bright white, platinum color. Not gray or pure white, but something different. Something unique. I pulled off my spectacles, adjusting my head for a better look, thinking maybe what lay before me was a trick of the light. But no. I put my glasses on. "How?" I turned to see Alejandro and Chloe next to me. Our neighbors, Fr. Flynn's team, and the research team were all observing us.

"Kyle." Fr. Flynn approached with the others.

"The stress of the situation," Dr. Chen pointed out and faced the others, adjusting her own glasses. "Extreme stress can cause people's hair to lose color, but not in minutes." She shook her head. "This… I don't know."

I ran a hand through my hair as I reviewed all the faces focused on me.

"Do I look awful?" I asked Alejandro.

"Never." He touched my arm. "Handsome as always."

Warmth radiated from his touch and moved through me, filling me with absolute peace and adoration.

"Kyle, how do you feel?" Dr. Thomas joined us, his quizzical gaze studying my face and the rest of me.

"Good." The words came out with barely any consideration, and I faced him. I peeked over my shoulder at the window again, seeing my new hair color. The change would take a while to get used to, but I wouldn't hide or cover up the new color, or try to change it. "Well, tired, but good overall. I don't think I understand what happened. And I wouldn't mind taking a shower to soothe my aching muscles." I chuckled. "Feels like I rode twenty-five miles, all uphill, on my bike."

"But is it over?" Mrs. Walker asked. "I'm glad you and your family are okay, Kyle, but doctor, is it over?"

"I don't think I can take any more of this," Mr. Harris added. "I had no idea things here were so bad. Deepa. Mercedes. How did you deal with all of this?"

"It's over," I proclaimed to everyone with 100% certainty. I spoke low enough for everyone to hear me, holding all the strength I had in my shoulders and head. "Leraje and Ipos are gone, and they can't return here. Ever!" Finality filled my words.

"Leraje and Ipos?" Fr. Flynn questioned, turning to Deacon Huy.

"Yes." I sneered at their names. Disgust and pity were a fifty-fifty mix in my emotions and thoughts. Their names held no fear for me any longer. They had been defeated and that was as much of a certainty as the sun beaming down on us, warming our faces and our bodies.

"Those were the names Kyle called out," Deacon Huy spoke with a peek at Deacon Sebastian, who shook his head in agreement.

"And you know they are gone?" Fr. Flynn asked me.

"Saint Michael came and vanquished them." I glanced at everyone before returning my focus to Fr. Flynn.

"You were in the presence of Michael the Archangel?" Michelle asked, her voice breaking as the others pushed closer to my family and me.

I shook my head. "No, but I heard him. At least, I believe

he spoke. Maybe I only sensed his words," I said, only partially interested in any of the questions, instead focusing on my family. I understood their need for clarity, but my need for my family and being safe held a higher place in my heart at the moment. "I don't mean to be rude, but I want to get Chloe and Alejandro home. We've all been through it today."

"Dr. Thomas, do you and your team mind assisting us in walking the area and ensuring everything is clean?" Fr. Flynn asked. "Kyle, I would like to check in on you. All of you. After you get some rest. Please?" he added.

"Sure."

"We'd be happy to help," Michelle spoke for the team and gestured to Zoe and Ethan.

"Maybe you can help shed more light on what happened, and how Kyle was able to get us all to move when he walked up to his family." Dr. Thomas ran a hand over the back of his neck, shaking his head. "I've never sensed anything so powerful, but also so controlled. It was as if all he had to do was snap a finger and we would have all jumped in obedience."

"Come on, everyone." Dannie signaled her hands to the group for them to move away. Her police officer mode kicked in, which I appreciated greatly. "Let's give some room to the Del Rosarios."

The sounds of resounding agreement from all those assembled made its way to my ears. I even caught a few 'thank yous', which was absurd since I didn't do anything. All the credit should be going to Fr. Flynn and his group, as well as Dr. Thomas and the researchers from the SVPRS.

I took Alejandro's hand in mine and pulled him closer to my chest as I pulled Chloe closer to us. If I could, I would have wrapped them in a bubble of protection. I huffed. Who knew? Maybe I already had. As a family, we made our way across the street to our home. For the first time as I walked to our front door, I viewed how beautiful our home was and how lucky we were to live in such a wonderful place.

After a long shower and one of the best home-cooked meals we had in a long time, exhaustion filled every part of my body. We were all tired. That night I slept better than I remembered. All of us did. Peaceful dreams of beauty and love filled my mind. All I remembered from that night's sleep are wonderful images one would associate with tranquility and affection. The next morning, as I showered, I noted how good the house felt. Something had drastically changed. The energy went from negative to positive, and the house and our family were better for it. Some of what happened yesterday slipped into a fog or haze of a dream. But there were aspects I would never forget. Hearing the voice of an angel speak, and the fear on the faces of the Demons trying to attach or possess Alejandro and Chloe when the angel spoke to them. Hearing life on our street for the first time since we moved here; another sign that our house was now a home. Knowing we would all be safe and, somehow, someway, we were all being protected, filled me with a greater joy than anything ever had.

"Hon," Alejandro called out from the stairs. "Fr. Flynn and Dr. Thomas are gonna stop by later and check in."

"Okay," I called out. Glad to know they would be coming over to hopefully shed more light on our experience.

*****

I lounged in our family room, savoring the peace in our home. Fr. Flynn, Dr. Thomas, and Michelle sat across from Alejandro, Chloe, and me. The words followed like a gentle stream making their way to the ocean, only to be added to the power of the sea. I finished telling them everything I experienced. I had moments where I assumed they might think I was insane, but they didn't.

"But why don't I remember anything?" Alejandro raked a hand through his hair, his words only a question for clarity, not frustration.

"I don't know." Fr. Flynn shook his head. "As I mentioned before, this experience was unlike any in all my years. The feeling of power, the blessed angels and Michael were present, I'm certain, but an interaction on that level…" He shook his head.

"It all feels like a dream," I closed my eyes, trying to clear my thoughts.

"Chloe, do you remember any of it?" Michelle leaned in, rolling her cup in her hands.

Chloe contemplated for a moment, working her bottom lip. She sported a streak of platinum hair similar to mine. It had appeared this morning. Alejandro also sported the streak. Still, I was the only one with a full head of platinum hair, which didn't bother me. I liked that we all shared this characteristic now. We were a family, after all, and this proved our link and signaled to others we were of one heart.

"I remember someone telling me that my gift was given to me," Chloe spoke. "Just like all our gifts are given to us."

Alejandro snapped his fingers. "And they were excited to see what will become of us… all of us." He scanned the group in our family room. "But how do I know that?" His hand moved to his platinum lock to smooth the hairs into place.

"Feeling the power and presence of the blessed angels," Fr. Flynn beamed as his lips parted, revealing a look of both reverence and exhaustion. "And what you describe is similar to the feelings my team and I have experienced, but what you all went through…" He shook his head. "I wish we could explore what occurred from a scholarly perspective.

There would be so much to learn." He reached for his tea to take a sip.

I shook my head. "I don't want to be some case study or some anomaly for the curious or worse…"

Dr. Thomas adjusted on the sofa. "May I play this for you?" He pointed to the laptop set up on our coffee table. He adjusted and moved closer to tap the device, bringing the screen to life.

"Ethan managed to catch your conversations on his camera," Michelle disclosed.

"I didn't think any of the smartphones or any of the tech worked," Alejandro questioned.

"He used his SLR Camera, and that worked." She shrugged. *Great. Video proof of ghosts, Demons, and angels. I hope this doesn't make it onto the Internet or social media.*

Anson typed on the keypad and hit play. We all leaned in to see what was captured on video. The image showed me standing, watching Alejandro and Chloe fall, everyone rushing to their sides, holding my husband and daughter down on the sidewalk. After a few moments, I walked over to Alejandro and Chloe on the ground being held by Fr. Flynn's team. I studied the teams holding down my family and waved a hand to the left. Everyone holding Alejandro down moved, or appeared to be gently nudged out of my way. I did the same to the right as everyone holding Chloe did the same. No words of protest came from either group, and my action cut off all conversation as they watched.

My husband and daughter lay prone where they were, struggling with no success.

The words that came out of my mouth were something I had never said before in my life. Each word I spoke was met in kind with snarls, growls, and hisses from Chloe and Alejandro. You'd think I'd be upset hearing them like this, but no. I know longer endured any fear from this event. Their reactions simply were their reactions, and nothing to fear. The conversation between us continued and, after a few minutes, a blast of wind blew our clothes and hair. The wind generated from me and spread out over the block. As the wind continued to tussle my hair about was when my locks shifted from red to platinum. At that moment, everything stopped. I viewed the screen as my image glanced to the sky, continuing to speak in this unknown language, and shortly after, I stopped speaking. Nothing more happened. Alejandro, Chloe, and I were hugging.

"We caught the whole exchange." Dr. Thomas beamed, proud of his team and their work.

I couldn't deny my own eyes. They managed to catch the exchange, but something appeared off, and I couldn't quite place what seemed different yet.

"You all were, in fact, speaking Aramaic." Dr. Thomas announced with a firm nod of his head. "We checked last night after we left."

"What are you going to do with the video?" Alejandro's tone filled with worry, and I moved over and squeezed his leg in support. Whatever happened, we would face as a family. Together. We survived a haunted house and neighborhood, so I had no doubt we had the ability to survive anything.

"You didn't notice?" Michelle leaned closer toward us, putting her glass down on the coaster on the coffee table.

"Notice what?" I asked. "Something did seem off about the video, but…" I shrugged. In reality, the whole video was *off,* but I didn't notice anything wrong with the video itself.

"Your faces." She paused and pointed to the screen. "Anything to identify who you are…"

"They are blurred over," Dr. Thomas revealed, rewinding the video and pausing the image. Where you should be able to see my face, Alejandro's face, and Chloe's face perfectly, the image had been blurred out.

I leaned forward, adjusting my glasses, and stared at the image. So did Chloe and Alejandro.

"We all look generic. Like AIs." Chloe frowned.

"How?" Alejandro asked.

Dr. Thomas shook his head. "This wasn't done by us. We tried to clean up the image, but we couldn't, and Ethan works with computers. He can't figure out what caused the distortion and…" He chuckled. "Well, he's not happy that the images can't be cleaned up."

"Even the metadata is blank," Michelle added, sitting deeper in the chair.

"And?" Alejandro asked.

Dr. Thomas closed the video file. "Basically, we can release the data, but there is no way for anyone to figure out who you are, or where this happened. Even if we gave them your address, the houses in the video seem off somehow, as well as all of our faces."

"Someone appears to be looking out for you," Fr. Flynn added, a bit of amusement crossing his lips.

"If I'm hearing you correctly, all your evidence is there, but our family won't be exposed." I couldn't help the excitement in my voice and tone.

"Pretty much," Michelle disclosed.

"If I may," Fr. Flynn began. "I would still love for you to share your story with the church, but I have to respect your privacy." He sat taller. "I won't tell them about you, but I will log my experience, keeping your names out of my report."

"Thank you." I checked my glasses on my face. "Who knows? Maybe at some point we'll be willing to share our story, but with everything Chloe's been through, not to mention us, the added stress of any media attention, or church attention…" I shook my head.

"You don't need to worry about me." Chloe beamed. "I'm not scared of bullies anymore."

My lips pulled in a grin as the smile bloomed over my lips, as well as Alejandro's.

"Good for you, Chloe." Alejandro praised. "We couldn't be more pleased, but I agree with your dad. The added attention is something none of us need… at least for now."

"We've had enough excitement." I added.

"Still," Michelle's gaze met mine. "I would love to explore options." She glanced at Chloe. "And we still have work to do."

Chloe sat in silence a moment. Finally her words filled our ears. "I know… but since this all happened, I feel different. Less scared, I guess." She shrugged.

"We'll see what happens in the days, weeks, months, and years ahead," I tried to put an end to this conversation.

After viewing the video, and hearing what Fr. Flynn, Dr. Thomas, and Michelle had to say, we all agreed we had been to hell and back. But given what we, and by extension our neighbors, had been through, coming out feeling this good about the future and our lives was something I don't think we would have attained on our own. Perhaps in time, but these events pushed us onto the fast track. Having a grateful spirit around this haunting wasn't ever anything I assumed I would hold in my heart, but as I observed our guests leave our home, for the first time since we moved here, I felt free and better for our experiences.

# ~ Chapter Twenty-Four ~

True to their word, nothing appeared in the media. Nothing online. No viral videos on social media. No interviews. No one coming to explore our neighborhood or camping out waiting for something to happen. Our lives were once again our own as we marched into fall. I glanced at Alejandro as he held me. Our quiet moments of intimacy these past few weeks were a level of closeness we'd never experienced. I'm not implying our lovemaking didn't bring us a peace or bonding on a higher level; it did, but since the cleansing of our neighborhood, we had achieved new heights, which, as we fell into climax, were unmistakable. Without sounding hokey, these moments were spiritual.

We spent the morning in bed enjoying each other, followed by a shared shower refreshing ourselves. By the time we had finished breakfast and a few household chores, a knock at the front door pulled us from our various escapes.

"It's them," Chloe called as she rushed by my office doors to the front door. "I'll be out front," she added.

"Okay." I pulled myself away from my office computer. Demons. Angels. Spirits. Hauntings. None of that kept work from needing to be done and, as the end of the year approached, my job ramped up. Given all that I had been through and how much time I missed from work, I was happy there had been no lasting ramifications from our experience. I think what helped my case was when people caught sight of my new hair. Without words, they each came to their own conclusion, my health and wellbeing, I'm sure, at the top of their internal lists. Even HR, after seeing me, never said a word. My boss wasn't sure what to say to me, or even how to look at me for weeks. Officially, the word in the office was we had family medical concerns to deal with. Unofficially, the co-workers that mattered to me got tidbits of our experience as I left the more harrowing parts of the story out. As for Alejandro, his streak of platinum told a story he didn't need to elaborate on. And, somehow, no one dared to question us. Even the school made no comments about the few days Chloe missed, but thankfully we ensured we kept things as normal for her as possible.

And really, it wasn't like we took huge amounts of time off, so there weren't many questions. Also, as time marched on, other things took priority and people went back to focusing on their needs and wants.

Even when Reza checked in with us, once we reconnected, I realized he had questions he wanted to ask, but thought better. We understood each other well enough to know when I was ready, and he was free. We would sit down and talk, but not until then. I was happy to call him a friend.

I took off my glasses, exchanging them for my regular glasses. Having perfect vision would have been nice instead of the new hair color, but that wasn't in the cards, and I didn't mind wearing glasses, especially since I'd been wearing glasses as long as I've been alive.

I stood, stretching, and walked to the door to open it. I believed Chloe would've left the door open for our guest, but clearly she had only seen them from her window upstairs before rushing off.

"Hiya," Deepa greeted me.

"Hi." I peeked over my shoulder to see if Alejandro was on his way. He had been in the backyard puzzling around with the new lights or something like that. "Has it been a month already?"

"Doesn't feel real, does it?" She smiled at me. "I'd be lying if I said I wasn't enjoying the silence. Everything's been so calm. Who dreamed life could be this normal… and good?"

I chuckled.

"Chloe seemed excited to see everyone," Deepa pointed over her shoulder.

"I think she likes them." I lowered my voice. "I wouldn't be surprised if she hasn't found her passion, but don't tell Alejandro."

"I heard that." We were joined by Alejandro. "Whatever makes her happy is fine with me…" He gestured to the front yard. "Now, let's do this." We stepped out into the bright sunny day, the warmth feeling amazing on my face. Today, like so many since our final encounter, was perfect. Cooler for sure, but still a sunny day with few clouds in the sky, showing some movement from the heavens above.

Fr. Flynn and his team organized everyone. He and Dr. Thomas shared a laugh, something I never thought I'd witness. The members of the SVPRS were getting things set up and passing out materials to all the neighborhood participants. They informed us on the day of their last visit that we would need to do a couple months of follow-ups—blessing the neighborhood to ensure nothing crawled its way in—but I wasn't worried about another Demon or bully spirit. None of the Demons would be able to return, and the only things here now were the love of our home, our neighborhood, and our family. Still, I appreciated having the added security. Plus, I had grown fond of all these people. They were there to help us when we were at our lowest.

As with our final battle, the whole neighborhood showed up, including the Chens. Since the cleansing, Dr. Chen and Mike had changed. They were lovely people. I appreciated them as neighbors, especially when homemade pot stickers or eggrolls showed up at our home for no reason. We even housesat for them when they traveled, and I had grown quite fond of Muffin, despite their yappy nature.

Chloe waved to us. She was already with the other neighbor kids as Deepa, Alejandro, and I walked over and greeted our friends and neighbors. I peeked up the street, then down it. This was a great home and a great place to live, and I couldn't wait to have Sara and Carter over for the official return of our dinners and game night. Heck, I was even excited to have Alejandro's family and my family over again. I wanted our home to become a real gathering place for everyone in our lives. And I believed now we could achieve that goal with ease.

# ~ Chapter Twenty-Five ~

Time is a funny thing. One day your teenage daughter is playing out with her friends in the neighborhood park, and the next day you're welcoming your twin sons, Lucas and Ezekiel, to your home, promising them they'll have a great life. Next you're having friends over for long overdue bar-b-ques. Or you're having family events that include more than your biological family. On another day, you're attending the wedding of the teenage boy who was so terrified he wanted his family to move away. Or, ultimately, you're watching a contractor tear down a burned-out home to replace the structure with something new. After the construction, you get to greet the new family as they move in. On a different day, you're saying goodbye to friends who move away because life has taken them in a better, or different, direction. All the while, here you are, watching life move forward, wondering where all the time vanished to.

Those first few months after the events in our neighborhood ended, some of our neighbors were still on edge. Who'd blame them? But like with a bad dream, the memories and fear faded as the call of daily life filled the space.

"Hey, handsome," Alejandro called from the door to my den, breaking my focus on the project laying before me.

I saved my file and peeked over at him. The streak of platinum was a beautiful accent to his already fetching, if not older, face.

"Hey there, yourself." I pulled off my glasses to swap them out. "Did you get the boys dropped off?"

"Yep, they're happy with my parents, enjoying time with their granny and granddad." He shook his head. "You know I don't remember Chloe, or us for that matter, having all this time off from school."

"It's an Inservice Day, and we had plenty of time off," I countered. "Remember those long summer breaks?"

"I suppose… still."

My lips pulled tight. "You think they'll be okay?" I questioned. I couldn't help but worry; they were so young, and I didn't like them being away from us.

"I'm pretty sure my folks can handle our boys and the rest of their grandkids for the next couple of nights."

"But Disneyland…" I glanced around, seeing the photos on the shelves, the collection of images that had grown over the years. "It's not right around the corner."

"No, but they did fine with Chloe and the others, so it's only fair." He crossed over and leaned against my desk. "Now, don't worry."

"Fine." I held up my hands in surrender. I didn't fuss so much about Alejandro's folks with all those kids. If I was honest, I missed the boys and the noise they would make when they played or ran around the upstairs, or downstairs, or backyard. With Chloe growing up so fast and the boys still young, I enjoyed having them around when they weren't driving me mental. I smiled at the notion.

"What are you working on?" Alejandro asked, peering at the monitor.

I ignored his question. "Chloe texted. She's gonna be working late tonight. Tonight is Flashlight Tours at the Winchester Mystery House, so she won't be home until after midnight."

"Fun." He laughed with a shake of his head. "I don't know how comfortable I am with her working there, given all that we went through and what Fr. Flynn told us about doorways and inviting trouble."

"Chloe and I both talked to Michelle about the job, and Fr. Flynn stated there shouldn't be any issues with her working there. Plus, he doesn't think there is anything to that place, except creative marketing and PR."

"Still." Alejandro sighed. "You both, her more so, have your *talents*."

"Talents that faded over time," I amended. "The more time that passes from the battle, the more those gifts seem to fade…"

"But they can return."

I shrugged. "It's fine." I'm not worried about these things any longer. We can deal with our PK abilities, assuming they became a problem again. Funnily enough, our proficiencies diminished, but I figured losing these aptitudes was possibly better for both of us. "Plus, Chloe is well-prepared and trained, thanks to both Michelle and Fr. Flynn. And if we can't trust them…" I didn't need to finish my comment. Alejandro understood.

"When did our baby girl grow up enough to have a job?" Alejandro switched topics.

*He never did like admitting Chloe was growing up.*

"When she passed her driving test, got her license, and decided she wanted to save for her own car." I sighed, reaching up and massaging my neck. I had been at the computer for a couple of hours and I hadn't moved much. My virtual meeting with Reza had been productive, and I was grateful for his and Micah's continued support and friendship over these last few years. It was something I had missed when life separated us. I cracked my neck again and shook my head toward the desk. I needed to move more. A practice my chiropractor was trying to ingrain in me. "When did we get so old?"

"Speak for yourself." Alejandro reached up and played with my mop of platinum hair. "I'm still young and beautiful, and I'm not the one with gray hair."

"Oh, really?" I stretched a hand over, running my fingers through his hair.

"Hey."

I laughed and glanced around my den. We had built so many good memories here. "Do you have any regrets?" He understood my question. I spoke about our house, and not about us as a family.

"Nope." He beamed at me. "Never. This is our home. The place we've raised our family. The place we fought and won to keep and enjoy."

I kissed him. "Good."

"Since the kids are gone and Chloe won't be home until late, what are your thoughts of maybe spending our free time over at the coast? Maybe a walk along the beach, dinner on the pier?" He winked at me. His eyes were hopeful and impossible to say no to. "Or, we could spend the evening upstairs, see how young we still are."

I laughed a good-natured laugh. "You are insatiable."

"It's the hair." He grinned, tussling my hair again and leaning over and kissing my neck. "Plus, I assumed you liked that about me… as well as a few other things," he whispered in my ear, giving my lobe a nip, which sent an electric jolt right to my groin.

I chuckled again, taking his hand and kissing it. I held his fingers to my chest. "True." I kissed his hand again. "Speaking of insatiable, I got a call from Michelle…"

"Oh, dear." He scrutinized me. "Let me guess, she and the group want you to go and help on a new case?" Alejandro asked, his gaze meeting mine.

"No." I smiled as I kissed his fingers once more. "She asked me if I was going to write about our experience," I uttered between kisses. "She thinks it's time…"

"Again? When doesn't she think it's time? I blame her and Reza for keeping after you." He pulled his hand away and stepped closer to me, his gaze studying mine.

I shrugged, meeting his stare. I had no intension of lying to him about the request. About once every six months or so, Michelle would check in and make an inquiry about where we're at with our thoughts on the subject. When I talked with Reza, he would ask the same.

"Our case is still one of the most unique Fr. Flynn or the SVPRS group ever worked, and they think our story might be good for people to hear, so they don't feel alone. They haven't experienced anything similar since." I sighed. "You remember how we felt when everything went mad? How alone. How crazy everything seemed." I examined his face. There were breaks there. Over the years, he had been glacially coming around to the idea. "How hopeless and scared we were."

He stepped closer to the desk, his arms dropping to his side. "I remember. But I don't want people coming and destroying our lives. Or Chloe's. Or the boys'. They weren't even with us when this all went down and, okay, fine, Chloe has thrived since. But the boys…"

I understood his concern, but these occurrences happened years ago and our lives were different now. The scars of the past have well and truly healed. We, as a family, were in a much better position. A much stronger place. A more prepared space. We understood the paranormal better. I believed we could handle the attention, assuming any came.

"I guess telling the story is up to you and Chloe." Alejandro's tone held more of a resigned inclination. Time had changed him—well, both of us, and writing our story was something I had talked about more and more. I believed I was ready to process the events and put pen to paper, in a manner of speaking.

"Hon, you were affected as well," I reminded him. "We all were, and I won't do this unless you're completely okay with the idea." I didn't want there to be any hesitation in his mind or heart.

"We'll see." His lips rose in a grin.

*You'll come around. That's part of why I love you. You are reasonable and willing to pass through your discomfort.*

"Okay, well, we can talk more about this book idea later. However, I do think I want to write our story, and I'm sure Chloe would love to be a part of the writing process. You know how passionate she is."

"Of that I have no doubt." He shook his head.

Chloe had found her calling in the paranormal. She was fascinated, but we told her schooling and a job first. Little did we know she would get a job at one of the most haunted locations in the country. The paranormal, in theory, may become a hobby, but not her focus, at least for now. Thank goodness she had a good head on her shoulders and, for the most part, understood we wanted to ensure she had a solid background. I think what helped her was Dr. Thomas and Michelle telling her the paranormal would always be there. Even when she spoke with Reza about his experience, he told her much the same thing. Fortunately, we all agreed and reinforced our message that a good education and maturity would be the best thing for her and any potential ghost hunting in her future.

But our daughter was clever, hence her current job.

Anson and Michelle both found Chloe getting a job at the Mystery House amusing, but had no concerns. She did have a job, after all, and being a tour guide would work around her school schedule. Plus, working for the Mystery House kept her from going out to abandoned places and locations like Hick's Road, where who knows what might happen to her.

I glanced at my computer, stepping over to close out the rest of the files and turn the damned device off. I licked my lips. I didn't have the heart to tell Alejandro that I had already pulled all my notes together to see if there might be something there. "Michelle also asked if I might be willing to come and give a talk at one of her courses."

"She wanted something more." He poked me in the side. "Hmm, feels like someone needs to hit their bike."

"Ass." I poked him in his own paunch. He wasn't as trim as he once was either, but his extra weight didn't matter. In my eyes he was still the sexy beast I fell in love with and had grown to love even more over the years. "How are the new renters?" I decided to change the subject before things got too stiff at my thoughts.

Alejandro glanced out my den window. "They seem fine." He raked a hand through his hair. "I still can't believe we bought the Williamses' old home."

"Well, someone had to buy the place." I followed his gaze. We focused on the single-story house out my window, the newness long gone, but the mature trees and yard made the house a home. "Better than letting the place sit and rot. No one wanted the house after hearing the odd stories that got out about the place." I shook my head. We figured that the tales and rumors came from the Williamses' realtor, or maybe the bank, but we weren't sure and the stigma didn't matter anymore now that someone lived there and the scars healed over. "And, because of those tales, we got one hell of a deal."

"Agreed. Plus, having the house gives each of the kids a place one day. The townhouse, our home here, and that house. Plus, I was thinking maybe… a house in the mountains?"

"Really? You think we can manage?"

"Owning property is the only way to create generational wealth, and we should be able to buy a new place through our LLC. I've been working the numbers," Alejandro added. "Anyway, the renters seem fine. Lidia and Juan don't seem impressed. They wanted to ensure that the family living next door to them wasn't loud and annoying and I agree. But the new folks seem nice. Considering everything, we've been lucky."

"Oh, I talked to Sara and Carter." I snapped my fingers. "They're gonna meet us at Hari's next Friday night. It'll be good to see them again. We haven't gotten together for a minute."

"Nice." He exhaled a smile. "How's Jackie?"

I laughed. "I think we got lucky; they've been living through a lot of teenage angst. I don't think Maggie's move with her dad helped matters."

"Probably not." Alejandro crossed his arms over his chest. "But getting away from her mother was the best call for Maggie that Dan could've made." He adjusted how he stood. "I only wish they didn't move so far away. Colorado Springs isn't exactly easy to get to."

"Nope, it's not, but I know Chloe and Jackie still chat with her and I think they're planning on asking about going out there this summer to see her."

"Oh, really?" Alejandro's eyebrows rose.

"Don't say anything." I shook my head. "We're not supposed to know. They were talking the idea over the other day and Chloe didn't know I heard. They were planning for next Friday night. A double date, I think."

"Hmm." Alejandro huffed. "What about the boys? That's the night with Sara and Carter, right?"

"We can get a babysitter? My parents?" I suggested.

"Or Chloe can stay home." Alejandro crossed his arms over his chest.

"Oh, come on, we can't keep her from her date," I countered. "It's the first Friday night she's had off in ages…" I tapped my lips, pulling out my phone. I checked the family calendar. "Yep, our poor daughter has been working like mad…" I slipped my phone into my pocket.

"Hmm." Alejandro frowned. The pinched lips, the furrowed brow, and crossed arms over his chest all showing his disapproval.

"Diego is a good guy," I beamed.

"I don't like her dating at this age. She's a baby."

"She's seventeen, that's not a baby."

"How are you okay with this?" Alejandro questioned.

"I didn't get to date as a teen and I love that she can." I surveyed him as his arms dropped from his chest, lowering his defenses. "She's a good kid and deserves to live a normal, happy and healthy life."

"But don't you remember being a guy at that age?" A hint of worry filled his words.

"Yes, I remember what being a teen was like. Always horny. Playing around whenever I was in the shower. Trying to find *alone time* three or four times a day. What's your point?"

"Our daughter." He huffed.

"And she knows how to handle herself." I added, crossing my arms over my chest. I wasn't trying to be defensive, despite my body language. "And I believe our daughter is as horny as any boy. Don't forget, sex is a two-way street."

He shuddered. "But… ugh… it's just… still, we should ask her about babysitting… can't hurt to ask." Alejandro sighed, changing the subject. He had no issues talking about sex in general, but when the matter came to Chloe being a sexual being, he wanted to ignore the topic and push away all those thoughts. She was his little girl and always would be.

*I get it. Her growing up isn't easy for me either, but I'm a realist when it comes to these matters. We've told her what we expect and we've given her all the information we can. The rest is up to her.*

"Come on." Alejandro pulled at my hand. "Enough talk. Let's take advantage of the quiet while we can. So, beach and dinner, or bedroom?"

I chuckled. "How about beach and dinner first, then some romantic alone time later?" I glanced at my computer and the files I had been working on. Who was I to say no to Alejandro, especially given that he was coming around to the idea of me writing our story and sharing past events with the world?

# Acknowledgements

This novel would not have been possible without the assistance of the Bay Area Ghost Hunters, Loyd Auerbach, Director of the Office of Paranormal Investigation, President of Forever Family Foundation, a Catholic Priest, and a retired Catholic Exorcist. Thank you for your knowledge and time.

# About the Author

M.D. Neu is an international award-winning inclusive queer Fiction Writer with a love for writing and travel. Living in the heart of Silicon Valley (San Jose, California) and growing up around technology, he's always been fascinated with what could be. Specifically drawn to Science Fiction and Paranormal television and novels, M.D. Neu was inspired by the great Gene Roddenberry, George Lucas, Stephen King, Alice Walker, Alfred Hitchcock, Harvey Fierstein, Anne Rice, and Kim Stanley Robinson. An odd combination, but one that has influenced his writing.

Growing up in an accepting family as a gay man he always wondered why there were never stories reflecting who he was. Constantly surrounded by characters that only reflected heterosexual society, M.D. Neu decided he wanted to change that. So, he took to writing, wanting to tell good stories that reflected our diverse world.

When M.D. Neu isn't writing, he works for a non-profit and travels with his biggest supporter and his harshest critic, Eric his husband of twenty plus years.